A MOTHER ALWAYS KNOWS

BOOKS BY NICOLE TROPE

NICOLE TROPE

A MOTHER ALWAYS KNOWS

bookouture

Published by Bookouture in 2024

An imprint of Storyfire Ltd.
Carmelite House
50 Victoria Embankment
London EC4Y 0DZ

www.bookouture.com

Storyfire Ltd's authorised representative in the EEA is Hachette Ireland
8 Castlecourt Centre
Dublin 15 D15 XTP3
Ireland
email: info@hbgi.ie

ISBN: 978-1-83618-011-1
eBook ISBN: 978-1-83618-010-4

For D.M.I and J

PROLOGUE

A knock on the head doesn't have to kill you. In fact, in most cases, it probably won't.

But perhaps a knock on the head with a full bottle of French wine might lead to more than just a headache, more than just a concussion, especially if it's swung hard enough and if it connects with the right part of the head. Human beings can be delicate creatures.

And if the person swinging the bottle is filled with fury and fear, then who knows how much damage they could do.

'Oh my God, oh my God,' the woman still clutching the bottle shrieks, looking down at the body on the floor of the office that now lies between us. 'I didn't mean to. I didn't mean to.'

Blood from a cracked skull is pooling on the ground, disappearing into the plush grey carpet, filling the air with a particularly acrid metal smell. I swallow and try breathing through my mouth, not wanting to give in to the need to run screaming from the room. I channel the best part of me, the strongest part of me.

'Of course you didn't mean to,' I say, stepping forward and reaching out to touch her but stopping before I actually connect with the fabric of her pale blue silk dress.

'What now – what am I going to do now?' She sinks to the floor, wraps her arms around herself, clutching the bottle of wine tightly to her. 'What now?' she keeps repeating.

I think fast, finding the best way to answer her plaintive cry, knowing that I need her to calm down. Speaking quietly, but firmly, I tell her what to do, amazed that she listens to me.

'Don't worry, it's going to be fine. I'm going to sort everything out,' I say when she's done as I've instructed. 'I promise you it's all going to be fine.'

I don't tell her that my heart is racing and my palms sweating. I need to seem cool and in control.

'You just stay there,' I say to her. 'I'll be back in a minute.'

'And you'll help me? You'll really help me?' she asks, looking up at me, tears snaking down her cheeks. She needs me, really needs me.

'Of course I will,' I say. 'Don't move.'

I open the office door, looking into the corridor, where all is silent. It's after midnight and everyone has gone home, which is fortunate.

'Think,' I tell myself as I step out of the office and close the door behind me. 'Think.'

I stand in the silence of the empty space for a moment and stare at the nameplate on the door: **ADMINISTRATION ASSISTANT**.

They don't add names to the sign because administration assistants come and go and they are never important enough to have their names noted. But assistants are more important than anyone realises. They get close to you as they take over all the irritating tasks at work, they learn about you, they know you. You see and don't see them and that can be a dangerous thing. I wonder who they will hire next, who will be the replacement for the current assistant.

And I wonder what they will say happened to the last one. I wonder how they will explain it all.

And as I move away from the office, I take comfort in the fact that I know the truth about all of it.

I think some part of me knew it from the beginning.

I think I knew it all along.

ONE

CORDELIA

The Week Before: Monday

Just letting you know I'm working late tonight.

It sounds like a reasonable text from someone who won't be home for dinner, who just wants to let his partner know that if she planned on cooking or them going out or anything at all that partners plan to do together on an average weeknight, he won't be there.

But all Cordelia can read is:

I will be with her.

I will be with her.

I will be with her.

And she wonders if he told the truth, if he just told the complete truth, would it make things easier? Instead, her questions, her pointed accusations, her straight-up requests for the truth have all been met with disbelief.

'What on earth is wrong with you, Cordy?'

'Why would you accuse me of something so tasteless?'

'How could you assume this about me? You know what they

say about the word assume, don't you? It makes an ass out of you and me.'

And finally, the worst one, the one that makes her blood literally boil as it heats up inside her.

'Do you think you might need to see someone about this? Isn't this exactly what your mother did to your father?'

And what she would really like to do is to tell him that she's done, simply done. That she's leaving him to whatever or whoever he is doing and getting on with her own life. She is only twenty-four after all. Her whole life is ahead of her, and he is nine years older than she is. Based on his age, Garth should surely be ready to settle down by now, should surely be thinking of starting a family.

But Garth is not ready for any of that. Instead, he is busy sleeping with someone, cheating with someone, secure in the knowledge that Cordelia will be at home, waiting for him when he's ready. And she hates herself for not having the energy, the impetus to just get up and pack a bag, walk out and consign the last four and a half years of her life to the scrap heap. Why can't she just do it?

She is lying on their bed, his bed really, his king-size bed covered in 1,000 thread-count sheets in a bedroom that has a city view from the floor-to-ceiling windows, where the electronic blinds are still open. She texts back:

That's fine. I have plans anyway. You go and do WHOEVER you want.

What are you talking about? I have to work.

No one in the whole world has to work this much, Garth. You're a shitty human being.

I'm not getting into this right now.

Of course not, and I don't care. I have drinks with friends anyway.

And Garth, clever Garth, doesn't respond to that because he knows it's a lie. Even after living in Melbourne for three years as she did her degree and after starting a job at a graphic design firm filled with people her age, Cordelia still has no one except Garth. Is that what he wanted? His disapproval of her friends from school, the slightly mocking way he talks about them as he points out their flaws – *Alex instantly takes over every conversation, leaving no room for anyone else. Has Cassie always slept with so many men? I mean, she's barely had time to get to know someone before she's with another one. Have you noticed that Sarah is jealous of you, of your looks? She's always saying something negative about your clothes* – has made her see her friends differently, and consequently, she knows she's pulled away a little. Her friends live in Sydney anyway, but any new person she has introduced him to, like Ben from her course, is instantly met with the same negativity. *He really thinks he's going to be a designer? The man is embarrassing and he dresses terribly and he's so boring. How can you spend time with someone who is so boring? And he's got such a pathetic crush on you. It looks like he's drooling every time he talks to you. I wouldn't be surprised if he turned into some kind of weird stalker.*

Garth's voice is in her head whenever she talks to someone and begins to consider them a friend. She views them as he would and instantly finds fault, so she pulls away.

She has no desire really to talk to anyone else, except perhaps her mother – but Cordelia refuses to do that. The push and pull over her mother goes on inside her all the time. Sometimes a memory will strike, an image of her and her mother shopping for clothes together or getting coffee and cake on a Sunday afternoon, and she will feel an intense longing to speak to her, to hear her voice. Then she will immediately squash the feeling and remind herself that she is not going to talk to her mother ever again. The irony of her replying to her mother's texts with 'stop talking to me' is not lost on Cordelia. But she can't seem to help herself.

But if she did speak to her, if she could make herself respond properly to one of her mother's endless texts, she would like to ask her some questions.

What made you think he was having an affair? When did you first suspect something was going on? And is that why you did what you did?

TWO

GRACE

Monday

I brace myself as the plane lands in Melbourne, feeling my body jolt as the wheels hit the ground. I am here. In the same city where Cordelia is.

I am only carrying hand luggage and so half an hour later I am standing outside the airport, waiting for my Uber.

It is an older man in a late-model Mercedes who pulls up. He's wearing a green corduroy peak cap, reminding me so much of Bert – my old driver, back when I had people who did such things for me – that I feel my voice catch as I greet him.

The sky is filled with threatening grey clouds and the wind is fierce as it buffets everyone it touches. It's the beginning of March, and while in Sydney summer refuses to give way to autumn, here in Melbourne, the coming rain has dropped the temperature.

'Terrible weather,' says my driver, and I smile.

'Yes, dreadful, but typical for Melbourne.'

'Well, it's only the start of autumn,' he complains.

'I imagine winter will be very cold,' I say as I take out my phone and read my last text to my daughter, sent this morning.

Hello darling. I hope you're having a good day.

She replied as usual:

Stop talking to me.

At least she still replies. She always replies.

I think briefly about Ava, the woman I was working for and who I have left behind in Sydney with only a short note of explanation – all of it lies. I think of her and her girls, wondering once again if I should have told her who I really am but instantly dismissing the idea. I don't want to hurt her or her children – my granddaughters. I let the word 'granddaughters' circle in my head, marvelling at the idea that those two lovely little girls are connected to me. I am so grateful I got to know them a little, and I close my eyes and wish my daughter, Ava, and her family well.

I try not to let my mind drift to the woman who lost her life because I don't want to think about Melody, but it inevitably goes there. I have to remind myself that I had to protect Ava and her family. I had no choice and I refuse to let the slight barbs of guilt hurt me. I did what I had to do for my daughter, as any good mother would.

'Fancy hotel,' says the driver as we pull up outside.

'It is,' I agree. 'I'm treating myself,' I add, thinking about the soft bed and large tub that await me.

'You deserve it,' he tells me as I slide out of the back seat.

'I do,' I agree with him again. Not that he'd know. 'I really do.'

Check-in is a breeze with everyone wearing their widest smiles and filled with the desire to help. Despite my taking an early-morning flight and despite it only being just over an hour of flying time, it's already close to lunchtime. Travel steals away hours impossibly quickly.

I decide to treat myself to a quiet drink at the bar before I go up to my room, and I order a glass of red wine, savouring the rich dark taste as I stare down at my phone. I sip slowly, enjoying the sensation of it in my mouth, making sure not to rush the one drink I am allowing myself. *I am not an alcoholic and I am in control of myself. I was an alcoholic but I am in control now.*

I click on the information for my new position, my new job.

The law offices of Harmer, Wright and Sing are looking for a temporary administration assistant while their current one goes on holiday. It's a week-long position only. But that's all the time I need.

I used up the last of my favours owed to me to get myself this job. I asked Bill, who owns a recruitment agency for temporary staff, to keep a lookout for something with Garth's company. I asked him two months ago and I told him I would only need a week or so, not something permanent. I just want to get in and see what kind of a man Garth is, see how he behaves at work, maybe even hear how he speaks about my daughter. I don't like what I have seen of the man, don't like the way he responds to Cordelia on social media or the number of women he seems to be speaking to. And one comment he made on Instagram, as a public reply to Cordelia, has me concerned. Not simply because it was rude but because it makes me suspicious of his motivations in dating my daughter.

It was just a quick, casual post with a picture of a pea-green coat that Cordelia had bought from a thrift store. She captioned it, *#goodbuy #onlyfortydollars #hadtobuyit #sorrycreditcardbill.*

Garth replied to that post with, *Says the girl with the trust fund.*

I saw that post a few weeks ago and it worried me. When I

went back to look at it again, Cordelia had deleted it so it must have upset her. Garth is much older than she is and successful at his job. Why would he make a remark about her trust fund? How much does he know about the amount of money that will be hers only a few short months from now when she turns twenty-five?

What kind of a man is my daughter involved with and do I need to protect her from him?

My mother's instinct tells me that the answer to that question is yes. And I always trust my mother's instinct. I hope I am proved incorrect and that my daughter is very happy with a lovely young man. But I have been watching them both on Instagram for a while now and his comment on her trust fund is not my only concern.

I need to make sure that he is not going to break Cordelia's heart. She has had more than enough trauma to last a lifetime.

Cordelia won't see me, so I had no option but to find a way to meet Garth without her knowing about it. My new position is the perfect way to get close to the man.

I will have to take my disguise up a notch to work in his firm as I'm sure he will have seen a picture of me. And even though I now look very different, I need to make sure he doesn't recognise me at all. I have a very expensive platinum-blonde wig and a pair of clear-lens glasses to create my new look. I will favour dowdy clothes, I think, nothing too pretty but rather a little baggy and dull-coloured.

I was so excited to hear about this position from Bill.

Before my life fell apart, before I burned down my house and had to sell my company, I threw a lot of business Bill's way when I needed temporary staff. I knew him finding me something was a long shot, and I couldn't believe it when I got his text. I had done what I'd needed to do for Ava, for my daughter who will never know that she's my daughter. The timing couldn't have been more perfect. I took that as a sign from the universe that I was doing the right thing. I had to leave Ava a little before I wanted to, but I had no choice. I would have liked to stay and help her settle into her new role, but I am sure she'll be just fine.

Tomorrow I will walk into Garth's office building and be shown around. I will be there to help everyone while their administration assistant is on leave.

But mostly I will be helping myself.

THREE

CORDELIA

Tuesday

She opens her eyes in the dark, her heart racing from a regular dream. It's her father, trapped behind a window, smoke swirling around him, his mouth open as he screams for help, his fists pounding on the glass. In the dream she is aware that she must break the glass and that there is a long metal pole in her hand that would do the job. All she needs to do is lift the pole and she will save her father but she cannot make her heavy arm move no matter how hard she tries.

It's just after 7 a.m. but any light outside is blocked by the blinds that shut out everything. She fumbles around on her side table for the remote, clicking it as her heart races. As the blinds open and autumn sunlight streams in, she takes deep breaths to calm her body, allowing the memory of the worst day of her life to wash over her, accepting it, embracing it, because that is easier than fighting it and trying to push it away.

Six years ago, when the cab she had caught stopped in front of her house, she was sure that a mistake had been made. The smouldering ruin surrounded by police tape could not possibly be her home.

She remembers that her skin was free of make-up, still smelling slightly of the lemon-scented face mask she had applied the night before in a hotel room with her three best friends.

'To us,' Alexandra had said and they'd sat on the bed, lifting glasses of mineral water to toast each other.

'Please, no alcohol,' Cordelia had said when she'd invited them, and Alex, Cassie and Sarah had happily agreed.

It had been a fabulous night, expensive as they'd ordered pizza and burgers and far too many indulgent desserts like the chocolate peanut butter pie covered in whipped cream. But her mother had told her to spend what she liked when she'd given Cordelia the gift of a night away to celebrate the end of final exams. It had been wonderful as they'd laughed about school memories and discussed plans for the future. Cordelia had managed, just for that night, to put aside her worry over her mother and her drinking and over the state of her parents' marriage. She had felt young and free and like the whole world was about to open up to her.

When everyone had gone home the next morning after a sumptuous pancake breakfast, Cordelia had caught a cab and arrived home to find... nothing. Everything had gone up in smoke. All their family pictures, everything Cordelia treasured like the fluffy toys she had kept since she was a child, mementoes of friendship given to her through her school years, her certificates of achievement, her computer and every item of clothing she owned was gone.

But none of that had mattered when she learned that her mother was in a hospital under police guard and her father was dead. Her father – whose last message to her had been *Have a lovely night, my darling, you've earned it xxx* – was no longer alive.

You shouldn't have been out enjoying yourself, she has admonished herself for years. *If you had been there, it wouldn't have happened.* For years she has played a scene in her mind where her mother tells her, *I've booked a night in a hotel for you and three friends to celebrate the end of your exams,* and instead of hugging her mother with glee and immediately calling Sarah, Alex and Cassie to tell them the delightful news, she instead says, *Oh, thanks, maybe I'll use it in a few months' time.* Because maybe if she had waited, her mother would have gotten herself into treatment or she would have stopped drinking or her father would have just moved out or, or, or. Maybe if she had waited, things would have been different and she could have gone to stay in the hotel with her friends and come home to a life that was exactly the same as it had been the day before.

Lying in bed, she knows that the air of her apartment smells vaguely of sandalwood, a candle she likes to burn, but she still inhales the smouldering smell, acrid and heavy, that greeted her that day as she stepped out of the cab. 'What?' she said to the policewoman standing outside the taped-off site as she explained.

'Last night,' began the policewoman again.

'No, I heard you,' Cordelia said, 'but I don't understand, I just don't understand.'

'Is there no one I can call for you, no relative who can come and get you?' the policewoman asked kindly, and Cordelia shook her head, again muttering, 'I don't understand.'

And then one of their neighbours, a lawyer, came over to her and took her to her own house. 'Sit down and let me get you something for the shock,' Marnie said.

She handed Cordelia a small whisky even though it was just after 10 a.m. The smell made Cordelia gag and Marnie frantically pointed to the guest bathroom, where Cordelia threw up her breakfast.

And then she called Cassie, who made her mother come

and get Cordelia and install her in their guestroom as she tried
to figure out exactly what had happened to her life.

At eighteen she had to arrange her father's funeral and talk
to insurance agents and figure out how to tell the whole world
that her life had been upended as her mother lay in a hospital
bed, insisting that what had happened had been an accident.
She refused to visit her mother, refused to see her at all, and
only glimpsed her at the trial to have her committed to the
psychiatric facility to be rehabilitated. Her beautiful mother
with golden blonde hair and lovely green eyes was diminished,
hunched, ugly with unwashed hair and pale, doughy skin.
Cordelia ached to hug her but she hardened her heart. Her
mother was responsible for her father's death and deserved no
sympathy at all.

You've broken me, Cordelia wanted to scream across the
courtroom, *you've broken us*.

She closes her eyes and pictures the memory fading, and
then because movement helps, she jumps out of bed and uses
the bathroom.

Returning to the bedroom, she sees that Garth's side of the
bed is still smooth, his pillow untouched.

He didn't come home. Again. This will be the third time in
two months that he's done this. And each time she worries that
he may never come home again because you can spend a night
in a hotel and come home to a hideously different world, so
Garth could easily stay out with whoever he is sleeping with
and simply never return. Being with Garth has helped her pick
up some of the pieces of her broken life. But now... now things
are changing in the most terrible way and she doesn't know how
to stop it.

There is a small tingle of fear inside her.

Everything okay?

She sends the text quickly, knowing that she shouldn't contact him at all, that he probably enjoys her worry and concern, but she needs to make sure that Garth is fine. She loves him deeply, too much for her own good. He doesn't reply, which is a little unusual. But their text exchange yesterday must have irritated him because he hates it when she doesn't simply accept his standard explanation of 'working late' without questioning it. He's probably sulking.

When he has done this little disappearing act in the past, staying away for a night or sometimes two, claiming to have slept at work when he is busy with a big case, he's always answered her texts immediately, driven, Cordelia thinks, by guilt. But her phone is stubbornly silent.

All through her breakfast of a scrambled egg and a piece of seeded toast, she waits for his reply.

She takes the phone into the bathroom while she showers, switching off the water midway through to check if she has heard a text notification, but there is nothing. In the bathroom mirror her skin looks pale, her blonde hair lank and her brown eyes dull. No wonder Garth prefers other women.

On the tram to work, she texts him again.

Is everything okay? Please text me back.

She scrolls back through their messages over the last few weeks in case she's forgotten that he has to be away on some corporate thing, and then she quickly closes her phone, conscious that she is on a crowded tram with people all around her. She wouldn't want anyone to see some of the messages she has sent him, particularly those over the last few weeks. They are horrible. She can be horrible, especially when she is angry and hurt and sitting on their sofa, stewing over everything because he's left her alone as he, once again, works all night. Just like last night.

Last week she was exceptionally nasty, on yet another occasion when he told her he wouldn't be home.

Do you think I don't know what you're doing? You promised we would go out together tonight. I know you're with someone else. Why won't you just admit it?

Cordy, please don't be ridiculous. The barristers need new arguments for the morning. They were demolished in court today. I need to work.

You're a liar. I know you're lying. Why don't you just tell me the truth? We can end this and you can get on with screwing her.

I am working!!!!!

I hate this. I hate you.

I can't keep having this conversation with you. I am at work and I will see you later.

Screw you, Garth. Your lies will catch up with you one day and then you'll see.

Then I'll see what?

She didn't reply to that text.

And when he did finally come home, they both simply pretended the conversation hadn't happened. Garth doesn't like confrontation, and if she tries to have a discussion about their relationship, he will simply walk out of the apartment and go to a bar or for a walk or to meet a friend. *Hello, red flag,* her friend

Cassie would say if she knew it was the case. But Cordelia rarely speaks to Cassie anymore.

The irony of her situation is not lost on her. The nights when her mother accused her father of sleeping with Tamara, her own assistant, were horrifying as her mother screamed and shouted and her father denied everything, eventually refusing to talk to her anymore and locking himself in the spare room. And then her mother would cry and drink more, and Cordelia would have to listen to her explain all the ways she had proven that her father was cheating and who he was cheating with.

But none of it was true. Her father died denying that he had ever cheated at all and her mother went to a psychiatric facility where she sobered up and got the help she needed. And Cordelia's whole life was blown out of the water.

Sometimes she wonders exactly who she would be now if her mother had not 'accidentally' burned down their house and killed her father. Would she be with Garth at all? He's good-looking and clever and he makes her laugh and she loves just being with him, doing anything at all, even something as simple as shopping for groceries, but would she still love him as much if she had not come home to a smoking ruin? And if she was still with Garth and her mother was at home, even divorced from her father because they both needed out of a toxic marriage, would she just pack up and go home and let her mother comfort her as she detailed her suspicions about Garth? Probably.

The desire to talk to her mother washes over her in a wave of longing but she pushes it away. Her mother is out in the world now, getting on with her life and texting Cordelia once or twice a day. Is she better? Is she happy? Does she feel guilty over the fire? Does she care that she ruined her only child's life? And what would she tell Cordelia to do about Garth? Cordelia doesn't even want to think about that because she would never follow her advice. Look what she did to her life, to their lives.

I'm not like her, Cordelia comforts herself as she often does. She is not drinking herself into a stupor and making ridiculous accusations. She knows the real truth. Garth has to work a lot, she knows that, and she even knows that senior associates at his law firm of Harmer, Wright and Sing sometimes work until the early hours of the morning. It's the job and Garth wants to make partner.

But she also knows that he's cheating. And she knows that it's serious, that it's something that matters to him and not just a hookup. She can feel it. There's no other explanation for the sense she gets when they are together that his mind is somewhere else and Cordelia knows exactly who Garth is sleeping with.

His law firm is filled with beautiful women, and a fellow senior associate in his medical negligence team is a woman named Natalie. Natalie and her boyfriend, Charles, have been to the apartment for dinner, and the two couples have been out for drinks and brunch. And each time they are together, Cordelia can feel a connection between Garth and Natalie, has been able to feel it since Natalie joined the firm six months ago. But she doesn't want to accuse Garth of sleeping with Natalie in particular, mindful that he will simply deny it. She wants to catch him out, to have him confess to it without meaning to, even if that means she will actually have to make a decision, actually have to do something.

As much as she hates to admit it to herself, she doesn't want to lose Garth. He was a strong, solid, capable and loving presence when she needed it most and she's afraid that if they do part, the collapse she feels she has kept at bay for six years will come and she will be destroyed.

And so, she stays. She believes he's sleeping with another woman but she doesn't have absolute proof, not proof that he couldn't deny. And some small part of her keeps hoping that she is actually wrong and that she is simply imagining the connection between the two of them, that Garth is telling the truth and the nights he spends away from her are only for work. Perhaps she's naïve or perhaps it's a form of self-preservation. Perhaps she is simply too afraid to be without him.

The tram stops near her office building and she gets off, pushing past people to get to the door. Still no text from Garth.

She sends another text.

Please just let me know you're okay.

He still doesn't reply, and all she gets is the usual text from her mother, which only serves to irritate her.

Good morning. I hope you have a lovely day, my darling.

Her head is down as she walks towards her building, willing him to reply, and she doesn't see the man stopped in front of her until she bumps into him.

'Oh, I'm so sorry,' she says quickly, not looking up because she's concentrating on her phone. She steps aside and moves towards the door, watching her feet as well.

'Careful, Cordelia,' he says, and it's only when she is inside that she realises the man used her name.

She darts back outside to see who it was but there's no one, and because she didn't even look at the man, she has no idea who he could be. Was his voice familiar? Maybe. But if he knows her, why didn't he say hello?

'Careful, Cordelia.' What a strange thing to say.

FOUR

GRACE

Tuesday

The building where Garth works is typical of any in the city centre. It towers in the air at least twenty storeys high with tinted glass windows.

I stop in the lobby, checking the board to see the floor I need to go to. The law offices of Harmer, Wright and Sing are on the seventh floor.

I cannot help but remember only weeks ago standing and checking a board in an office building where I was going to apply for a job with a woman who I knew was my daughter. I only left the clinic three and a half months ago, and I feel like I've been on a treadmill, running to keep up with everything going on in my life, with everything I need to do. But I know how quickly life can change and I feel a sense of urgency when it comes to my daughters. I cannot allow their lives to turn out like mine did, and isn't that what every mother wants? For her children to live a better life than she has? It seems impossible in this day and age, but I left Sydney certain that things are on the right track for Ava, and now I just need to make sure I can say the same of Cordelia.

As I wait for the elevator, I indulge myself in a small fantasy of introducing Ava and Cordelia, of seeking out similarities between them and finding myself surrounded by family.

It won't happen, of course. I would never do that to either of my daughters. They can never know of each other's existence. Both their lives would be thrown into chaos.

The elevator doors open directly into the law offices. I know it's a large practice but you would be hard pressed to tell that there was anyone here at all. Two receptionists sit behind a grey stone counter, answering the phones in low voices. I peer down a hallway but every single timber door is closed. The slightly stale smell of manufactured air from the air conditioner and the plush grey carpet contributes to the feeling of this being a place where a lot of money is made and spent. I know that Garth charges seven hundred dollars an hour for his time.

I approach the desk and a young man with neatly slicked-back hair and deep blue eyes looks up at me, smiling brightly. 'Good morning. How may I help you today?' he asks.

'I've been sent over by the Staff in a Moment recruitment agency,' I say. 'Apparently your administration assistant is away for a week?'

'Oh,' he says, his fingers flying over the keyboard. 'Of course, yes. Give me a moment and I'll get Peter to come and just show you through. You can take a seat. He won't be long.'

He gestures to a buttery brown sofa and I sit, touching the soft leather with my hand.

Waking up this morning, it took me a moment to realise where I was. The bed was so soft and the room so dark. I can't get used to the luxury of the hotel. Strange when I was once surrounded by such luxury as part of my everyday life.

But when I was fully awake, I ordered a room service break-fast and scrolled through my phone, contacting Cordelia first with my usual message of love and then checking in on Ava and the girls. Ava's Instagram page, which I follow using a fake profile, had a picture of her standing in front of an office door, a wide smile on her face as she pointed to a handwritten sign that said, AVA GREEN, CEO. 'Well done, my darling,' I murmured as I imagined the nameplate to come in brass with engraved lettering. She will do a fabulous job; I know she will.

There were no pictures of her little girls but I checked on Finn's website and saw that he had added something: NOW TAKING COMMISSIONS. I was delighted. One day he will have a show for all his lovely portraits, but until then, he can help Ava by taking commissions. Life in Sydney is very expensive. I know that the two of them have a long way to go after Finn's cheating and the fallout from that, but I feel like they will make it. I know they will. Not every marriage needs to end when a partner cheats. Finn never denied what he had done and he was filled with remorse.

So very unlike Robert, who lied until the very end. But I'm not going to think about Robert and what he did now.

Today is a new day and the one thing I want more than anything is to reconnect with Cordelia. I will make that happen. Something is bothering my child. Something is wrong. I can feel it. Approaching her directly would be counterproductive. I need to see what's wrong first so I can help her fix it. That's what mothers do.

'Grace?' I hear, and I look up to see a portly man, his suit pants held up by red suspenders, not a choice you see too often these days.

'Yes,' I say, standing, noting that he glances at me quickly and then away. I am wearing a shapeless brown dress that billows around me, the glasses I have chosen are black-rimmed and make my green eyes bulge slightly, and I have used only the tiniest amount of make-up so I appear older than I like to. Combined with the wig, I believe I look nothing like Grace

Morton at all, nothing like Grace Enright either – which is the name I used when working for Ava.

I am still using Grace Enright's name though. Because she is a woman who gets things done.

'Come through here,' he says. 'I'm Peter, head of HR.'

'Nice to meet you,' I reply. I follow him to an office, where there is a desk piled with papers and a sign, **ADMINISTRATION ASSISTANT**, on the door. 'Now I think she's left everything in pretty good order and she put together a manual for you to follow so it should be easy,' he says, gesturing to the desk.

'I'm sure I'll be fine,' I say, knowing that the most important thing for a temporary assistant is to be able to simply slot into place without disturbing anything. It is not my intention to disturb anything, unless it needs to be disturbed.

'Oh, excuse me,' he says as his phone buzzes in his pocket. 'Look, just find me if you have any questions but anyone here is able to help. Kelsey, the intern, is around somewhere and she's pretty good with everything. I'm sure you'll come across most people over the course of the day.' He swipes his finger across his screen and answers, 'Yes, Jack, thanks for getting back to me,' and then he turns and walks away, leaving me in the office.

I quickly find a blue file that the permanent assistant has left for me. It's neatly arranged with clear typed instructions and I am grateful that she seems to be very organised. Glancing around the office, I search for any pictures of her. There is one of a couple, at least ten years older than I am, wide smiles on their faces. The woman has neatly bobbed grey hair and blue eyes and her husband is balding. They are pictured in front of a bright blue ocean, sitting at a small table with elaborate cocktails in front of them. She must be close to retirement age and is obviously very good at her job. She seems like someone I would know or be friends with. I wonder if she is on holiday with her husband and then I have a moment of sadness for the retirement years I looked forward to, for the travelling that Robert and I would have done. *Let that go*, I admonish myself. I need to concentrate.

I sit down and get to work, filing and setting aside invoices that need to be paid. After an hour, I get up to use the bathroom and take the opportunity to look around a little. I walk down one corridor, reading the names on the doors, but I can't find Garth. I turn and walk in the opposite direction. The law offices take up an entire floor.

When I find Garth's office, the door is closed and I knock gently, thinking that I will introduce myself and ask him if he needs anything. He doesn't need to know that I will not be doing that with everyone.

There is no reply from inside the office and I push down on the handle slowly, glancing around to see if anyone is watching me, but I am alone.

Garth's office is silent and dark, his desk empty of everything except for a leather-bound notebook and a pen. I don't want to turn on the light but I step forward and open the book, using my phone screen to give me a little light. There's nothing written in it, except a single sentence: *Monday 6 p.m. Meeting with J.* It's Tuesday today and I wonder if the meeting went ahead, who J is and why he would have written it down when everything is stored on phones these days.

'Garth,' I hear and I step away from the desk as a woman walks into the office.

I know immediately this is Natalie.

I follow Garth on Instagram the same way I follow Cordelia, and Natalie, who is very pretty with white-blonde hair and deep green eyes, makes more than the occasional appearance on his page. It astonishes me how easily my follow requests are accepted despite my Instagram page having very little information. I mostly put up pictures of delectable-looking dishes, like a seven-layer chocolate cake and a Mexican-inspired taco salad, with recipes to accompany them in the comments. I obviously seem harmless enough but I am always surprised by the amount of information people are happy to share with the general public.

I don't comment on any of Cordelia's or Garth's posts, but Natalie comments on just about everything Garth puts up. Another reason why I am concerned about his relationship with my daughter.

Hope it was worth it, she commented on a picture of him holding a tall beer in his hand, white froth streaming down the side of the glass, followed by a whole lot of winking emojis. What was she referring to? His drinking? Something he did?

If only they knew... she commented on a picture of him at his desk, which he hashtagged, *#neverends #bigdayincourt.*

There is also a picture of her and Garth together at a bar with some other lawyers, glasses raised in celebration of their *#bigwin.*

'Oh,' she says when she sees me. 'Who are you?'

'I am sorry, I'm Grace, the temporary admin assistant. I got a little lost and I thought I might find a map or something in the office.'

It's a lame excuse but Natalie doesn't even stop to think about it. 'Well, why don't I show you to where you need to be.' She is dressed in a tight black suit with a cream blouse, every inch the professional.

I nod and follow her out. 'Oh, of course,' I say after she has walked a few steps. 'I know where to go now.' She nods and leaves me with a smile.

Back in my office, I take a few deep breaths, reminding myself that I need to be careful and not rush into things. I will meet Garth soon.

It's nearly lunchtime and I pick up my bag to leave. I have an hour, according to the manual, and I intend to use it to see my daughter.

She won't see me, but I need to see her.

I have not actually seen my daughter in the flesh since my trial six years ago.

I would like to get close enough to her to see if she's still wearing the same perfume she always wore. I would like to be able to touch her, even just by bumping into her, but I won't do that. Instead, I will keep my distance and I will just watch her.

Her office building is close to Garth's, so I have time to get there and wait to see if she leaves for lunch. She has only worked at her graphic design firm for the last few months, her first job since she graduated from her course. She is a very talented artist. As a teenager she would often design dresses for herself, and of course I had the means to pay a dressmaker to get them made for her. I am surprised that she has chosen the world of logos and adverts as a career but it is a safer space perhaps, not as subject to the vagaries of luck as fashion design would be. I imagine my daughter would seek out safety as much as possible after everything that happened and I will always carry a heavy burden of guilt for that. If she will only speak to me, I can change things for her. I would pay for her to open a design studio, to hire people to work for her. I would give her everything to make her happy but she doesn't want me in her life and I can't blame her. It doesn't mean I won't keep trying. Selling my company, Wax to the Max, my chain of waxing salons, for well below its market value was galling but I still have more than enough money to do whatever I choose to do with my life. And what I choose to do is to make sure my daughters are safe and happy and thriving.

It's just after 1 p.m. and I am standing on the pavement outside the café opposite the building where Cordelia works when I see her come out. I gasp, unable to help touching my chest. There she goes, my darling child. She looks around and then starts walking and I quickly cross the road to follow her at a discreet distance. She is wearing a light, black trench coat, belted tightly around her small waist, and her golden blonde hair is held back in a loose ponytail. She is so beautiful.

Images of her as a baby, a toddler and a young child come to me and I feel like I am looking at a stranger but at someone I know with every part of my body at the same time.

She stops in front of a sushi restaurant and goes in, emerging with a bag in her hand, and then she turns and starts walking back to her office. We used to share sushi dinners often before life changed. We would delight in trying new dishes, and even as a young child she was never squeamish around raw fish. She's an adventurous eater but sushi is a favourite, and I'm glad to see that something is still the same, that there is something, even something as simple as a mutual love of sushi, that connects us.

I had hoped she would eat in a nearby park or somewhere I could watch her, but the wind in the city is fierce and I don't blame her for wanting to be indoors. Like everyone in her generation, Cordelia walks with her head down, her eyes on her phone, occasionally shaking her head as she texts with her thumb.

There is something about her hunched posture, about the way she is texting, that makes me think she looks worried.

I drop back because I know where she's going, but as I do I see a man, tall and broad in a black leather jacket, his phone at his ear as he nods, and I notice that he is only a few people behind Cordelia, and when she stops to look at a dress in a shop window, he stops too. He looks quite young, but I can't tell much about him except that he has brown hair because of the sunglasses he's wearing. When she starts walking again, he does as well. He walks behind her right up to the door of her office building and then he crosses over the road to the café where I was going to sit. I watch him get a table right by the window. He takes off the glasses then smiles up at a waitress who comes to serve him. I can't tell if he's the same age as Cordelia or younger, but as I watch he looks out of the café window and I turn away.

It could be a coincidence but I don't think it is. That man is following Cordelia.

And I really need to know why.

FIVE

CORDELIA

Wednesday

'Harmer, Wright and Sing, how may I direct your call?'

'Yes, hi... um hello, could I please speak to Garth Stanford-Brown?'

'And who shall I say is calling?'

'It's Cordelia Morton, he'll know what it's about.'

She should be working on the logo for a sandwich shop but so far all she's managed to come up with is a smiling burger and that's definitely not what's needed, but exactly how many ways are there to sell a sandwich? Every morning, on her way into work, she pretends she's heading for her own design studio, stopping to study displays in clothing store windows if she has time, thinking about how she would change or improve the designs she sees. Arriving at her real work is always hard as she sits down and opens her computer to start her day. This is not the life she imagined for herself but then so little of her life is what she imagined – being in the wrong job is just one more thing.

It's hard to concentrate anyway. Garth has been gone for

two nights now, something he has done before, but he hasn't replied to any of her text messages, which is something he has never done before. He must be really angry with her.

Cordelia's messages to him have grown increasingly desperate, so desperate she feels embarrassed when she looks over them.

Please just call me and let me know you're okay.

I'm sorry I was so awful to you. I know you had to work. Just call me.

We can sort this out if you call me.

This is ridiculous, just call me, Garth.

What is wrong with you? Why would you be such an arsehole? Call me.

Please just call me.

Last night when she got home, the apartment was empty. But she imagined that he would be back late, probably sliding into bed after she was asleep. She had planned to not let him get away with his behaviour. She had a whole speech ready, and no matter how late he got back, she was going to give it to him, telling him that he was selfish and manipulative and rude. *You know my history and you know how much I worry about people I love and yet you chose to not reply to my messages. That's cruel.* She had even been able to see how he would look, to see how his handsome face would fall and he would apologise when he realised how upset she was.

But Garth did not come home last night, and at some point, well after midnight, Cordelia was unable to fight sleep anymore and she succumbed. And this morning, his side of the bed wasn't slept in. She leapt out of bed as soon as she realised, hoping to find him on the sofa or to at least find some evidence that he had been in the apartment. But the kitchen looked the same way she had left it, neat and tidy with the white marble surfaces wiped down. And there were no extra clothes in the laundry hamper either. Garth hadn't been home and he hadn't texted her.

I can't believe that you didn't come home again and that you didn't message me either. You are being such an absolute shit, Garth. I don't understand why you are treating me like this but you're not going to get away with being an arsehole forever. Don't be surprised if you get home and I am gone!!!!!

She'd imagined that text would get a response but he still didn't reply so she, much to her humiliation, returned to trying to placate him.

Look, I'm sorry. I was angry. I just need to know you're okay. Just send an emoji, anything. Please.

She didn't want to call his work, didn't want to give him the satisfaction, but now she just needs to know he's okay. And she wants him to admit what he's doing by not contacting her. Is he hoping that she will just move out? Just break up with him and leave? It's a dick move whatever way you look at it.

The hold music gets to the end of the instrumental and loops back to the start, and Cordelia realises she's been on hold for more than five minutes.

'I'm sorry,' comes the receptionist's voice. 'Mr Stanford-Brown is not in today. Can I take a message?'

'Oh... no, no, but um... can you put me through to Ian Chen?' she asks.

Ian is close to Garth. They both began working at the firm at the same time but Ian specialises in insurance cases. Cordelia likes Ian and his partner Mack, who are always fun to go out with. Unlike others in the firm, Ian always seems to be watching for when Cordelia grows bored with stories about the firm and their cases and he smoothly switches topics, asking Cordelia about her work or talking about binge-worthy television.

She hears the receptionist click her tongue at the new request but the hold music comes back and Cordelia looks around her office, checking if anyone is watching her. It's her lunch hour so she has every right to be on her phone, and there are only a few people at their desks. And no one is looking at Cordelia. She hasn't really exchanged more than work talk and a few mild remarks about weekends with anyone at work. She spends all weekend with Garth when he's home and she likes to be available during the week in case he finishes work at a reasonable time, so she has refused the one or two invitations for after-work drinks that she's received.

You are such a doormat.

She bats the thought away and picks up a pen, doodles on the paper in front of her while she waits.

'Cordelia,' she hears finally.

'Ian,' she says, relieved to have actually found someone to speak to and scrambling for what to say because 'my boyfriend refuses to talk to me' would sound ridiculous but how else could she explain to Ian why she needs to speak to him?

'It's um... look, I'm just going to be honest with you, Garth and I had a bit of a fight and he hasn't been home and I just need to know he's okay.' She feels herself flush, humiliated at having to do this, but she's struggling to do anything except worry about him – and if she knows he's okay, she can start thinking seriously about what to do.

'Um... yeah, well, we work on different floors and I haven't seen him but... let me go and see if I can get hold of him, okay?

I'll call you back or I'll get him to call you.' Ian speaks so kindly that Cordelia can't help a rush of tears that she quickly wipes away. Screw Garth for doing this to her – it's so manipulative and it's actually downright mean.

'Thanks so much, Ian, do you have my number?'

'Just a sec, let me grab a pen.' She gives Ian the number and they hang up.

She looks back at her computer screen, hoping for some inspiration about a sandwich, but her mind won't focus. She hates this stuff. She should be designing clothes, spending her day surrounded by soft fabrics in fabulous prints and colours, but this just felt easy and safe. All she really wants is to feel like one day will follow the next and there are no hideous surprises waiting around the corner.

A therapist she went to see for a few sessions told her she was stuck. 'You're still there, on that terrible morning, realising that your whole life has changed. You need to find a way to move forward,' he said.

Cordelia focused on his ears, where grey hair poked out, as she replied.

'My mother set fire to my home and killed my father. Then she went into a psychiatric facility because the state declared her just a bit mad and an alcoholic and therefore not really responsible for what happened. How exactly do you think I should move on?' She sounded like a petulant child, which was exactly the therapist's point.

'You'll move on when you're ready,' Cassie said when Cordelia told her about the session. 'Screw the old fart – what does he know?' So Cordelia stopped going to therapy, unwilling to confront what had happened every single time.

Her boss, Jacinta, walks through the office, purposeful strides and a large container of the same salad she buys every day in her hands. Cordelia leans forward and taps at her computer keypad, hoping that she won't be asked when the new logo will be ready, and mercifully, Jacinta goes into her office and closes the door.

She picks up her pen again, returning to her doodle that has become a design for a wedding dress as she thinks about Garth and the start of their relationship.

When she first met him, in a London pub, the best way she can describe how she was feeling is 'bruised'.

Her skin felt more sensitive to the air, as though someone had physically hurt her. She was exposed and vulnerable, depressed and sunk in grief as she mourned the loss of her father and the mother who she used to love and trust.

Once the trial was over, once her mother had been sentenced to a stay in a psychiatric facility over what she and her lawyer kept calling 'the accident', Cordelia had not known what else to do with herself – except run. There was no more house, no home to go to, no relatives she wanted to be with. She could have gone to stay with her mother's parents but even though she knew they loved her, they were difficult people, angry and sad all the time, judgemental of everyone and every-thing, even of Cordelia as she got older. *Why would such a pretty girl need to wear so much make-up? What do you mean you want to design clothes, that's not a job. You should come to church with us if your parents are not able to understand why it's so important. We hope you're not dating. You mother's whole life was upended by the wrong boy.*

Since she was fourteen, Cordelia had been visiting them on her own and stretching the time between visits as much as she could. Each time she'd gone, she'd had the feeling that her mother had just been waiting for Cordelia to tell her that her parents had asked about their own child, but they never had. Cordelia had sent them messages to keep in touch but she couldn't imagine living with them in the state she was in, pretty certain that they would both tell her she was better off without her mother. There was a lot of history between her mother and her parents, not all of which Cordelia knew. She'd imagined that her grief would only be compounded if she lived with them. She'd chosen to stay in a serviced apartment, rented for her by her mother's lawyer until the trial was over.

There had been no one she really wanted to speak to except her friends, and most of them had had little idea of what to say to her. *Sorry your mum killed your dad?* They don't make a card for that. The only thing she did have was enough money to leave the country. And so, when the trial had ended and she'd been free to go, she had run. Cassie was spending a year in the UK, travelling around and working in a pub to earn money. *Come over here*, she had texted. *You can share my grotty flat and I'll get you a job in the pub.*

Cordelia hadn't needed the money but she'd needed to do something, to feel something different when she woke up every morning.

And for a few weeks, it had been better. It was eight months after her father had died and London was heading into summer, the air getting warmer.

Cordelia had been to London before with her parents but never alone, tethered to no one and allowed to do whatever she pleased.

Everything was new and exciting and, most importantly, no one knew that she was the daughter of a woman who had set fire to her own house. She was just Cordelia Morton – or, 'Hello, love, can I get a pint?'

Perhaps the newspapers had carried the story when it first happened, but no matter how many people Cassie introduced her to, or how many people she met herself serving behind the pub counter, there was never even a flicker of recognition when she told them her name.

Not until the day that Garth walked into the pub.

It was the middle of August and London was in the grip of a heatwave, people struggling to deal with soaring temperatures.

Cordelia loved the heat so a thirty-four-degree day was perfect for her.

At lunch the pub was full of people, and both she and Cassie felt like they would never get through serving the queue of customers.

'Excuse me, miss,' she heard, the voice deep and perfectly English, and she looked up to see a tall man with sandy-blond hair and brown eyes, the tip of his nose red and sunburnt.

'Sorry, what can I get you?'

'Australian?' he asked with a beautiful smile.

And she smiled back and nodded, used to being asked the same question again and again. 'One of the chaps with us is Australian. We're sitting in the beer garden at the back. You should come and say hello when you have a moment. I think he's a bit homesick for the beach on a day like today.'

'I will if I get the chance,' Cordelia said, not expecting she would. 'Now what can I get you?'

He reeled off a list of drinks and she wrote them down so she could keep them all straight.

Half an hour later the pub emptied as everyone went, reluctantly, back to work and suddenly there was nothing for Cordelia to do as Cassie cleaned up. 'You can clock off now,' said Cassie. 'Go home or go and sit in the sun. I'm happy to finish up here and then I have a date with Paul,' she said, referring to her latest boyfriend. Cordelia didn't want to go home alone but she did want to enjoy the sunshine.

'Thanks. I'm absolutely starving. I may get some chips from Mick if he's willing to make them for me,' she said, referring to the chef in the kitchen.

'I think he already made you a plate and is keeping it warm. He knows what you like,' Cassie said with a laugh.

Cordelia poured herself a big glass of Diet Coke and filled it with ice, going through the kitchen to get her chips and thank Mick for making them. She had actually forgotten all about

Garth but she went to the beer garden to sit in the sun. As soon as she was outside, she heard someone call, 'Hey, hey, Australia, over here.'

It was the man with the sunburnt nose.

Stifling a sigh because she really wanted to sit quietly by herself, Cordelia made her way over to the table where she was introduced to Garth, another man named Liam, a woman named Susan and an Australian man named Gill.

She smiled politely, wondering how quickly she would be able to get away, certain that this group would have to head back to work soon even if they seemed to have all the time in the world.

'We're celebrating being made senior associates,' said Garth, 'and Gill is waiting for the right time to call his mum because he misses her and Australia, don't you, mate?'

Gill nodded. 'I haven't been surfing for months.' He looked like a surfer with blue eyes and scruffy blond hair.

'I'm not a surfer but I miss the beach,' said Cordelia.

The conversation turned to all the ways she and Gill missed Australia and then it became a comparison between the two countries – Tim Tams versus McVitie's, Christmas in the sun versus Christmas with snow, meat pie versus bangers and mash – with a lot of laughing and more drinks.

'Just Diet Coke for me,' Cordelia kept saying, even as those at the table moved on to wine and the sun dipped in the sky.

Finally, Gill said that he had to leave, and the others went with him but Garth stayed, talking to Cordelia about plans she and Cassie had to travel around Europe in a month's time. And when Garth asked for her number, she was happy to give it to him. When he asked for her surname – because, 'I like to have everyone's full name and I know two other Cordelias already' – she gave it to him without thinking. Later he confessed that he had never met a Cordelia before but wanted her surname so he could google her. As it turned out, he hadn't needed Google because he immediately recognised it.

'Cordelia Morton, Cordelia Morton,' he said, mulling over the name. 'You're not related to Grace Morton, are you?'

Cordelia felt her face colour, wanted to lie but she just shrugged. 'I am. She's my mother.'

'That must have been just awful for you, just awful,' he said with absolute sincerity, and Cordelia found herself, shockingly, in tears. Kindness was harder to bear than a raised eyebrow, a sideways glance or a whispered conversation – something that had happened often in Australia with people she didn't know very well.

'Hey, hey,' he said, coming around the table to sit next to her and putting his arm around her shoulders, wrapping her in his woodsy aftershave.

She got a hold of herself pretty quickly and he moved away. 'Sorry, I don't normally cry. I mean, I'm mostly done crying.'

'I wouldn't be,' he said. 'I would be an absolute mess. I think it's amazing that you're here and functioning. You're very brave.'

His words loosened something inside her and she was able to smile. Everyone, all her friends, the therapist, wanted her to put it all behind her. Even Cassie was getting tired of hearing the same story and Cordelia didn't blame her. It was nice to meet someone who understood that what had happened was impossible to move on from.

'Do you want to talk about it or should it just be something I never mention when I see you again?' he asked.

'How do you know you're going to see me again?' she said.

'Oh, I definitely am, Cordelia Morton, I definitely am,' he said as he offered her another perfect smile.

They were together from that day. On their first proper date, she found herself sharing things with him that she usually didn't share with anyone else. He was happy to listen, interested in who Cordelia's mother had been before the terrible year Grace had trashed all their lives with alcohol and a mad obsession over a cheating husband. He wanted to know all about her company and how she had built it, and some part of Cordelia enjoyed remembering her mother as the successful businesswoman and wonderful mother she had been before alcohol had taken hold of her life.

Cordelia was instantly smitten. No matter where she went or what she was doing in the UK or travelling around Europe, she always came home to Garth and he was always there for her, listening to her tales of visiting Scotland or Italy and happy to wait for her to come back. When she told him she wanted to go home, he excitedly shared that he had always wanted to work in Australia and his law firm had an exchange programme with its sister company there.

Cordelia thought they would be together forever, despite Garth's sometimes scathing humour and the age gap. He was her safe place, the person she could count on.

But now they are in this situation where she knows he's sleeping with someone and they fight all the time. She just can't leave him because he knows her, and he knows everything she went through, and she's afraid to be alone with only her thoughts and her questions about her life.

Her phone rings, startling her out of her thoughts as she drops the pen.

'Hello?'

'It's Ian.'

'Ian, hi, thanks for getting back to me. Did you see him?'

'Um, that's the thing, Cordelia. He wasn't there.'

'Oh.'

'And he hasn't actually been into the office for the last two days. No one knows where he is. He hasn't called or sent a message, nothing, and no one can get hold of him. He's just... gone.'

'Just gone?' she asks, confused.

'Yes, according to Natalie, he hasn't been in at all.'

'Natalie,' says Cordelia.

'Yes, you know, they work together, you've met her,' he says, sounding concerned.

'Yes, of course, yes, I have. I know Natalie.' If Natalie was also away from the office, it would have been an awful revelation, confirmation of the affair, but somehow the fact that the woman is there and has not seen Garth is more worrying.

'You haven't heard from him at all?' asks Ian.

'No... I haven't,' says Cordelia, and she feels the room swim a little as the whole carefully built tower of cards that is her life comes tumbling down.

SIX

GRACE

I am troubled by the man who may or may not be following Cordelia and I spend the night trying to convince myself that I'm being paranoid. It would be so easy to change my thinking if my gut wasn't involved, if my mother radar wasn't buzzing. But I know something is wrong, and I only get a few hours of sleep. The next morning, I am up early, my wig, glasses and a baggy black jacket in place as I stand outside the building where she lives with Garth.

I am hoping that she leaves promptly because I would hate to be late for my own job. It's fortunate that our buildings are so close together in the city and I wonder how often she and Garth meet for lunch or if they ever do.

I didn't see him yesterday, which I found a little strange as during the course of the day I came across most of the lawyers, learning that the firm is actually spread out over two floors. On the sixth floor there is a whole other suite of offices filled with lawyers in different teams. I am, I have also learned, not the only administration assistant but rather one of five. My role is just to deal with the day-to-day paperwork and other annoying little tasks that need to get done. I am different to the legal assistants, who actually have some knowledge of the law. It's easy enough work, and when I set up a plate with some pastries in the conference room for Joel, one of the partners, when he had a meeting with some clients, he barely acknowledged me, which suits me. I want to get in and out and find what I need, if there is anything to find at all. It's strange not directly working for one boss but that works in my favour as well.

Glancing at the time every minute or so, I wait until Cordelia comes out and then I wait a little longer, expecting or hoping that nothing will be out of place, but within moments of her leaving her building and heading towards the tram stop, there he is. The same man. This cannot be a coincidence. Is he a stalker, someone who follows her on social media who's developed a weird crush on her, or something else? Young women have to be so careful these days.

I follow behind him but it's hard because he seems to be very suspicious of everyone around him, stopping constantly to check his surroundings.

I keep my phone out, the camera open. If I get a chance, I'm going to snap a picture so I can try and work out exactly who this is. Aside from the fact that he's tall and has broad shoulders, there is little to distinguish this man from any other young man on the street.

I hop on the same tram she does but at the back, concealing myself in the crush of people on their way to work. I notice that the man gets on the tram too, but much closer to Cordelia.

Once Cordelia is safely inside her building, I keep following the man, sure that there will be an opportunity to snap a picture of him.

He turns down an alley and I am so intent on following him that I don't think about it, I just keep going, and it's only when I look up and see that I am actually trapped with no way out that I realise my mistake.

I turn quickly and start to leave but he is suddenly in front of me, looming over me.

'You're not following me, are you, ma'am?' he asks, his emphasis on the word 'ma'am' making me feel old. Looking at him now, I can see that he is probably the same age as Cordelia. He has bright blue eyes and he gives me a lazy, dimpled smile as he waits for me to answer.

I feel my heart in my throat because he may be young but he is much bigger than I am, and something about the way he is standing with his legs wide apart and his hands in his jacket pockets feels threatening. But before I can give in to panic, I quickly find Grace Enright, the survivor, inside me and scoff. 'No, I was lost. I'm looking for the Hilton hotel.'

'The what?' he asks.

'The hotel,' I say, my voice rising so that people walking past the alley can hear. 'Do you know where it is?'

'No, but then I can't afford the Hilton,' he says with a laugh and then he lingers for a moment, staring at me as I feel my body heat up inside the ridiculous jacket I am wearing to help conceal myself.

He turns and leaves and I know better than to try and snap a picture. There is something frightening about him and I'm not going to put myself in danger without knowing exactly who he is.

I arrive at the office just in time. 'Morning, Grace,' says the young man, Tristan, who sits behind the desk. 'Good night?'

'Quiet, thank you,' I reply. 'What about you?'

'In bed by nine,' he says and then he takes a call. The woman who works alongside him is Leah but we haven't actually had a conversation yet. People are friendly enough but everyone is busy with their own work.

In my office I open up my banking app, where I can still see Cordelia's credit card. She probably has no idea that something she gave permission for me to be able to access at seventeen is still available to me, something that I only realised after I downloaded it when I left the clinic. Once, I was the one paying off her card and so had a right to see where the money went, and she's never changed it. I have tried to avoid looking at it, not wanting to invade her privacy, but now I need to know if my daughter is in some kind of trouble.

I can see that she's fond of a coffee every morning from the same coffee shop, that she buys small amounts of groceries and that she, unusually, has recently paid an electricity bill. I assume it's for the apartment she's living in and I'm sure that she and Garth have their own arrangement but he should be making a lot of money. There is a trust fund for Cordelia but she doesn't have access to the funds until she turns twenty-five. Obviously, she has shared this information with Garth, something that bothers me because it's a lot of money. Has Garth known about the trust fund from the very beginning? Regardless, she has to live on her own wage for the moment, especially since she refuses to speak to me. I would give her money for everything she needed if she would speak to me.

I made sure she had money before I went to the clinic. But she was in the UK for some time and she also came home to study, not working while she did so. Surely on her junior designer wage, she doesn't have enough to be supporting herself and Garth in that very expensive apartment?

I scroll back further and find that the enormous rent on the apartment has also been paid by Cordelia on more than one occasion. I don't like this at all. Garth is a senior associate. Why is he making his much younger girlfriend pay rent?

This morning, I sent her a message, just like every day.

Good morning, darling. I hope you have a good day.

But she has not responded as she usually would, which is to tell me to stop contacting her.

I send another message.

Hello, darling. I just want you to know that I'm here for you if you need me. If you need anything at all. Please contact me.

This time, she replies.

I don't need anything. I don't need you. Stop contacting me, please, Mum.

I stare down at the message, rereading the last words: *Please, Mum.* She hasn't called me Mum for years. She certainly hasn't used the word 'please'.

Something is very, very wrong. I can feel it.

A mother knows. A mother always knows.

'I was asked to give you this,' I hear, pulling me out of my worries, and I look up, pushing my phone to the side. A pretty young woman with her black hair in a pixie cut is standing in the doorway holding a file filled with papers.

I stand up, holding out my hand to take the file, which she gives me.

'I don't think we've met,' I say. 'I'm Grace, the temporary assistant.'

'Kelsey,' she says, smiling. 'I'm just here for a summer internship, although that ended a week ago but I don't have university every day and my dad wants me here whenever I can be. My dad's one of the partners, Joel.'

'Thank you,' I say, assuming she will leave the office, but she stands studying me so I attempt a conversation even though I have no desire for one.

'And are you enjoying it?' I ask politely, and her brown eyes darken.

'No, my dad wants me to be a lawyer... but I have my own plans.' She shrugs and then she turns and leaves, and I sit down, opening up the folder filled with client meetings in the conference room that I obviously need to make sure are all scheduled correctly. I am longing to somehow force Cordelia to talk to me but I find the right screen on my computer and get to work.

At lunchtime, I grab myself some sushi and make my way to Cordelia's building, hoping to catch a glimpse of her and to see if the man is still following her. I position myself on a bench across the road from her building and wait but she doesn't leave for lunch. I am disappointed as I eat my sushi but also glad that I can't see the man loitering in front of her building waiting for her to come out as well.

It's possible that I may have just imagined that he was following Cordelia. He could just be someone who lives in the area and leaves the same time she does and also works in the city. I shake my head as I remember how I would do this after I first discovered my husband had slept with my assistant. On its own, a text on her phone should not have made me jump to the conclusion that they were sleeping with each other, and sometimes in the middle of the night, as the alcohol started to wear off, I would try and add logic to the situation. *Perhaps her boyfriend calls her his 'sunshine girl' as well. Maybe I have this all wrong and it's just the alcohol. Maybe this is all my fault and I'm just paranoid.*

But first instincts are usually the best instincts and I should have just trusted those from the very beginning. Grace Morton questioned herself. But Grace Enright trusts herself. The man is following my daughter and I need to find out why.

My lunch hour ticks away but I don't move, craving a glimpse of Cordelia.

When someone sits down next to me on the bench, I don't move. I don't even look to see who it is in case I miss Cordelia coming out.

'What are you waiting for?' I hear a voice ask, and I am forced to turn away from the building.

'I'm...' I begin and then I see who it is, instantly cursing my stupidity for not finding a way to conceal myself. I have been watching Cordelia's building, waiting for my daughter and waiting to see if he is there, and at the same time, he has been watching me.

I know I could just get up and walk away. There are lots of people on the street and he probably wouldn't follow me. But I need to know exactly who I am dealing with here.

'What do you want?' I ask.

'Me?' he says with a shrug. 'So many things, Grace – you don't mind if I call you Grace, do you? Nice disguise, by the way.' He smiles. His teeth are perfectly white. 'I want to stay at the Hilton hotel for one thing. But just right now it's out of my reach; won't be for long, though. You ask Cordelia when you see her, ask her about her man and what she should be doing right now, what needs to happen to keep everyone's lives humming along nicely.'

He offers me another lazy smile. I have no idea what he's talking about, no idea how he's recognised me and how he knows I'm connected to Cordelia. What does he want Cordelia to do? What does he think she should be doing?

He stands and steps right in front of me. 'Go ahead, take your little picture,' he says, gesturing at the phone I am holding in my hand. 'I have no secrets.'

I lift my phone to snap a picture so I can try and figure out who he is, but as I do, he grabs it from my hands, turns it around and snaps a picture of me, and then he throws the phone back at me when he's done. I don't catch it and it lands on the ground, where I quickly bend to retrieve it. When I sit up again, he's casually sauntering away.

I am wearing a wig and the glasses and an oversized jacket but he has seen easily through my disguise to the woman I am trying to hide. He knows who I am and who Cordelia is.

He obviously knew I was following him this morning. Even without my wig and glasses, I am unrecognisable from who I was before. So how does he know who I am? How is it possible that he has recognised me as Grace, Cordelia's mother?

I look at the picture he has taken of me with my phone, noticing a small chip on the glass screen that I touch with my thumb, feeling the rough edges. In the picture I am startled, my eyes wide with shock and some fear. I hate the way I look. I hate that he has taken me by surprise, whoever he is.

Inside my jacket, I can feel my whole body shaking. The air is warm enough and I'm not cold at all but I am afraid. I bite down on my lip as anger grows inside me. How dare he threaten me? How dare he threaten my daughter? He has no idea who he's dealing with. No idea at all.

Before I return to my office to get to work on what seems to be endless timesheets, I knock on Garth's office door again and, receiving no reply, I open it after a quick look around me. If Natalie catches me here a second time, she will not so easily buy my excuse.

His office is dark, the same notebook on his desk. Nothing has been touched or moved. I find that very odd. I step inside and move around his desk, opening the top drawers that are filled with stationery. I don't have time to search properly. I can hear people talking, their voices getting louder as they get closer. I need to get out of here and I move quickly, but as I do, I step on something lying just under Garth's desk. Leaning down,

I feel around with my hand because it's too dark to see what I've just stepped on.

I pick it up and realise, even in the dim light, that it's an earring. Clenching my fist with the earring inside, I take it back to my office and study it.

I have no idea how long it's been lying on Garth's office floor but it looks quite expensive, and it's very pretty with a small cluster of diamonds surrounding a tiny sapphire.

I wonder who it belongs to as I place it on my desk where it can be seen. And I wonder who exactly will claim it and what that will tell me about Garth.

Returning to my work, I bury myself in timesheets, in which all the clever lawyers in the firm have a tendency to make a lot of mistakes.

My mind keeps wandering back to my encounter with the young man; everything he said runs on a loop through my head as I dissect every word, searching for clues as to who he is. What should Cordelia be doing and what will happen if she doesn't do it? Exactly what is going on with my child?

Every terrible scenario runs through my head as I think about what Cordelia could be involved with. I remember her testifying at my trial. She looked so lost, so despairing. What might a person who feels that way do? What might she get herself into?

SEVEN

CORDELIA

Wednesday

Even though she knows that Garth hasn't been to work, she is still hopeful when she gets home that he might be there, that he will simply be in the kitchen, mixing up a drink. Maybe he needed some time off? He has been working very hard according to everything he's been saying. Could he have had some kind of mental breakdown, leading him to just need a few days away? But he texted her on Monday night and said he had to work late. He was lying. He hadn't been to work at all. So where was he? Where is he?

She is angry with herself over all the text messages she sent him. She is just like her mother: paranoid for no reason. Maybe something was really wrong and Garth didn't feel he could talk to her. She is a horrible person.

The apartment is dark, the air slightly chilly because the evenings are growing colder. She turns on all the lights and the television, just needing some sound.

Garth has not been to work and he has not been home. She

simply hung up once Ian told her, panic taking over her body. What was she supposed to do?

Somehow, she managed to get through most of the rest of the day, telling Jacinta she felt sick and leaving at 4 p.m., just walking into the autumn air with no clear plan. She wandered around the city, looking in dress shop windows and checking her phone constantly until the sun dipped and she got too cold to be outside anymore.

She makes herself a cup of tea and sits on the sofa after kicking off her shoes, grabbing a soft orange furry blanket to cover herself.

Where are you?

She texts Garth and she doesn't expect a reply so when her phone rings she nearly drops it, relief rushing through her body at the idea that this will be Garth.

But it's not Garth; rather, it's his mother, Evangeline.

'Hello,' she answers. Evangeline and Cordelia have only spoken on the phone a couple of times, and both of those times, it was only because Evangeline couldn't get hold of Garth.

'Cordelia,' says Evangeline, her tone clipped and her irritation obvious.

'Hi Evangeline,' she responds.

'What on earth is going on over there?'

Cordelia can picture Garth's mother in her expansive living room, staring out of a window at mist-covered grounds. It's morning in the UK and Evangeline has probably just returned from walking the dogs, two golden retrievers who are friendly and sweet.

Evangeline is not friendly or sweet but tall and rail-thin with bobbed brown hair and a fondness for tweed trousers. She shares Garth's brown eyes but her face is all angles and her lips permanently pursed in distaste.

On the few occasions she has met Cordelia, she has made her disdain for Cordelia's lack of education, *oh, an art degree*, her age, *you're terribly young aren't you*, and her family, *I am so sorry about all that terrible mess with your family, dear*, completely obvious. Cordelia walked around the large cold house, terrified to touch anything and hoping to just get through the weekend visit without upsetting Garth's mother.

Evangeline was against Garth coming to Australia since he had a wonderful future in the UK, and while the woman stopped short of calling Cordelia 'a whore who stole my son', it was implied in every conversation, especially ones where Garth's ex-girlfriend, Katherine, was discussed. *She was just such a lovely, easy-going young woman, but you can't choose your children's partners, can you, darling? Of course, if you and Katherine had stayed together, there would be none of this running off to the colonies nonsense. Now Katherine did a degree in law as well, didn't she, darling? She was your equal in every way. I believe she's doing splendidly in a large firm in London. Her mother and I catch up for a cup of tea at least once a month but then Emma and I always did get on so well. Perhaps I could meet your mother, Cordelia, when she's over her... difficulties.*

'I'm not quite sure what you mean,' Cordelia says now in reply to Evangeline's question.

'Well, allow me to explain, my dear. Garth phones me every single day at 7 a.m. your time. Since he left me to come and live down there at the bottom of the world, he has not missed a day.'

Cordelia doesn't doubt that. At seven every morning, Garth is on the treadmill in his study. He hates to be interrupted during his workout and he is always on the phone.

But not for the last two mornings. Was he on the treadmill on Monday? Cordelia is usually asleep when he is. She didn't hear him leave on Monday.

She remembers feeling him getting into bed very late on Sunday night and there was evidence of his being in the apartment on Monday morning. He had, as usual, left a half-drunk cup of coffee in the sink. Was the coffee from Monday morning or Sunday night? And had she actually felt him get into bed or just imagined it because his side of the bed was rumpled from their Sunday afternoon nap?

'Oh,' says Cordelia, unsure what Evangeline is expecting her to say.

'He has not contacted me for three days now. So, I repeat the question, what is going on down there?'

Cordelia files away the knowledge that Garth didn't phone his mother on Monday either, something that is very out of character for him. He always calls his 'mummy'. Perhaps he was in a rush and decided to forgo his workout. But in a rush to get to where? Ian said he hadn't been in at all. Cordelia curls up tighter under the blanket, shivering.

'I don't know,' she says. 'He hasn't been home.'

'So where is he?'

'I have no idea. He hasn't been at work either.' Cordelia feels her hand tremble, nearly spilling her cup of tea, and she leans forward and places it carefully on the coffee table, hearing Garth's voice, *Use a coaster, Cordy*, even as she does so.

'What? That's ridiculous. Garth would never miss work.'

'I know,' says Cordelia, gritting her teeth. 'I don't know where he is.'

There is a minute of silence and then Evangeline clears her throat and lowers her voice as she says, 'I know you've accused my boy of cheating and I know what that mad mother of yours did to your father, and let me tell you, Cordelia Morton, if anything has happened to my son, you will surely suffer for it.' And then she hangs up the phone.

Cordelia cannot even process what has happened.

If Garth has not contacted his mother, something is terribly wrong. Should she report him missing? Is that what needs to be done? What if he's just staying away from her? He would be furious.

But he wouldn't miss work. Work is everything. And he wouldn't miss calling his mother. She made such a fuss about them leaving her to die without her only son that he will always carry guilt about leaving. But Cordelia knows that he was also anxious to put some distance between himself and his mother, who can be very demanding. A phone call every day is over the top but, as Garth explained, 'It means that I don't have to hear about how I've neglected her, and I enjoy talking to her, so why not? It's only ten or fifteen minutes and then we both get on with our lives.'

Picking up her phone, she googles, *What do I do if I think someone is missing?*

According to the internet, she doesn't have to wait twenty-four hours, she can simply go into any police station and report Garth as missing, but reports will not be taken over the phone or by email. It's been way more than twenty-four hours anyway.

She looks outside, where there's still some end-of-summer light left but storm clouds are gathering. She knows that the wind outside will be fierce.

It's late, but she has no choice. The nearest police station is only a block away, so there's no point in taking her car. She barely uses it anyway because they are surrounded by shops and restaurants and it's easier to get into work on the tram because parking in the city is always impossible.

Grabbing her jacket, Cordelia sets off for the police station.

She walks with her head down against the wind, pushing forward without looking at anyone as she rehearses exactly what she's going to say.

Should she tell them about the fight? Will they ask to see her phone? Maybe she should delete the messages, but then can't they find them anyway? Shaking her head, she looks up and realises that she's in front of the police station. *I haven't done anything wrong*, she reminds herself.

Pushing open the front door, she finds herself in the reception area where all is quiet, only a woman in uniform standing behind the counter.

'Going to be a big storm,' she says as a greeting, and Cordelia nods, shrugging off her jacket.

'What can I help you with?' the woman asks as Cordelia approaches the counter, and suddenly this is all very real. Garth is missing. He is actually missing. Maybe he's been in an accident or had a heart attack, even though he's too young for a heart attack. She should have done this days ago. Why did she wait so long? She's a dreadful person.

'My boyfriend is...' she begins and then she is crying and the policewoman is handing her tissues.

'Take your time,' she keeps saying, 'take your time.'

Finally, Cordelia gets a hold of herself and explains.

The policewoman takes notes, nodding her head.

'And have you contacted any of his other friends? Even those in the UK?'

'No, I mean, if he hasn't talked to his mother or been into work...'

'And you have no idea of any reason why he might have just... left of his own accord?'

'No... I mean, we had a fight and... I think he's seeing another woman and...'

'Right, right,' says the policewoman, nodding, and Cordelia can see that all the pieces are falling into place.

'But he's left everything he owns and he wouldn't... miss work... or not call his mother,' she repeats as she scrunches up yet another tissue and shoves it into her pocket.

'Okay, and how has he been lately? Has he seemed like himself?'

'He's... yes.'

'And there's no history of mental illness or anything like that?'

'I don't know, really. It's never come up.' Has it ever come up? She searches her mind for any mention of anything like that but Garth rarely discusses his family outside of his mother. He has an older sister who lives in London but Arabella and Garth seem to lead largely separate lives. Arabella looks like her mother, tall and thin, but she has been lovely to Cordelia on the few occasions they have met. She has twin boys who are both at boarding school and she's married to a heart surgeon. She doesn't actually have a job, but rather serves on a lot of charity boards. Cordelia always finds herself searching for things to say to her, since they have very little in common. Garth has a cousin who lives here but they aren't close at all, and Cordelia's only met him once so she would be uncomfortable contacting him. But maybe she should? Does she even have his number?

'Never come up?' asks the policewoman, pulling Cordelia back to the conversation.

'No... it's just, not something we've discussed. He's very... British,' she says, hoping that this is somehow an explanation for why they have not had this kind of discussion. Garth is very reserved, and even now she is still hearing things about his childhood for the first time, like about getting beaten up at boarding school. Garth didn't delve into the emotion of that experience but rather brushed over it with bravado and a quick laugh: 'I deserved it. I had a very smart mouth.' And in truth, Cordelia appreciated that. By the time she met him, she felt she had been mired in an endless emotional rumination about her life for years. It was a relief to be with someone who just waved away an experience or chalked it up to 'lesson learned'. It felt like a much easier way to be in the world.

'But you've been together how long?'

'Four and a half years,' says Cordelia. It's the second time the policewoman has asked the question.

'Okay, leave it with me. I have your number. I'll check the hospitals and everywhere else.'

'And you'll call me if you find anything out?' asks Cordelia desperately.

'I will, absolutely, I will,' the policewoman says, and there is nothing left for Cordelia to do but leave.

By the time she gets home, Cordelia is exhausted and dealing with a pounding headache.

She heads for the fridge, grabbing a tub of peanut butter chocolate ice cream. Her eyes fall on the knife block on the counter and she reminds herself to ask Garth where the missing knife is. It's been missing for a few days, or maybe longer than that? She can't remember but she will ask him about it when he comes home.

When will he come home? Will he come home?

She can't bear thinking about it anymore. Taking the ice cream to the sofa, she turns on the television. Slumped under a blanket, she watches sitcom reruns for hours as she finishes the ice cream and then a bag of crisps and a chocolate bar. She eats without thinking, without tasting, simply moving her hand to her mouth, the same way she imagines her mother used to drink.

She remembers watching her mother once from the doorway of the living room. She had just come home from a late-night study session at the library and Cassie's mother had dropped her off. Cordelia had been about to greet her mother when she just stopped and watched her, watched the glass of wine going to her mouth and down again so quickly that it was done in less than a minute. And the worst thing was the way her mother was muttering, even as she watched the news on television, 'I know what I know. Don't tell me what I'm supposed to think. Bastard, bastard, bastard. You should both rot in hell.'

Cordelia left then, scampering up to her room and shutting the door. During her mother's trial, she kept that particular incident to herself, even though it painted her mother as crazy, like Janine, her mother's lawyer, wanted her to be.

Cordelia hates that memory and she shakes it away as she takes another bite of the chocolate bar, crunching through nuts and sticky caramel.

Every few minutes she lifts up her phone and looks at the screen, convinced that she may have somehow missed a call from the police.

She doesn't try Garth again.

Something tells her there is no reason to do that.

The next day she calls in sick for work.

And she's not in the least surprised when the detectives knock on her door. Not in the least.

EIGHT

GRACE

Thursday

Last night I went to Cordelia's apartment building after work and stood outside for an hour, debating with myself over whether to just ring her bell and demand to be let in. But I was conscious, the whole time, that it was possible that she would just send me away.

I am scared for my child, and last night I allowed myself more than one glass of wine, desperate to be able to let go of my worry for a bit. I need to stay away from alcohol for a few days now, if only to prove to myself that I can.

If I had a picture of the man, I would be able to google his image and try to find out who he is, but I have nothing, and until I talk to Cordelia, I am stuck, not knowing what to do. None of what he said makes any sense to me.

In the morning, I send Cordelia my usual message and get no reply from her so I go to her apartment building, where I once again wait outside. I have gone back through her credit card history over the last four years and have started to see that, in the last five months, she's been paying for a lot of things in the apartment. She also pays for dinners out and has paid for an expensive weekend in the country even though she has only been working full time for a few months. I am beginning to get a picture of the kind of man Garth is, when it comes to money at least. I was aware that he was a flirt, and very full of himself from his Instagram posts, but this is something different.

If he had no idea who Cordelia was when he met her, he must certainly have learned soon enough that she comes from money. He's a lawyer and it would not take much for him to find out exactly how much I got for selling my company.

Last night I looked up his family, who seem wealthy, but I studied their big house in the countryside on Google Maps and then found it on a heritage site. It's old and badly in need of repair. Perhaps Garth assumed that Cordelia has access to her trust fund already. Or he assumes that she will have access to many millions soon enough.

Is this some con man playing the long game?

It's a hideous thought. And what does the man who spoke to me have to do with the two of them?

Looking at the time on my phone, I see that Cordelia is late. She'll miss her tram if she doesn't come out soon. And I will be late for work.

She lives in a busy building and there are people in and out all the time, but when she hasn't come out for another ten minutes, I begin to debate with myself about going in, just going in and knocking on her door.

And then, from around the side of the building, the man in the leather jacket appears, the scary young man who knows my name and Cordelia's name. I am standing near a wall and I feel myself shrink back, not wanting him to see me. But I take out my phone, lifting it up and holding it as steady as my trembling hands will allow. I snap away, taking as many pictures as I can, hoping that he won't notice me and praying that one of them will be clear enough for me to search for him on the internet.

He paces up and down in front of the building as though he is waiting for her to come out as well.

And then another car stops and two people climb out – a man and a woman, badges on lanyards around their necks – and the man in the leather jacket stops pacing. He moves his phone away from his ear and shakes his head as he walks away quickly.

The two people now walking into Cordelia's building are very obviously the police. Detectives.

I pull at the zip of my jacket, needing some fresh air on my skin as I remember my interview with detectives after the fire. I was in a hospital bed at the time, hooked up to an IV as I detoxed from alcohol, my body sweating and shaking.

They charged me as I lay in bed, reading me my rights as I leaned forward to grab a bowl so I could throw up.

I am so far from that struggling, pathetic woman now, and yet as I stand watching the entrance to Cordelia's building, I realise that I would give anything for a drink. That delicious cool burn of vodka or the sensual mouthful of a good wine would make everything disappear for just a moment. Instead, I can only stand here, worrying about everything that could possibly have gone wrong in her life.

A lot of people live in the building so perhaps the police have nothing to do with her. But somehow, I feel that's not the case. And when I look to see where the man in the leather jacket is, he has disappeared.

Whatever fears I held for my daughter are now magnified.

And I am not really sure what I do now.

I have no choice but to leave. I am running late so I hail a cab and get driven to work so that I will be there on time.

In the lobby, I glance in the mirror, checking that my wig is on straight.

The office seems to be busier when I get upstairs. Usually, I don't see anyone until they begin making themselves coffee later in the morning, but as the elevator doors open, I see Tristan speaking to another man who is leaning over the desk.

'Good morning,' I say to Tristan, who nods and smiles.

'Oh, Grace,' he says, 'this is Max, who works in medical negligence along with Natalie and Garth.'

Max is a nice-looking man, tall and very thin with a neat beard. He holds out a hand to shake mine. 'Sorry, I don't think we've met, you sorted out my timesheet for me.'

'Hello,' I reply, taking his hand. 'Yes, it was just a small error.' This is Max Blum, who somehow had himself down for fifteen billable hours on one day and zero on another. 'I feel like I've met everyone through their timesheets,' I add, 'except Garth Stanford-Brown. I was going to ask you to introduce me because I haven't seen anything from him,' I say to Tristan.

'Well,' says Tristan, and then he looks at Leah, who is busy on a call, 'Garth actually hasn't been in this week.'

'Oh, right,' I say. 'Is he away?'

'No,' says Tristan, and Max raises his eyebrows at me.

'We haven't seen him,' says Max. 'It's a bit strange, to be honest. No one has seen him. And we can't actually get hold of him.'

I realise that this is why the office seems buzzier than usual. People are standing in groups talking and they must be talking about Garth. It's not possible to not be able to get hold of someone these days, not unless they really don't want you to. I feel my body break out in a light sweat. Where is Garth? Is Cordelia even in her apartment? What is going on?

'Anyway, nothing for you to worry about,' says Tristan, and I get the feeling that my being new and only temporary means that I am not to be included in the discussion about what may have happened to Garth.

Kelsey walks past reception and Max straightens up and steps away from the desk, moving a finger across his lips to Tristan, telling him to keep quiet. Kelsey scowls at us and then walks away.

'I imagine this can't be good for the firm,' I say, looking for any other information that might help me to understand what's happened here.

'No,' agrees Max, who leaves the desk, and Tristan bends his head back to his work.

I am grateful to get away anyway, needing the peace of an office with a closed door so that I can calm my racing heart. Garth hasn't been into work? No one can get hold of him? Does Cordelia know where he is?

Taking out my phone, I go through all the pictures I have of the man and use one that has his profile from the side in an image search, but nothing comes up. Irritated, I throw my phone down on my desk, wishing that my daughter was not so stubborn, that she would just talk to me so that I could help her with whatever is going on.

I pick up my phone and text her again.

I hope you're okay, darling. I am here if you need me.

She doesn't reply, which is of no comfort. Even her usual angry text would have made me feel better.

She may be in more trouble than I thought. Do the people in the office know about his relationship with Cordelia, and if so, have they contacted her to ask about Garth? Do people do that? The man in the jacket, Garth missing, and the fact that she didn't go to work today all swirl in my mind as I try to concentrate on work. Did Garth leave first and Cordelia has gone to meet him now? Is my daughter still in the country?

I open the banking app and check to see if she's bought a plane ticket – or tickets – but there's nothing new.

Every now and again I glance at the picture of the woman whose position I am covering and envy her, her holiday, wherever it is. She feels very familiar to me now after seeing her all day as I work here. I can't seem to keep myself on track because I am agitated and craving a drink but I will have to settle for a coffee, which I know will do nothing to calm my nerves. I open my office door just as Natalie is walking past with Max. I don't want to speak to anyone so I quickly close it almost all the way and wait for them to go into their offices, but not before I hear Max say, 'It's going to come out, you know. It's better if you tell them first.'

'Not a chance,' says Natalie. 'There's no way I'm going to say one word. Maybe this has nothing to do with that night. I'm keeping my mouth shut until I know what's what.'

I freeze right where I am, straining to hear if they say anything else at all, but all I hear is the sound of an office door closing, and when I pull open my door, the corridor is empty.

I make my way to the kitchen, where I make a strong cup of coffee. What were they talking about? A client? Garth? It seems logical that it was Garth. The mystery of his disappearance seems to be hanging in the air in the office. I can almost feel people speculating about it.

What is Natalie keeping a secret and what does it have to do with my daughter's boyfriend?

NINE

CORDELIA

After calling in sick, she gets up and dresses in a tracksuit, determined to go through Garth's things, determined to find something that will tell her where he is and why he hasn't come home. She knows he would be furious if he caught her.

When they moved in together, after he found the apartment, he was very clear with her that she should not touch any of his boxes. 'I'll do my stuff, just leave it all.' Cordelia had hated the apartment on sight. It was too cold, all angles and glass with polished concrete floors, and too high up, making her feel weird when she stood too close to the edge of the balcony. 'The railing isn't very high – it would be so easy to fall over it,' she said to Garth.

'Don't be such a child, Cordy,' he responded and so she kept quiet about her other complaints about the apartment. Garth loved it and she loved Garth and she wanted to live with him.

Perhaps looking through his things is childish and certainly an invasion of his privacy but he's not here to complain. She starts with his bedside table, sliding open the drawer and looking down at the neat arrangement of dental floss, the same detective fiction novel he's had for over a year already because he always scrolls through his phone when he has time, a collection of pictures featuring his mother, his late father, the dogs and his home, a mobile phone charger and some hand cream because he always complains that his skin is dried out by the Australian weather. She lifts up the photos and pages through them but there is nothing out of the ordinary.

Underneath the pictures is an overdue tax bill from the UK from last month. She stares down at it. Why didn't he pay that?

His bedside table drawer is so different to Cordelia's, in which she has a collection of different creams from hotels, keychains given to her by her friends over the years, two novels, both of which she is reading, make-up samples that she has collected and so many other things. Since the fire she has a hard time of letting go of anything, finding herself holding on to everything, from half-empty tubes of cream to generic birthday cards from stores she likes to shop in. So much was taken from her that night that she feels like she has to collect more stuff than most people so she has something to show for her life. It's ridiculous and means her cupboards and drawers are always a mess but she can't seem to stop herself.

Would Garth have left without the stuff in his drawer? Maybe not the pictures. She checks his closet as well but his identical white shirts and navy blue suits are lined up perfectly. Nothing is missing except for the clothes he was wearing when he left the apartment on Monday morning or Sunday night. Because she suddenly remembers he *did* go into work on Sunday night. He went in despite her being angry about that. She sits back on her haunches, going over that night, the memory returning in a flash.

Chinese takeaway on a Sunday night was a tradition of theirs and they had ordered from their favourite little restaurant just a few steps away from their building.

They were watching television as they ate. The story on television was about a football player, and Cordelia can't even remember his name because in truth they were both on their phones and she wasn't even paying attention, but then she put down her phone. 'Should we find a real movie to watch?' she asked Garth and he shook his head.

'I want to see what's happened to him now.'

'Why do you care? You don't even like football,' she said and Garth shook his head again.

'That bastard and his drug problem cost me thousands.'

He didn't seem upset, not really, but she was shocked at the mention of the word 'thousands'.

'Did you bet on a game he was playing in or something?' she asked him.

'Something like that,' he said.

'Well, gambling is stupid and you deserved to lose money if you're betting thousands. I hope you don't do it again.'

'Cordelia,' said Garth, standing up, 'don't lecture me like I'm a child.'

'Well, if you're spending money on silly things and asking me to pay the rent, then I have a right to say something,' she sniped, regretting it because she knew that the whole weekend would end with a fight and that it would feel like it had spoiled everything. They had so little time together as it was.

'Oh, please,' he said. 'I pay for way more stuff than you do and you'll have millions from your mother one day very soon when that trust fund kicks in.'

'I don't even know if I want to take money from that. I don't want any of my mother's money. I don't know if I will ever speak to her again,' she replied, and she knows she was ashamed of how hot her eyes grew as tears threatened.

'How nice to have the luxury of just refusing money,' he sneered and Cordelia burst into tears.

She remembers now how quickly Garth changed tack,

immediately comforting her. She thought the night could be rescued, but only half an hour later he got a text that he said was from work.

'I have to go to the office quickly and help Natalie with something,' he said before changing into work clothes, something she found odd but no odder than the idea that he had to go to work on a Sunday night. He even put on aftershave.

'Really? On a Sunday night? Just how stupid do you think I am?' she asked him and he sighed.

'I'm not doing this now. I need to go. I'll be back soon.' He dropped a kiss on her head before she could say anything else and left.

She was asleep by the time he got back. Had he even come home at all or did she just imagine the feeling of him climbing into bed?

Was he even here on Monday morning? She reminds herself of the coffee cup in the sink, but she hadn't cleaned the kitchen on Sunday night, instead going to bed in a huff after he went into work. The coffee cup could have been from Sunday afternoon. He texted on Monday night that he was working late, although that was an outright lie.

Cordelia moves to the bathroom, where Garth's shaving cream and aftershave sit next to his electric toothbrush, all things that could easily be bought again, but why leave without them? Garth wouldn't waste money on a whole new wardrobe. He is always questioning her spending habits, asking her if she *really* needs another pair of shoes. He wouldn't just leave and buy everything new. She checks the laundry hamper again. Garth put on a white shirt to go to work on Sunday night. He never wears his white shirts more than once but there's no white shirt in the hamper. *Did you come home on Sunday night? How long have you been missing?*

The intercom buzzes, startling her so she jumps. The sound makes her heart skip because perhaps it's Garth and he lost his keys; maybe he's been on some sort of drunken bender for a few days or he's been with another woman. She doesn't care right now as she hastily smooths her hair back, conscious that she's not wearing any make-up.

She runs for the intercom and presses the buzzer. 'Yes?' she says, sounding a little breathless.

'Ms Morton?' a woman says.

'Yes,' answers Cordelia, disappointment making her sag.

'My name is Detective Ashton and I'm with the department of missing persons. I'm here about Garth Stanford-Brown.'

'Oh,' says Cordelia.

'Would it be okay if we came up and just had a chat with you?'

Cordelia's hand trembles as she pushes the button to allow the police into the building and then she stands by the door waiting for them to knock. This isn't what she wanted. She wanted a call to say they had found him and everything was fine. Maybe he's in the hospital with something that will mend like a broken arm or something but then why didn't he call her? This isn't what she wanted but she's not surprised. This was coming, of course it was coming.

The knock at the door is rapid and loud, conveying authority, and Cordelia pulls the heavy door open quickly.

'Ms Morton,' says a woman, and Cordelia nods.

'Come in,' she says, stepping back and allowing the woman and a large balding man into the apartment. They are both dressed in suits – the woman's black, the man's an unattractive brown – that look like they may have come from the same store. Cordelia wonders if it's some kind of uniform.

'Can I offer you some coffee?' she says, clearing her throat because she's not sure what to do. Don't people on television offer the detectives coffee?

After her father died, she spent a lot of time with detectives but then it was two women and they were so kind, offering tea and tissues as Cordelia cried and tried to talk about what life had been like before the fire. Then she was supported by her mother's fierce lawyer, Janine Saunders, a woman who seemed able to stop a line of questioning with only a look. Janine sat next to Cordelia, dressed in chic dresses with tight jackets, her hair neatly wound in a bun. 'You tell them all about your mother's drinking, Cordelia, don't hold anything back,' she instructed each time Cordelia was required to talk to the police. 'Your mother is an alcoholic and suffering from delusions induced by her abuse of alcohol and they need to know that.'

'Please don't talk about her like that,' Cordelia said once.

'I will talk about her in a way that saves her from prison, Cordelia, remember that.'

She has a moment of wishing that Janine was standing here right now. Janine would know what to say and do. Why did she offer them coffee?

'Nothing to drink, thank you. As I said before, I'm Detective Ashton and this is my partner, Detective Jameson. We're from the department of missing persons. We're here to talk about Garth.'

Cordelia nods. 'Can I just use the bathroom?' she says, her gaze on the balcony door, wishing she could simply open it and escape. But they are sixteen floors up. There is no escape.

'Of course,' says Detective Ashton.

In the bathroom, Cordelia sits down on the edge of the tub and takes out her phone. She never wanted to do this, never wanted to have to do this, but she has nowhere else to turn. She has no one else to ask for help. Cassie is still in the UK, and her friends in Sydney wouldn't understand, and she barely speaks to them anymore except online.

She types a text but doesn't send it because maybe, just maybe, she won't have to send it. And then she washes her hands. 'Time to face it,' she tells herself in the mirror.

She has no choice now.

Back in the living room, the detectives are standing awkwardly next to the white leather sofa. Cordelia hates the colour, is always terrified of staining it with something, but once again, it was Garth's choice.

'Please sit down,' says Cordelia.

Detective Ashton does and then she looks expectantly up at Cordelia, and Cordelia sits down as well.

'I know you reported Garth missing last night and I should let you know that his mother also reported him missing.'

Of course Evangeline called the police. She probably called half of Australia demanding that someone find her son. Garth comes from a family that used to have money and position in society. Now they are struggling to hold on to their large old home but Evangeline still thinks she is entitled to special treatment from the whole world.

'Oh,' says Cordelia, instantly cursing her stupid response.

'Yes. And at this point I should let you know that we have been in contact with all the major hospitals and there are no records of an unidentified man matching Garth's description being brought in over the last four days.'

'Four days,' says Cordelia because surely it can't be that long. But it's Thursday and she only knows he left the apartment on Monday morning or Sunday night. She has no idea where he went, what he did, no idea at all.

'Yes, it took you a bit of time to report him missing. Were you not concerned for him?'

'I was... I just...' She may actually be in trouble here. Real trouble.

'Apparently you think he may be having an affair?' the detective says. 'Do you have any idea who with?'

'I don't...' Cordelia shakes her head, not willing to say anything because she can only imagine the kind of trouble she could get into for bringing Natalie into this. Natalie is a lawyer and surely this is slander if Cordelia is wrong. 'I just think he might be, that's all,' she mumbles and then she rubs her nose, wishing she had never told the policewoman last night about her suspicions.

'Right, and when was the last time you saw him?'

'I told the other policewoman, on Sunday night.'

'I thought you said he was here on Monday morning?'

'He... I assumed he was because he left his coffee cup in the sink, but he went to work on Sunday night. He went to meet a co-worker, another lawyer.'

'On a Sunday night?'

Cordelia shrugs. She has no answer for this.

'And you didn't see him after that?'

Cordelia shakes her head. 'I was asleep when he came home.'

'If he came home,' says the detective, typing on her phone.

Cordelia swallows, bites down on her lip. *If he came home.*

And then there are more questions, and an hour later, they are still going and Cordelia's head is pounding and she desperately needs the bathroom but she's afraid to ask to use it since she only used it an hour ago.

'So can I just go through this again?' the detective says to Cordelia, who nods, just like she did the first and second time the detective asked this question.

'You didn't call the police because he often just disappears for a day or two?'

Cordelia nods and then clears her throat. 'Well, not often, but in the last few months –and, I mean, he doesn't disappear, he just doesn't come home because he says he... sleeps at the office.' *Sleeps at the office? Really, Cordelia? Where? On the sofa? What about showering and changing clothes? How have you allowed yourself to believe something so ridiculous?*

'Right, but you are in contact with him usually?'

'Usually, yes,' says Cordelia. She shifts on the sofa, wishing that the detective was not sitting so close to her. She can see a tiny spot of something, maybe coffee, on the detective's shirt and she keeps wanting to point it out. She would like to move away but is worried that if she does, she will look guilty of something.

'So did you text him when he didn't come home the first night?'

'As I told you, yes, I have texted him quite a lot.'

'Right, yes, I can see from your phone that you have.' Cordelia didn't want to show the detective her messages and knew she could simply refuse when the detective asked her, but it was easier just to do it. This morning, before she got out of bed, she deleted some of the messages between the two of them, an understanding in the back of her mind that things were going to escalate. And if Garth was hurt, in hospital or something, she didn't want to have to look at how horrible she had been again.

'And you called his office?'

Cordelia grits her teeth, not wanting the detective to see she's getting to her.

'I did, yes, and they said he hadn't been in for three... four days now. I didn't call again this morning.' She concentrates on the detective's eyebrows, two sharp, thin lines, plucked into submission. Part of Detective Ashton's skill seems to be in her ability to lift these eyebrows only slightly to convey disbelief without her actually having to say anything. Her black hair is tied back, which emphasises how small her dark brown eyes are. Perhaps she thought extremely thin eyebrows would make her eyes look bigger?

'No, we've called his office this morning. He's not in. We will be going over there today as well.'

Cordelia reaches for her glass of water in front of her on the coffee table. It's left a mark on the timber, something that Garth would point out and immediately be angry about. *Two thousand dollars, Cordelia. Have some respect for my objects, please*, he would say, tapping his finger on the table and then pointing to the coasters. He has a thing about his objects. His leather sofa, his coffee table, his expensive bamboo sheets, his oversized bed. His objects are beautiful and expensive and they matter to him. Surely he wouldn't willingly leave all his objects?

But she ignores the ring because Garth is not here and he hasn't been here for four days now. 'So are you going to... put out an alert or something?'

'We will be doing everything we can. Is there any reason why you might be worried about his mental health?'

'No, I mean... he works hard but I don't think so.'

'And how long have you been together, again?' asks the detective.

'Four and a half years,' sighs Cordelia.

'And the argument you had was about...?'

The detective has asked this question three times already.

'It was just about him working so much,' she lies, just as she did the first few times.

'Not about him possibly having an affair?'

'No,' says Cordelia, and she looks down at the water mark and then pulls her tracksuit top over her hand and wipes it away.

'But if he were having an affair, who do you think it might be with? It would be helpful for us to know.'

'I don't know,' Cordelia says, thinking again that surely it will be worse for her if she brings Natalie into all this. 'I don't know,' she repeats and then she stares out of the balcony door to the blue sky, wondering how warm or cold it is outside. She would like to be outside.

Detective Ashton's colleague hasn't asked any questions. He hasn't even sat down. He just keeps moving around the apartment occasionally picking up one of Garth's precious 'objects', like the ugly little fertility sculpture of a woman with enormous breasts. 'Why did you buy that?' she asked when he came home with it one night.

'It's art and it will increase in value,' he told her.

Cordelia had come home from the UK and rented a small apartment to start studying while Garth got himself organised to come over. She had assumed that they would just share her apartment but Garth saw himself a certain way and so had insisted on this very expensive apartment, and then he had filled it with stuff, and it has always been more his than hers, even though he has asked her to pay the rent a few times when he's said he's a little short. 'I have to keep up appearances, Cordy, and dinners with people from the firm can get expensive.' Lately he has seemed to be 'a little short' more often than not.

'Then maybe we should move somewhere cheaper until I'm earning enough money.'

'Well, that trust fund will kick in soon enough, won't it?' he said when they had the conversation, and she instantly regretted telling him about the trust fund.

She will get two million dollars when she turns twenty-five. She realises this is life-changing. A fortune. More money, as a lump sum, than most people will ever see. And it will be enough to buy a nice apartment and travel a little without having to worry about bills. Garth also knows that her mother sold her company for a lot of money and he has, in fact, been encouraging her to forgive her mother for some time now.

'She made a mistake and she's paid for it,' he has said. 'You need to forgive her.'

It is the one thing in her life where Cordelia will not allow Garth's opinion to influence her decision. His opinions influence enough of her life as it is, from what she wears to who she spends time with. She has been determined to never speak to her mother again. In any situation over the past four years, she has sought help and advice from Garth instead.

Now he's missing. Or dead. She blinks away the thought.

She feels a momentary desperate need for her mother, something she always tries to avoid feeling. But she does wish she was here now. Not the drunk, paranoid, accusatory mother who Grace became, but rather the mother who would listen when she talked and offer sound advice without judgement. The mother who baked cookies with her and lay next to her on her bed and talked about Cordelia's day.

'So is there any reason why you think he might have stayed away for so long?' the detective asks again.

Just leave, just get out of my home and go away, go away! she wants to shout as her face burns with the realisation that the detective knows she's lying about why she thinks Garth has left.

'Can't you like... trace his phone or something?' she blurts out, desperate to move the conversation along. 'I mean, isn't that what you can do these days, just trace his phone and find out where he is?'

'It's interesting that you say that,' says Detective Ashton with a small smile. Her two front teeth are slightly crooked. 'And we can do that but it actually takes a lot longer than people think because we have to get a warrant and then we have to talk to his provider and use cell phone towers, and it can take weeks, but interestingly...' The detective lets the word hang in the air and Cordelia can't help rubbing her arms, her skin itching.

'Interestingly?' she prompts.

'His mother has a location app for his phone. Lots of people have one for their families – you don't have one for Garth?'

'I... no,' she replies. *This is not good. This is not good.*

'Well, his mother does have one so she was able to provide us with the location of his phone.'

Cordelia nods, waiting for the answer, a hundred scenarios running through her head. With his mistress, on a holiday, dead? Why has the detective taken so long to tell her this? Why not just start with where his phone is because that's where Garth is, obviously.

'It's here,' says the detective. 'It's here in the apartment.'

What? What? What? Cordial feels her stomach twist as the detective continues speaking.

'His mother says she called you yesterday and asked about Garth. When you told her he wasn't home, she got worried and then when she checked her location app, she saw that his phone was here, in the apartment, and that's when she called us. I'm sure you can understand why that would worry her.'

'But why didn't she just call me back?' asks Cordelia, the notion that Garth's phone is here making her feel almost dizzy. 'Why didn't she just call me and tell me?'

'It seems she doesn't really trust you,' says Detective Ashton, enunciating the words slowly and, it seems to Cordelia, with some pleasure. Cordelia would like to look away from the detective but the woman holds her gaze and then one eyebrow moves slightly upwards. 'Why do you think that is?'

'I...' Cordelia gives in to the desire to scratch her arms and attacks her skin with her nails as the detective watches her. 'I need the bathroom,' she says and she gets up without waiting for permission, darting away and slamming the door shut behind her. Afterwards, she washes her hands twice, trying to still her racing heart.

And then she sends the text she had typed. There is no maybe about it, she has to send it.

As she goes to leave the bathroom, she gets a response, and she is so shocked she quickly replies:

What? No. You have to wait. There's something happening. Come tonight. Only tonight.

Confusion jumbles her thoughts. That wasn't what she expected at all but she can't even take time to process it.

When she opens the door, the detectives are standing right there, waiting for her.

'You don't mind if we have a quick look around, do you?'

asks Detective Jameson, finally finding his voice as he looms in front of her. And she realises that this has been where they were heading all along. They have questioned her for nearly two hours and only now told her that they know where the phone is. If she says they can't look around, if she demands that they come back with a search warrant, she is immediately suspect number one.

She can only shake her head, alarm bells ringing in her ears.

Garth never, never leaves home without his phone.

Never.

TEN

GRACE

Thursday

The only thing I can do is concentrate on my work. I turn on my computer and access what I need, even as my heart pounds and my mind swirls. Somehow the monotony of timesheets and scheduling manages to take my mind away from the man for a few hours. Close to lunchtime, I realise I am thirsty and sit back, rubbing my eyes behind my fake glasses.

In my pocket, my phone vibrates with a text and I pull it out slowly, assuming that it's spam since no one but the hotel and Cordelia have this number.

Mum, I need you. You have to come.

The phone slips from my hand and lands on my desk with a clank. I pick it up and read her words again. I take a shuddering breath, not wanting to cry.

She has asked for my help. And that must mean that things are so much worse than I thought.

I want to go to her immediately.

Tell me your address. I'm in Melbourne.

What? No. You have to wait. There's something happening. Come tonight. Only tonight.

I agree and she sends me the address that I don't really need. I don't want to wait. I want to go and be with her right now but my daughter has reached out to me for the first time in six years. I cannot screw this up by barging in and trying to take over and sort out her life for her. I need to do as she says.

But it's so hard to be patient and wait. I've struggled with patience my whole life and especially when I was serving my time in the clinic. 'Just take each day as it comes,' my therapist told me. It's a trite little saying that I actually laughed at. I found it easier to be patient once I had written down my reasons to get better, my reasons for getting out. One of those reasons is my daughters but the other is karma.

The twelve-step programme that can be found all over the world, designed to help addicts with their recovery, encourages participants to seek out something bigger than themselves: be it God or the universe, anything that allows us to feel that there is something greater than ourselves at play. I settled on the idea of karma.

You cannot do bad things and not expect to be punished for it in some way.

I am aware that I have done terrible things, even if I know my reasons behind everything I did, but I feel like I was punished before I did anything awful. I lost everything because of what Robert and my assistant, Tamara, did to me. But sometimes, karma takes its time. It allows awful people to be happy, to experience success and joy and to live full lives. Sometimes karma doesn't seem to be paying attention. But I am.

I feel that way about Tamara whenever I look at her Instagram page. She looks different now, six years later, as though she has somehow grown into herself as a woman with sharp cheekbones and a fabulous sense of style. She travels the world, always with a different, older man. She has lunch and dinner at expensive restaurants and in general seems to be living her *#bestlife*.

Instinctively I click on her page now, checking her out as I do regularly. Her latest picture is just her hand holding a glass of champagne, captioned, *#tomylove #futureplans*. She doesn't seem to be displaying a ring so I assume she's not engaged, but she's obviously referring to someone and I cannot help but seethe at the idea that she has someone to love her. She doesn't deserve that.

That's not karma, and when I'm done helping Cordelia with whatever this is, I will turn my attention to Tamara. I will be karma and I can't be stopped.

I don't care how long it takes me. They say revenge is a dish best served cold, but if you ask me, all that matters is that it's served.

I look at the time on my phone. If I let my thoughts take over, I can sometimes lose an hour or two. I push Tamara to the back of my mind, reminding myself that I will see my daughter soon. I will actually get to be in the same room as her. I am buzzing with joyful anticipation and I keep checking my phone, willing time to speed up.

Mid-afternoon, I realise I'm starving. I'm so distracted by thoughts of my daughter that I've worked through lunch. Leaving my office, I bump into Kelsey, who is on the phone, her pretty face lit up as she giggles at something that the person she is talking to is saying. 'Can't wait,' she says, hanging up when she sees me.

'Planning something special?' I ask her and she nods.

'I'm going to take some time off from university. My dad will go mad but I don't care.'

I open my mouth to offer some advice and then close it again. I'm not going to get involved with telling this young woman that she's making the wrong choice. I have my own child and her choices to worry about.

'I'm only nineteen,' she says, as though intuiting my judgement, 'I have years to do the boring stuff.'

'I'm sure you do,' I agree because this is not my business after all. I leave her to her plans and head to the exit.

But as I go to leave, I see the two detectives from this morning outside Cordelia's building standing at reception, and I dart back inside my office, my heart pounding. It's definitely the same ones. I recognise their suits.

Why are they here? It must be something to do with Garth not being at work, it has to be. What do they know? Will they want to speak to everyone here too? And if they speak to me, what will they know then? I'm not sure how I will manage to lie to detectives. My driver's licence still says Grace Morton. They will make the connection between me and Cordelia, of course they will, and I can't have that happen.

I open the door to my office slowly, touching my wig to make sure it's secure, and then I move quickly, getting myself to the bathroom.

I wait in a stall for a few minutes, trying to decide what to do. It's possible that I can get out of the office without speaking to the detectives. I've only just started here after all, and I'm temporary. As far as anyone knows, I'd never even heard of Garth until I began working here.

But I don't want to take a chance and have to speak to the detectives.

I take a deep breath and open the stall door, into the bathroom, where I wash my hands just as another stall door opens and Natalie comes out. She startles when she sees me. 'Oh, I had no idea anyone else was in here,' she says.

'I'm just getting ready to head out for a late bite to eat,' I say, not looking at her but noticing that she seems agitated as she begins washing her hands.

When she's done, she doesn't leave, just stands there, watching me.

'Is something wrong?' I ask.

She shakes her head. 'There are police here.'

I know this but I feel suddenly it would be better if she thought I didn't. 'Why?'

'Garth, one of the senior associates, has been missing since Monday. He didn't come in on Monday and he didn't let anyone know why.'

'I did hear that from Tristan this morning. Perhaps he's ill,' I say.

'No,' whispers Natalie, 'I don't think that's it. I think something has happened to him.'

'But why?' I ask, attempting to sound confused.

'He's...' she shakes her head, 'he's not a good guy. He's just...' I wait for her to finish, holding my breath for what she is going to say, but she seems to realise that she's speaking to me and she shrugs her shoulders. 'Sorry, I shouldn't be saying anything. I'm sure everything is fine.'

'You can talk to me if you want, Natalie. I don't know him but you seem concerned about the police being here. Perhaps you need to tell them something?'

I *knew* Garth wasn't a good guy, knew it from the moment I first saw a picture of him with his fake smile. I'm happy for Natalie to tell the police exactly what he's done so I can get him out of my daughter's life.

'I... No... no, I don't really know anything,' she says and she leaves the bathroom quickly.

I wash my hands again, allowing the cool water to focus my

thoughts. And then I open the bathroom door and check who's around. I see the two detectives talking to Natalie, who glances around her, as though looking for some support. And then they move off into an office and the door is closed. I need to get out of here now.

At reception, Tristan is on a call. I wait patiently, my eye on the office where the detectives have taken Natalie.

When he's done, I lean forward and whisper, 'I have to leave, Tristan. I'm feeling really unwell. My... stomach,' I say, feeling my face colour at the implication but it works because he sits back quickly.

'Of course, off you go. I doubt there will be any work done here today.'

'Why?'

'Well,' he sits forward again, delighted to be able to share a bit of juicy gossip, 'Garth, you know, the one you asked about this morning?'

I nod.

'He hasn't been in all week and now his girlfriend, a lovely girl who is way too young for him if you ask me,' he says, waving a hand, 'but she's reported him missing and there is some stuff being said about him...'

'What stuff?' I ask.

Speaking in a whisper, he says, 'Let's just say that Garth has wandering eyes and sometimes they wander in the wrong direction. Lots of tongues wagging about that today.' He gives a knowing nod.

'What do you mean the wrong direction?' I ask.

He sits back again and I must look more ill than I thought because he shakes his head.

'You really should go, Grace, the last thing we need is for the office to come down with some sort of nasty bug.'

'Of course. I'll see you in the morning.'

'Feel better,' he sings as I turn to leave and then he answers a call.

In the corner of my eye, I see the door to the office where Natalie and the detectives are swing open, and I dart for the stairs instead of waiting for the elevator, running down the seven flights and emerging sweating into the strong wind of the city.

I hail a cab to take me back to my hotel, where I will shower and have something to eat before I go and see Cordelia. Looking down at my watch, I see that it's after 4 p.m. I will leave my hotel to see Cordelia at 5 p.m. Only an hour to go.

Only an hour until I know exactly what has been going on with my child.

Tristan must be talking about Garth cheating. Wouldn't any cheating be the 'wrong direction' if he has a girlfriend? Putting this together with Cordelia paying the rent and other bills makes me wonder exactly what this man has been up to. But where is he?

I am going to sort this out because that's what I do for my children, that's what I will do for my child. And no matter how dangerous the man in the leather jacket is, or what Garth is doing or has done, they have nothing on a mother protecting her child. Nothing.

ELEVEN

CORDELIA

Thursday

Her mother is in Melbourne and will be here soon. Cordelia cannot believe it. Why is she here? Did she somehow know Cordelia would need her?

It's just before 5 p.m. and she told her mother to come tonight. She should be here soon.

She paces around the apartment as she waits. Walking over to the glass doors, Cordelia slides them open and steps out onto the balcony, automatically crossing her arms over her chest in the wind. The apartment balcony is lovely in summer when the weather is fine, and it's possible to sit out here on the outdoor sofa and sip tea as you gaze over the city and the river. But most of the time, it's too cold and windy because it's so high up, and the balcony doors remain firmly shut.

Looking down, she studies the street, sixteen storeys below, and then shakes her head. It's not like she's going to be able to see anything anyway. Turning back, she goes inside and to the kitchen to make herself a cup of tea.

She was never going to speak to her mother again.

Her hands tremble a little as she decides on coffee instead, needing the caffeine kick.

She was never going to speak to her mother again and yet she has called on her for help. Why?

Because she will understand.

Taking a sip of her coffee, she looks around the apartment, wishing she had told the detectives that they could not look around, that they had no right to open drawers and cupboards, however carefully they did so. The apartment is not large and it didn't take them long to find Garth's phone.

It was under the bed, the ringer on silent, the battery on seven per cent. Cordelia had not even thought to look for his phone because Garth never leaves home without it and he had texted her from it on Monday night.

'I didn't know,' she said when Detective Ashton showed her.

'Unusual for anyone to leave home without their phone these days,' said the detective, her eyebrows rising as she looked at Cordelia.

'I don't... I didn't know,' Cordelia repeated.

'He's never left it at home before?' asked Detective Ashton.

'No, never,' said Cordelia. 'Why would he have done that?' Cordelia wasn't actually asking the detective, but rather herself.

'But you say that he was texting you from the phone on Monday?'

'He was,' insisted Cordelia.

'Right,' replied the detective and then she cocked her head as though something was confusing her, 'but you're not even sure he came home on Sunday night.'

'I mean... I thought,' Cordelia stumbled.

'And if the phone has been here all along it would be easy enough for you to send yourself a text from it.'

'Why would I do that? I wouldn't have done that,' snapped Cordelia.

'Of course not.' The detective nodded, her disbelief obvious in her tone.

'There must be a reason why he left it here,' said Cordelia. *But he texted me from it on Monday. He did.*

The detective shrugged. 'If someone wants to disappear, it's something that I have seen before – I mean, if he just wanted to.'

'But why would he want to?'

'You tell me,' said the detective, her gaze locked on Cordelia, making her feel almost naked with the intensity of her scrutiny.

'Why are you asking me all these questions? I didn't know the phone was here and I'm really worried about him now. Surely you should be out looking for him.'

'Oh, we are looking, we are definitely looking. Is it okay if we take his phone with us?'

'Well, he might... I mean, I don't think he would like it.'

'Perhaps you can unlock it for us and we can just check to see if he's had any messages that might tell us what's happened.'

'I don't...' The words caught in Cordelia's throat. 'I don't know how to unlock his phone. He uses a pattern and I'm not sure of what it is.'

The detective nodded but again, Cordelia could see that the woman didn't believe her. 'We'll manage to get it opened if you're okay with letting us take it.'

Cordelia stared at the detective, aware that all this strict politeness was a ruse. If she refused, she would look guilty of something.

It will be worse after they do manage to open the phone. She didn't count on anyone having Garth's phone except Garth.

'It's fine,' she said, unable to stop herself folding her arms across her chest.

'You're not planning a holiday anytime soon, are you?' said the detective, moving towards the door of the apartment.

'Of course not,' exclaimed Cordelia. 'Garth and I are talking about going away next summer but...' She stopped speaking, the enormous weight of her fear for Garth heavy on her shoulders. 'But now...' She scrunched her eyes shut, feeling a tear escape.

'We'll find him, I'm sure,' said the detective, a touch of gentleness in her voice, and Cordelia understood that she had finally behaved the way she should.

She walked to her front door, pulled it open, desperate for them to be out of her space.

'Oh, and just checking, your mother is Grace Morton, isn't she?' the detective asked as she stepped through the open front door into the hallway that led to the elevator.

Cordelia felt her jaw tense. 'Yes,' she replied.

'Right,' the detective said, nodding. 'Right. We'll be in touch, and of course if he contacts you, please let us know immediately.'

'Obviously,' Cordelia replied. She closed the front door, leaning her forehead against it, waiting to hear the sounds of the detectives' footsteps moving away. And after a few minutes, she understood that the detectives were waiting outside, probably with their ears pressed up against the door, waiting to hear if she called someone or said or did something.

She walked slowly away from the door, sneakily quiet in her own home, and then she closed herself in the marble en suite and reread the text from her mother, convinced that she might have imagined it.

According to her mother, her father cheated and lied; according to her mother, her father was gaslighting her. And if Cordelia is honest with herself, she knows that's exactly what Garth has been doing as well.

Did the detective mention her mother because she knows?

Like mother, like daughter?

She thought her mother was in Sydney, hiding in an expensive apartment. But her mother is here and now she's on her way and Cordelia has no idea what to do with herself.

If Garth wanted to disappear, to run away, he might leave his phone, but what would he want to run away from? If he had walked in three nights ago and said, 'I'm in love with someone else and I'm leaving you,' or, 'I want you to leave,' Cordelia would not have been surprised. She would have accepted that what she had suspected was the truth and she would have packed a bag and left, just left.

She vowed, as a teenager, watching the arguments between her parents, that she would never be as pathetic as her mother, turning to alcohol to numb the paranoia, screaming and shouting and needing Cordelia's father to confess to something. She promised herself she would just leave if her marriage or relationship fell apart, but it hasn't been so easy now that she actually suspects Garth of cheating. Love makes people do crazy things, and feeling you've been betrayed by the person you love the most in the world is not as easily dealt with as Cordelia imagined when she was a teenager.

She is ashamed of herself, for acting the way she has acted with Garth, for judging her mother, for thinking that her life would be impervious to something like this because she already suffered the loss of her father. There isn't some kind of scale where it all balances out. Shit happens and then more shit happens and hopefully you figure out how to survive it.

Now she just wants to know that Garth is okay and that whatever has happened, they will both survive it. She thinks, she hopes.

The bell for the doors at the front of her building rings, the sound loud in the apartment. Her mother is here, outside right now. Her mother is here.

TWELVE

GRACE

Thursday

It will only be minutes now until I see my child.

I press down hard on the bell for her apartment, unable to believe that I will soon see Cordelia, face to face, for the first time in six years.

'Mum?' Her voice sounds tinny and far away. 'Mum,' she repeats as though unable to believe it.

'I'm here, sweetheart,' I say. 'I'm here.'

A buzzer sounds and glass doors slide open. And then I am in the world's slowest elevator as it moves from floor to floor, and I have to bite down on my lip to stop myself from screaming as it stops on the seventh floor and an old man shuffles inside slowly. 'Oh, I thought it was going down,' he says when he presses the symbol for the ground floor on the panel.

'Up,' I say and then I look down, not inviting any conversation.

'I guess I'll just ride up,' he sighs.

Finally, we are here, and as soon as the doors open, I dart out and find her apartment. I raise my hand to knock, but the door opens before I can do that and there she is, my beautiful girl.

'You're here,' she says.

'I'm here.' I want to reach out to her, to grab her and hold her tight. She looks so thin and pale.

'You're so skinny,' she says.

'You're too skinny,' I say and she nods, stepping back to let me in. 'Garth... my boyfriend... my boyfriend doesn't like overweight women,' she says and then she shakes her head, regretting the words.

'Can I... can I hug you?' I ask because she is standing at least two feet away from me. Close enough to touch but her shoulders are back, her fists clenched. Her whole body is ready for a fight. She has only called me because she is desperate, I know that, but at least she has called me. I have a moment of heavy sympathy for her because there is no one else she could call. Robert wanted a second child but I knew that would make it harder to build my business. Cordelia was enough for me, but after everything that has happened, I regret that she has no sibling she can turn to for help. Not one that she knows about.

She nods and then steps towards me and I put my arms around her, feeling her resistance to being touched by me. I hold her close, breathing in the same sweet perfume she has always worn. I hold her tighter and, finally, I feel her relax into my arms, feel her body meld to mine and then she is crying and I am crying and the two of us are holding each other tight.

Finally, we break apart and she goes to grab a tissue for each of us. I look around the apartment as I blow my nose. She lives here? There is nothing of her in this space. Instead, it looks like a bachelor hired a designer to furnish it. The sofas are white leather, the coffee table a dark timber and the rug on the floor a Persian design in orange and red. None of this feels like Cordelia, whose favourite colours are pale blue and grey, but it has been years since the last time I saw her, and then she was in court, testifying. Perhaps she has changed?

'Do you want something to drink?' she asks me and I can hear in the tentative nature of the question that she is worried I might ask for an alcoholic drink.

'A cup of tea would be lovely,' I say. I wander over to the sliding glass door that leads to the balcony. I stand and gaze over the city of Melbourne, where all the buildings are lit up and it has begun to rain. Down below, colourful umbrellas under streetlights bob along, seemingly moving on their own.

I know how much this apartment costs to rent, and for something so small in Melbourne, it's a sizable sum. I also know how much money Garth makes, and while, as a senior associate at a law firm, he is making a large salary, this still takes a reasonable chunk. Is that why she's occasionally paying rent? Or is it something else?

'Here you go,' says Cordelia, and I turn to see that she has a tray with tea and a plate of chocolate biscuits.

Sitting down, I take a sip from the mug she hands me and then I grab a biscuit. I would like a drink but I will never drink in front of her again. The secret that I have returned to drinking is something I will take to my grave. Cordelia's eyes are red-rimmed and she is biting her lip, a habit she has had since she was a child when she is worried about something.

'Tell me,' I say as she takes a bite of her own chocolate biscuit.

'Garth is missing,' she says. 'My boyfriend, the man I've been with for the last four and a half years, is missing.'

'Oh, when... Why don't you start at the beginning, darling?' What I feel is mostly relief. Garth is missing, so what? I knew that already. He is missing and she is safe and that's all that matters. I know that I cannot tell her that. She obviously loves the man, but if he has left her, then I know she is better off without him.

Unless something terrible has happened. I think about the man in the leather jacket again, the one who told me Cordelia was supposed to be doing something, and I look at my child, my daughter, wondering exactly how much I don't know about her. Does she know about Garth's wandering eye?

'The police were here today. They searched the apartment. They found his phone under the bed.'

'His phone? He left his phone?'

Cordelia looks at me. 'He did,' she says.

'That's... unusual for anyone these days.'

'It is,' she agrees, 'and when the police unlock it, they will find out what's been happening.'

'And what has been happening?' I ask.

She shudders a little, and then she brings her knees up to her chest and wraps her arms around them, the way she used to as a teenager when she would come and tell me that something was bothering her. 'He cheated. I mean, I thought he cheated; I think he's cheated. I thought he was sleeping with a woman at his firm named Natalie but now I'm not so sure it's her. I'm not sure he did cheat or if I just... I'm not sure about anything.'

'Oh, Cordelia,' I say. I have a thousand questions but I take another bite of the biscuit, concentrating on the crumbly sweetness as I caution myself to be patient.

'He denied it, he always denies it when I ask him.'

'Well...' *Of course he denies it. How many men deny it and instead turn it around on their wives and girlfriends?* Finn, who cheated on Ava, crosses my mind. Finn is a different kind of man. Not every man is toxic and awful. There are plenty of strong men in the world. But there are also plenty of Roberts and Garths.

'And the detective who came to interview me this morning asked if I was your daughter.'

'He did?'

'It was a she, and yes, she did.' Cordelia looks around the

apartment and then she shrugs. 'Perhaps she was worried I'm going to burn this all down. And if she wasn't worried before she looks through his phone, she will be when she does.'

The words are filled with cruelty and meant to hurt me and I can't help flinching slightly, but I also know that she is in crisis right now and is hurting me because I am here. Mothers often become punching bags for their children, listening as a teenager screams that they hate them because of something that happened at school or with a friend. But I am so grateful to be here, so grateful she contacted me, that I will accept her anger and her pain. We stare at each other, my daughter and I, two women cut from the same cloth. And I know in that moment that whatever she has done and whatever it takes to save her, I will do it.

'Why will they think that?' I ask, hastily taking a sip of tea because my mouth is suddenly dry.

'I sent him... nasty messages, called him a liar and...' She drops her head onto her knees. And her shoulders shake. She is crying. I put my cup down, shift over to her and wrap my arms around her.

'It will be fine, it will be okay,' I tell her as I pat her back.

She pushes me away and stands up, moving away. 'I need a minute,' she says and I watch as she walks over to the small bathroom near the kitchen.

I have no idea where to begin with this, what questions to ask, but I finish my biscuit and tea and then take the cup to the kitchen. A half-drunk bottle of wine, dark red in its green bottle, is standing on the counter and my hand moves towards it, but the bathroom door opens and I quickly drop my hand and turn to the kettle, flicking the switch to boil it again.

'I'm starving,' says Cordelia, coming into the kitchen. It's just after 6 p.m. and I realise that I am hungry as well.

'Shall we go out? Or would you like to order in? Or I could make something. I don't know what you have here.'

'Can you…' She stops speaking and looks down at her feet in thick grey socks, biting down on her lip. 'Can you make me your special grilled cheese?' she asks. 'I think I have everything to make it.'

'Of course. You go sit down,' I say.

I used to make her my special grilled cheese – which is just a combination of cheddar and mozzarella with a sprinkling of tomatoes, fried up in a pan – all the time when she was a child, but as she grew older, it seemed that she only wanted it when she had something she really needed to discuss, like an argument with a friend, a bad grade in a class she wanted to do well in, a break-up with a boyfriend.

I open her fridge and find the ingredients I need, navigating my way around her small kitchen easily enough.

I am done in ten minutes and place it in front of her on the coffee table, putting my own in front of me. She has covered herself in a soft orange blanket and is staring at the balcony doors, where the rain is heavier now.

She lifts the plate and takes a bite of a triangle of grilled cheese, closing her eyes and savouring the flavour. 'I'm sorry I stopped speaking to you,' she says when she has swallowed her first bite.

'You don't…' I shake my head. 'You don't have to be sorry. I understand your anger. I'm just glad I'm here now, and I will help you, Dee Dee,' I say, using her childhood nickname.

'I've missed you, Mum,' she says, more tears appearing, and I nod.

'You have no idea how much I've missed you. But now you must tell me everything because I will help. I will find a way to help.'

Cordelia takes another bite of her sandwich and then she begins to speak, starting with how she met Garth and then telling me about his strange behaviour in the last few months and about her suspicions that he's cheating.

I listen as I eat my own grilled cheese, the man in the jacket on my mind, waiting for my child to reveal everything she knows. I want to show her the pictures I have of the man who has been following her, but something tells me to wait, to let her speak, to take some time. I need to know everything she knows, and I need to know if she's hiding things.

And I have to be careful so that she doesn't find out about everything I am hiding. Not now, not yet and, hopefully, not ever.

THIRTEEN
CORDELIA

Friday

Cordelia wakes at dawn and lies staring at the ceiling in the manufactured dark. Finally, she can't take it anymore and she turns on her bedside light and grabs her phone, not wanting to open the blinds. It's so strange to not be able to text Garth, not to be expecting a text from him.

If she could, she would delete everything she has texted him over the last few months but there's no point. The police have the phone, they have it.

Do they look at everything? Will they go through his pictures and see the ones she sent him when she was in Australia and he was still in the UK and she was missing him so much? Even alone in her bedroom, Cordelia feels her face colour.

It's too early to call the detective and ask her if they have any news on Garth – the woman won't even be at work yet. And her mother left here so late that she doesn't want to wake her.

She turns on her side, closes her eyes and thinks about her

mother, here, last night. It was surreal to see her, surreal to touch her after all this time, and Cordelia's first instinct was to just tell her to go. She didn't want her back in her life after everything she had done. Her mother ruined her life, completely ruined it.

But when she stepped forward to hug her, Cordelia allowed it, and then somehow, she felt her resistance crumble.

Her childhood had not been all bad. Her mother had read her stories and baked with her and loved her and always been on the other end of the phone even though she was always working. Cordelia had known she was loved. She had known that, and only in the year when her mother began to accuse her father of cheating had it all been awful.

Her mother is different now – not the same person she was during the terrible year when everything crumbled, and obviously not drinking and paranoid like she was back then either; but different. She seems stronger, more resilient, like nothing will faze her. And Cordelia needs someone like that right now.

She's changed the colour of her hair, turned it a lovely shade of copper, which goes nicely with her green eyes and she looks... well, thinner, but fit and well. She looks like Cordelia would have wanted her to look all through her seventeenth year when she was drinking every night, eating junk food and only paying attention to her business or, eventually, her delusions about Cordelia's father.

Her mother had listened carefully to everything Cordelia had to say and Cordelia kept nothing back. Can she trust her now? Can she trust her to actually help if Cordelia needs her? Because she has a feeling she will need someone.

Her theories about Garth go round and round in her head.

He's left her for another woman – not Natalie, or it is Natalie and he's just hiding out until he has the courage to come and tell Cordelia the truth? But why?

Something bad has happened to him, like a heart attack or

he's been mugged or something like that and he's lying some-where hoping for help but no one knows where he is. Cordelia shudders at this idea.

Maybe he's gone home to the UK, just left Cordelia with everything to sort out and gone home. But then he would have called his mother. Men don't just disappear, they don't. She has no access to his credit cards or bank account but the police will probably look into that today.

As time moves slowly forward, Cordelia sends a message to Jacinta.

So sorry. I'm still not well. I can't come in today.

Jacinta is obviously awake, probably doing an early-morning yoga class or something equally impressive, and immediately texts back.

So sorry, hope you're better soon.

She gets out of bed and into a hot shower, closing her eyes as the water soothes her body and silently pleading with Garth to contact her.

Her phone starts ringing as she gets out of the shower and she grabs it with a wet trembling hand, swiping her thumb across the screen.

'Garth?' she says. She didn't recognise the number but Garth doesn't have his phone so any number could be him.

'No, I'm sorry, Cordelia. This is Detective Ashton.'

'Oh... have you...?' She can't finish the sentence.

'We haven't located Garth but we were wondering if we could take a look at your car?'

'My car?' says Cordelia, not understanding.

'Yes,' says the detective without adding anything else.

'But I barely drive it because I catch the tram to work and Garth doesn't drive here. I mean, he can, but he doesn't.'

'Right, but you do have a car?'

'I do, it's parked downstairs.'

'Then you won't mind if we take a look at it.'

'I don't... I don't understand why you need to look at my car.'

'Cordelia, do you drive a 2017 red Toyota Corolla?'

'I... yes,' says Cordelia, remembering arriving home from the triumphant passing of her driver's test when she was seventeen years old to find the car, brand new and a shiny red, sitting in the driveway wrapped in a big pink bow. When she left the country, she gave it to Alexandra to use while she was away but she took it back when she moved home, even though she rarely used it.

'And when last did you drive it?'

'I don't really... maybe a few weeks ago. I went to a big shopping centre to get new towels and I didn't want to carry them back on the tram.' It feels ludicrous to be giving these details to the detective and she thinks she should just keep quiet now, stop answering questions.

'We're on our way over to you now. Would we be able to take a look at the car?'

'Why? I don't actually understand why or what this may have to do with Garth.'

The detective sighs. 'Cordelia, we are actually outside your building and we will shortly be in the garage. We would like you to voluntarily come down and allow us to look through the car. We have a forensics team with us.'

'What?' shouts Cordelia, dropping her towel and grabbing the clothes she was wearing last night so that she can pull them on. 'You can't do that.'

'We can. Your building manager told us he has a record of the car leaving at 2 a.m. on Monday. Your boyfriend hasn't been seen by anyone but you since last Sunday because he didn't go into work on Monday.'

'But he was here on Monday morning, he left his cup in the sink... I mean, I think...' says Cordelia in protest. 'He went to work on Sunday night. He went to meet Natalie, his co-worker, ask her, have you asked her?'

'We have and she says that she did not call or meet with him on Sunday night. No one at the firm called him or met with him on Sunday night.'

'What?' yells Cordelia. 'But he said—'

The detective continues talking over Cordelia. 'The car left the garage at 2 a.m. and returned two hours later. Please meet us in the garage with your keys.'

'Do you have a search warrant or whatever it is you need to do that?' spits Cordelia, beyond furious now at being spoken to like this and commanded to do what this woman says.

'We do, Cordelia,' Detective Ashton says softly. 'We do.'

Cordelia is dressed now and finds her knees feeling weak. She sits down on the edge of the bed. 'I'm coming,' she says. She has no choice.

They're making me give them access to my car, Mum. They saw it leaving the garage early on Monday morning. You need to come.

I'm on my way.

A few days ago, she was worried about Garth cheating on her, leaving her, or her having to make the decision to leave him.

But whatever has happened to Garth, it is so much worse than that. It is becoming obvious that something else has been going on.

Cordelia finds her keys where she usually leaves them in a glass bowl by the front door. They are sticky with something for some reason and she grabs an antiseptic wipe and cleans them before taking the lift down to the garage, where the detectives, two men in white jumpsuits and the building manager are standing next to her car.

Cordelia throws a scowl at Lionel, the overly familiar building manager who feels the need to greet her every time he sees her with something like a leer and a statement about how pretty she looks today. He's creepy and weird and Cordelia does everything she can to avoid him.

'The police asked me for the CCTV from the last week and of course I had to tell them what I saw,' he says earnestly.

Cordelia ignores him and turns to look at her car, parked in its usual parking space, which is the one that comes with the apartment she and Garth rent.

It's filthy, covered in mud splatters all up the side, the wheels caked in thick clumps of dirt, and there's a scratch on the driver's door. Her car looks like it's been driven through the bush, not something she would ever do.

This is bad, very bad. How did that happen? Did he take the car without telling me? Why didn't he get it cleaned? Where would he have gone? Did someone steal it and bring it back? What's going on here?

'I don't know how that happened,' says Cordelia, gesturing to the dirt and the scratch as she swallows a lump of panic in her throat. She never drives the car anywhere except in the city, and even with the rain, there's no mud to get on the car.

'Don't you?' asks Detective Ashton, her hand outstretched as she waits for Cordelia to hand her the keys.

Cordelia feels like she's watching some police show on television and any minute now there will be a witness who saw her dragging a body away from the car in the middle of the bush. It's ridiculous.

'Do I need a lawyer?' she asks, because isn't that something you should ask?

'Let's not jump to conclusions just yet,' says the detective with a small smirk. But Cordelia can see the woman has already made the leap. And everything in her life is about to go up in flames again.

She hands the detective her keys and the detective studies them, then brings them close to her face and sniffs, something that looks so strange Cordelia stifles the urge to laugh.

'Did you clean these with some sort of antiseptic?' asks the detective.

The urge to laugh evaporates and Cordelia nods, her heart skipping in her chest.

'You can return to your apartment,' says the detective, and it doesn't sound like a suggestion but rather an order.

Cordelia turns and heads back to her apartment to wait for her mother

She has no idea what to do with herself. It's only just after 7 a.m. and barely light but the detectives have been up early, just waiting to speak to her. When did they find out about her car, and why didn't they say anything last night? It feels like they are playing some sort of cat and mouse game with her, like they are withholding information. She is definitely the mouse in this scenario and she hates feeling like that. Do they actually know where Garth is? Do they know something and they're keeping it from her?

And what do they think she's keeping from them?

FOURTEEN

GRACE

Friday

I hold my daughter tightly when I arrive at her apartment and she returns my hug. I can feel how thin she is through her track-suit top. Cordelia only stops eating properly when she's unhappy, turning to junk food as stress burns inside her. I suppose I am the same way, except I turned to something else.

She explains why the police are looking at her car and details the dirt on the sides.

'Perhaps it's just mud from the road,' I suggest without actually believing that's the case.

'No, Mum,' she sighs, 'it looked like the kind of dirt that comes from driving in the bush.'

'Garth could have taken it out without telling you.'

'Yes, but why would he have done that?'

'And where would he have gone?' I ask.

'I don't know,' she says. 'If he is having an affair, it can only be with someone he's met through work, I'm sure of it. He only really knows the people at his work. He hasn't made any other friends since he got here and he has never mentioned anyone else to me. Maybe whoever he has been sleeping with will know something about the car.'

I take a deep breath. It's time to tell her because I can't hide this any longer, and because it's nearly 8 a.m. and I really need to get to work if I want to keep this job. And of course I do. Now more than ever.

'Let's sit down,' I say and she obliges, pulling the soft orange blanket she has draped on the sofa over her.

'I have something to tell you,' I continue, and I watch as her body curls up tighter, her arms going around her knees. She is afraid of what I have to say, and once again, I am reminded of what I have done to this young woman, this young woman I love with all my heart. 'I'm actually working at Garth's firm.' I speak quickly.

She shakes her head. 'What?'

'I wanted to... Okay, this is going to seem terrible to you but I wanted to see what kind of man he was. I just wanted to know that he was a good person and he was treating you well.'

'But you only just... found out about him,' she says and she moves away from me, pushing her body along the sofa.

'I...' There is nothing for it but a complete confession. 'I've been following you on Instagram. You wouldn't talk to me and I had to know that you were okay, and when pictures of him began turning up, I needed to know who he was and so I followed him and I've been watching, and I was worried because he's so much older than you and he doesn't seem very nice sometimes.' The words come out in a stream, and I speak so fast I feel like a movie being sped up so you can get to the end. I don't look at Cordelia until I'm done, and when I do, her face is white and she is biting down on her lip.

'No, no, oh God, that's so... How could you do that? How could you just stalk me like that? It's so creepy, so weird.' She shrugs off the blanket and gets up. 'I need you to go,' she says, 'just get out. I'll deal with this myself.'

I touch my chest as a sharp pain pierces me. I have messed this up. I stand, nodding my head as my eyes spill over with tears. I can't believe I have blown this chance. She is staring at me, horror on her face as I go to pick up my bag. I think I will never see her again but as I get to the door of her apartment, something inside me, Grace Enright perhaps, tells me not to leave, not to just accept this.

'There's more you need to know,' I say, because I have to tell her.

'Good God, I don't want to hear one more thing!' she shouts. 'Just go and leave me alone.'

'Someone is following you,' I say.

'What? What, are you crazy?' she asks, and then before I can reply, she yells, 'No, no, no, you're making stuff up now so I'll let you stay here and I can't, I just can't deal with you and all your...' she circles her hands, 'all your everything.' She sneers as she shakes her head.

There's no way she's going to listen to anything else I have to say. I will always be on the back foot with her, even when I'm trying to help her, even when she's in desperate need of help.

She doesn't understand how desperate I am too, desperate to help her. She doesn't understand what it's been like for me, not really.

'You know, Cordelia,' I say, 'I understand your anger but I want to tell you that you have no idea what it's like to have your child, the child you have loved since the moment she was conceived, reject you.'

'With good reason,' she yells.

'I know that,' I shout back, my heart pounding now. 'Don't you think I know that? Don't you think I have tortured myself with what I did to your life every single day for the last six years?'

'You killed my father,' she yells back again, tears falling as she backs away from me even further, crossing her arms over her chest.

'It was an accident,' I say, lowering my voice because we can't just stand here shouting at each other. The police are in this building. 'And I have paid for that accident every single day for six years. And if you think that cutting me out of your life will make it better, then I have to accept that. But I want you to think about this, Cordelia June,' I use her full name, 'I got myself a job as an assistant so that I could see what kind of a person you had chosen to be with. I have to wear a wig to do that job so that no one recognises me. I have to call myself by a different surname. You know the kind of person I am. I wouldn't have done something so drastic without good reason and now it seems that something has happened, something that could change your life again, and I just want you to be safe, Dee Dee, safe and secure and living a peaceful life.'

'You made sure that was never going to happen when you burned down our house with Daddy inside it,' she says, the words whisper-soft, and then she turns away from me, going into the bedroom and closing the door with a purposeful click, which is somehow worse than if she had slammed it.

I lean down and pick up my bag from the sofa where I've dropped it. It's probably better if I give her some space now. That's all I can do. I tried to tell her about the man following her but there's no way she will listen to me now.

I will leave and hope that she will call me when the detectives contact her about anything they find in the car.

As I make my way to the door, someone knocks, a fist rapping sharply on the wood. It's followed by the chime of a bell.

I stop, unsure what to do, but then the bedroom door opens and Cordelia comes out. Her red-rimmed eyes tell me she's been crying.

'Shall I open it?' I ask her and she nods, seeming very young right in this moment, and I wish that I could take this all away from her. I know she is angry with me, will always be angry with me over her father's death, but I can't go back in time. I can only help her now.

I pull open the heavy door to find the two detectives I saw yesterday standing there.

'And you are?' asks the woman without even introducing herself.

I push my shoulders back, irritated. 'Grace... Morton,' I say, knowing there is no point in using Enright. 'Cordelia's mother.'

'Oh, yes, you've been released,' says the detective, with a quick glance at her partner.

'Are you done with my car?' interrupts Cordelia.

'No,' says the detective. 'It's being towed so that it can be examined more thoroughly.'

'What? Why? What if I need it?'

The detective turns to her partner, who is standing quietly behind her. She takes a plastic bag he is holding and turns back to us, lifting it up so we can see exactly what's in it, so that we can see the knife.

'Do you recognise this?' she asks Cordelia, whose gaze swings immediately to the kitchen, where there is a knife block sitting on the white marble counter, one knife missing. The knives are stainless steel, a common collection found every-where. Usually there is one knife with a serrated edge, the rest with smooth edges. Cordelia turns back, and I see her clench her fists. The knife in the plastic bag the detective is holding has a serrated edge, and it has dulled, rust-brown spots on it, the dull rust-brown colour that blood turns when it dries. It could be something else of course. Anything is possible. But I don't think it is something else. I think it's exactly what it looks like.

I clutch the strap of my handbag tightly, feeling a light sweat bead my upper lip.

What have you done, my darling girl? I think, a desperate fear coursing through my veins. *What have you done?*

FIFTEEN

CORDELIA

Friday

Cordelia knows that she must be looking at what the detective is holding because her eyes are focused right there. She is here in her apartment, standing next to her mother, looking at a detective holding a plastic bag containing a serrated knife, stained with what definitely looks like blood. But she can't quite comprehend that this is actually happening. She has a moment of feeling like she is actually looking down on herself, dressed in a blue tracksuit hoodie, loose matching pants and black socks with her blonde hair tied back. She can see this for a second, can see how she is staring at the plastic bag. And she has a vague unbidden thought: *I wouldn't want to be her*.

'Do you know where this may have come from?' asks the detective, even as her glance moves to the kitchen, which can be seen from the front door. Cordelia doesn't answer.

She knows the knife is missing, has, in fact, thought about taking a proper look for it in all the drawers in the kitchen because sometimes – rarely – Garth will unload the dishwasher and put things back in the wrong place. She thought about asking him where it was only days ago or was it weeks ago? Time feels elastic right now, stretching and pinging back without warning.

How long has it been missing? She has no idea.

'Can we come in?' asks the detective.

'Um... yes,' says Cordelia, stepping back. Does she have a choice? Just like yesterday, she has no idea whether or not she can say no even though she would like to scream the word and run to her bedroom, climbing into bed and burrowing under the covers until all of this just goes away.

'Just a moment,' says her mother. 'I don't think that's a good idea.'

'Oh, why?' asks Detective Ashton, sounding genuinely curious.

'Look, I don't know if you showed my daughter your search warrant for her car and I know she allowed you to search her apartment yesterday, but right now, I don't think she wants to speak to you anymore, at least not until you make it clear why you are questioning her.'

'Well,' says Detective Jameson, and Cordelia watches her mother lift her head to look up at him. 'As you may or may not know, Ms Morton,' his emphasis on the word 'Ms' making him hiss a little, 'we have your daughter's car leaving her building at 2 a.m. on Monday and now we have a knife, with what looks like, I think you will agree, blood. I'd say there is quite a lot to discuss, especially since I can see that knife block from here and I can see that one knife is missing, unless of course you know where that is,' he asks, looking at Cordelia. 'Not in the dishwasher, is it?'

Cordelia cannot help a shake of her head because she knows the knife is not in the dishwasher.

Her mother folds her arms and throws her shoulders back, and Cordelia recognises that the Grace Morton who built a company up from one store to fifty all across Australia has appeared. In truth she had almost forgotten that this Grace existed after everything that happened. Her anger at her mother, at her getting herself a job at Garth's firm so she can spy on him, and by extension Cordelia, is still there, simmering. But her fear over what the detective is holding, over what seem to be a lot of awful things pointing to Cordelia somehow being involved in something dark, is greater.

Where are you, Garth? What's going on? Why is this happening?

'My daughter will not be speaking to you at all without the presence of a lawyer,' says her mother.

Detective Ashton frowns. 'But surely there's no need for that. All we want to do is have a conversation.'

Her mother turns to look at her. 'Cordelia, what do you want to do?'

And Cordelia suddenly feels very, very young, and completely unsure. She has no idea what the right answer is. But her mother seems certain and she hopes she can rely on that.

'If you decide to engage a lawyer,' Detective Ashton warns her, 'it means that any other conversations we have will have to be conducted at the police station.'

Cordelia risks a quick look at her mother, who nods slightly.

'I want a lawyer,' she says and Detective Ashton shakes her head, her shoulders dropping slightly. Detective Jameson looks disappointed as well and Cordelia takes this as a sign that she has made the right decision. She was bullied, however politely, into allowing them to search the apartment and take Garth's phone. She will not allow them to bully her into another 'conversation' again. Not now that her mother is here and seems so sure of what to do. She doesn't let the thought form of why her mother would know what to do in a situation like this. Whatever her mother did in the past, Cordelia needs her strength now.

'Now, unless you are going to formally arrest my daughter for something, I think she would like you to leave.'

'We will require her to come down to the police station for a formal interview,' says Detective Ashton.

'We need time to find a lawyer and it's Friday, so she will not be in a position to speak to you until next week,' says her mother, and Cordelia would like to return to her bedroom and curl up in bed and just leave the grown-ups to it. Only five days ago she felt like a fully functioning adult, and now she has been reduced to a child because her mother is here and the police seem to be accusing her of something.

'Fine. Take my card,' says Detective Ashton. 'We need you to come in as soon as possible, Cordelia.' She is looking at her mother rather than at Cordelia. 'We want to take that knife block with us,' she adds, pointing towards the kitchen.

'Not unless you have a search warrant for the apartment,' says her mother, and then she steps back, ready to close the door.

'We will need Cordelia to surrender her passport when she comes in for an interview,' says Detective Jameson.

'Fine,' says her mother.

'It would be odd, wouldn't it?' says the detective.

'What would be?' snaps her mother, her irritation with Detective Ashton obvious.

'If another man connected to a Morton woman was dead.'

The horror of this sentence, of what it might mean, of what it could mean, shocks Cordelia into a maelstrom of fear and fury. 'What are you saying?' she yells.

The detective seems to realise that this was entirely inappropriate and she raises her hands. 'Nothing, nothing,' she murmurs.

'Then perhaps you shouldn't have said it,' snaps her mother and she closes the door, forcing the detectives to step back.

'Rude woman,' says her mother.

'What now, Mum?' asks Cordelia, feeling a jittery hysteria rise up from her toes, making her whole body tremble. 'What now?'

'Now I'm going to go to work and I'm going to contact Janine and hopefully find you the best criminal defence lawyer in Melbourne.'

Cordelia feels her body sag and her shoulders round. She cannot fathom what has happened to her life and how everything has fallen apart again.

SIXTEEN

GRACE

Friday

I find I am exhausted. It's still early in the morning and I am ready for bed again but my daughter is looking at me with such despair in her eyes, as though I may know exactly what to do about this. I can't fall apart now. At least she is no longer yelling at me but I know she is still angry. Her anger is just being trumped by her fear and confusion.

'What do I do? cries Cordelia, her body hunching over.

I grab my daughter by her shoulders and hold on tightly. 'Cordelia, I want you to listen to me, really listen to me. We are not going to get hysterical because that will lead us nowhere. We are going to take things one step at a time and we are going to figure out a plan.'

She shakes me off and turns, walking away from me to the kitchen. 'What plan, Mum? What kind of a plan are we going to come up with? That knife was from my knife block,' she says, gesturing at the one empty spot in the block. 'I haven't been able to find it for... I don't even know how long because I wasn't paying attention. I thought Garth had just put it somewhere.'

She shakes her head and starts opening and closing drawers. 'Maybe it's here somewhere, maybe that knife is not from my kitchen, maybe...' She opens a bottom drawer in the kitchen and grabs a whole lot of utensils, picking them up and throwing them out onto the floor, pushing them one way and then the other, the sound clattering through the apartment.

'Stop it, just stop it,' I command and she stops abruptly, throwing me a look of dislike, which I ignore.

I move away from the door and sit down on the sofa, taking out my phone and checking the time. I have ten minutes until I need to leave for work. I would like to have the time to talk about this slowly and carefully with my daughter but it's more important than ever that I keep this job. Natalie knows something; in fact, there are probably quite a few people at work who know something more about Garth. I need to get that information before the police do.

But I also know that I need to make sure Cordelia is genuinely as confused by this whole situation as she says she is.

'Please come and sit down so we can talk, just talk,' I say and she moves out of the kitchen.

'Is there anything you're not telling me, Cordelia?' I ask her as she sits down on the sofa. I ask gently but I am mindful of the man in the leather jacket and what he said. 'Anything at all? Because it doesn't matter what it is – I can help you or at least I can try. We can get through whatever it is together.'

'No, Mum,' she says, shaking her head. 'Why wouldn't I tell you everything?' She grabs an ugly orange cushion, hugging it to her.

I don't say what I really want to say. *Can I trust you? Do I have the right to ask that? What are you hiding?* Instead I try to tell her again about the other danger she is in.

'I know you don't want to believe me but someone *has* been following you,' I say.

'Mum, please—' she says.

'It's a man,' I say. 'He wears a leather jacket and he's young, maybe the same age you are, and he... said something to me about you and Garth.'

'What? What exactly did he say? When did you speak to him?' she demands.

'He said that I should ask about your man and about what you were supposed to be doing now.'

'I don't understand,' she says, standing and pacing back and forth by the coffee table. 'Why would he speak to you? How did you know he was following me?'

There is no point in lying to her because she is going to find out anyway. 'When I first got to Melbourne, I wanted to see you. I just wanted to see you and you didn't want to talk to me so I... went to your work and came to this building and I just... followed you.' I swallow as I say these words, realising how it must sound to her. I don't want her to think I'm crazy.

'So you stalked me on Instagram *and* in real life? There's no one following me, Mum. *You're* following me.'

'I have a picture,' I say, taking out my phone, but she doesn't want to listen anymore.

'This is so disturbing, I can't even...' She throws her hands up and goes to stand by the glass balcony doors, folding her arms over her chest. 'And you got a job at Garth's firm. What is wrong with you?' she asks as she shakes her head. 'This is completely crazy,' she mutters.

I open my mouth to respond but I find I have no words available to help. Probably because she's right.

'Look, I think you need to leave. I can deal with this myself. I should never have asked for your help, never have trusted you. Just go, please.'

And here we are again. I stand and grab my bag. 'I know you're angry and I'm sorry... about all of it, but I just wanted to see that you were okay, just that, and I noticed him, and then a couple of days ago, I sat on a bench across the road from your building and he sat down and he spoke to me.'

'He spoke to you? How did he know that you knew me?'

I shake my head. 'I don't know, that's the thing... I was wearing a wig.'

'The wig you said you have to wear to work?' she asks, curiosity and concern overriding her terrible fury at me.

'Yes, I didn't... Look, I just wanted to see you and I didn't want you to recognise me. I know it was wrong but I have been trying to speak to you for years, Dee Dee, and you just wouldn't and I had to see you.'

'I think you're... I don't believe there is anyone following me. I don't know why you're making things up,' she says as she shakes her head, and she no longer sounds angry, but she does sound sorry for me. She slumps down onto the sofa, hugging the cushion to her chest again. 'You need to go, just leave, please.'

I nod sadly. There is nothing more I can do. 'I will find the name of a good lawyer and text it to you,' I say.

'I can find a lawyer myself,' she says, not looking at me, instead staring out at the sky filled with clouds, weak sun struggling to peep through.

Responding to her, arguing with her, will do no good so I just keep quiet. I move away from her to leave and pull open the front door.

'Let me ask you something, Mum,' she says and I stop.

'Anything,' I say, turning back to her.

'Do you know what happened to Garth? I mean, you said you don't like him, even though you've never met him, and you've been sneaking around and spying on us. You've been in Melbourne for the same amount of time he's been missing so do you know where he is and what's happened to him?' She doesn't look at me as she speaks the words and her tone is soft and neutral as though we are discussing the weather, but I can hear what she's actually saying, actually asking.

My mouth feels dry and I swallow quickly. 'Why would you ask me that?' I remember this about Cordelia from when she was a teenager, her ability to get under my skin, quickly and without even thinking about it too much. When she was fifteen, she went through a stage of pushing back on every single thing, from the time she was supposed to be home, to homework, to the way she spoke to me. We would argue about it all, and in every argument there would be shouting on both sides, and then suddenly, her tone would lower and she would say, 'Let me ask you something,' and inevitably I would just nod and be quiet and she would say something cutting and mean like, 'Do you think that you have a right to tell me what to do when you're barely here as a mother?' or, 'Is it possible that you don't like Sarah just because you've never spent any time with her because you only have time for work?' and I would wilt and just walk away.

She shrugs. 'Just curious. And I would like an answer.'

'Of course not,' I respond, not allowing myself to be reduced by this question. Instead, I allow myself to get angry again.

She's an adult, not a child, and she's the one in trouble, the one who needs my help. I would like to tell her this but I know it would serve no purpose so before she can say anything else or I can say something I regret, I finally leave her apartment with my heart hammering in my chest. When the door shuts behind me, I check to make sure there is no one around to witness me putting on my wig and place it carefully on my head. I feel better with it in place, as though some of the heaviness I carry as Grace Morton has disappeared. I am now Grace Enright again.

The reunion I had planned and the things I hoped for in coming here have not happened. It has all gone quite horribly wrong and I'm not sure what's going to happen now. And I hate feeling like that. I hate it.

I leave Cordelia's apartment building and try to get a cab

but can't find one. I try my Uber app but the nearest car is twenty minutes away. As I wait, I glance around me, my eyes darting back and forth as I try to spot the man in the jacket. I didn't see him when I arrived this morning but then he may just be staying away because the police have been here. I hate the idea that he's out here and my daughter is alone in her apartment. Why wouldn't she look at the picture? Does she actually know about him already? I hate having to question my child's integrity but I have to be honest with myself. If she thought Garth was cheating, it would have been terrible for her. I know how terrible it was for me and what I did when I found out about Robert.

I start walking, knowing that it will take me at least twenty minutes to get to work.

Frustrated, I call the firm.

Tristan answers. 'Harmer, Wright and Sing, how may I direct your call?'

'Oh, Tristan,' I say, 'it's Grace. I'm running terribly late because my car has broken down. I am hoping to get there as soon as possible.'

'Oh, Grace, I thought you might have to call in sick but how dreadful for you. You are having quite a week. Don't worry, I'll tell the powers that be for you.'

'Thank you so much.'

'The police are here again anyway, interviewing all the senior associates who work with Garth – you know, the lawyer who's disappeared,' he whispers into the phone.

'Oh,' I say, squeezing my hand into a fist, reminding myself to tread carefully. I'm grateful that Tristan is a bit of a gossip. I can tell he's just dying to discuss things, especially with someone not really connected to anything and who is willing to listen.

'Do you think... do you think they're going to speak to everyone?' I need to know if I have to just not make it to work today, because there's absolutely no way I am going to speak to the detectives. Detective Ashton will recognise me instantly. Cordelia is angry with me, and with good reason, but I need to see what else I can find out, and for that, I need to talk to the people Garth works with. But that may have to wait until Monday.

'I shouldn't think they'll talk to anyone else. I mean, they had a quick chat with me but I didn't have much to do with Garth. He's a bit of an arrogant dick, you know. Everyone knows he's got a girlfriend but he's still constantly on the prowl and he thinks he's so smart but he's too stupid to know where not to stick his...' Tristan stops speaking as though he's just realised what he was going to say.

My stomach clenches and I feel slightly sick.

'You know what I think has happened?' he continues in his dramatic whisper.

'What?' I ask as I walk faster, my breath short.

'I think that little girlfriend of his found out that he's been cheating on her, and something... well, I don't know, I'm not the jealous type. Maybe she is, and you know her mother was a little mad as well.' The urge to reach into the phone and slap Tristan makes me walk faster. But he has no idea who he's speaking to and so I can't blame him for the things he's saying.

I *was* a little mad and I did a terrible thing and I am still trying to make up for that.

'Is that what the police think?' I ask.

'Who knows what they think – that Detective Ashton is borderline rude to everyone. Still, it's the most exciting thing to happen around here in months.'

'It's a bit sad,' I say. 'I wonder what happened to him.'

'No idea,' says Tristan. 'Oh, they're talking to Natalie again... Sorry, Grace, I should go.'

I am nearly at the office, and when I get there, I stand across the road, watching the front of the building and just waiting.

Tristan will have told anyone who asks about my car trouble, which I will tell everyone was a flat battery, something so banal that no one ever questions it. That's the good thing about the position of assistant. No one cares where you are or what you're doing unless they need you.

I cannot be in the building at the same time as the detectives. Even with my wig on I am sure Detective Ashton will know who I am and I cannot imagine what will happen then.

Despite it only being the start of autumn, it's actually cold in the city, the wind furious and sharp. I wish I had a proper coat, but I didn't expect to stand outside for this long.

How long will they be there? How long can I stand here?

Finally, after about half an hour, I see them come out of the building, both of them on their phones. They cross over the street and I move back further against the wall where I am standing, dropping my head.

They walk right past me without even glancing in my direction, and I hear Detective Jameson say, 'Guilty as sin, I'm sure of it.'

And Detective Ashton answers, 'I know, and we'll get her, don't worry.'

And then they are gone and I dart across the road, my stomach twisting as I keep swallowing so I don't throw up.

Are they talking about Cordelia or Natalie? They must be talking about one of them, and I wonder, once again, if my daughter is hiding anything from me and how exactly I will ever find out what it is.

It might be easier to talk to Natalie, ironically. Natalie has no idea I am anything more than a slightly nosy temporary assistant. No one cares what they tell someone they may never meet again. Secrets spill out more easily to strangers than they do to those who are close to us.

I take a deep breath and enter the temperate air of the office building, relieved to be out of the wind tunnel of a city. 'Right,' I mutter as I get into the elevator and channel Grace Enright.

I'm ready to find out the truth.

SEVENTEEN

CORDELIA

Friday

When the door closes, Cordelia is suddenly very alone in the apartment. And everything crowds in on her, threatening to overwhelm her completely. Garth, her car, the knife, her mother following her, the man following her – if she can even believe her mother's story – her mother working at Garth's firm. She pushes the cushion against her face and just screams, long and loud until she cannot scream anymore.

Curling up on the sofa, she gives in to tears of frustration and anger and fear, not even trying to stop herself until she sinks into the black hole of an exhausted sleep.

She is woken by her phone ringing insistently on the coffee table next to her. She gropes for it, finally getting her hand on it and putting it to her ear after she swipes the screen. 'Yes,' she says, and she is shocked by how rough her voice sounds, as though she hasn't used it in days. It's the screaming and the crying.

'Cordelia,' says Jacinta, 'I thought I would see how you were,' and Cordelia groans. Work has suddenly become the least important thing in her life. She moves the phone from her ear and stares at the screen. It's Friday and there's usually a staff meeting over lunch. Jacinta likes to 'touch base' with everyone once a week.

'I'm so sorry, Jacinta, I'm really not well,' she says.

'Well, you do sound awful, Cordelia,' says her boss, a touch of sympathy creeping in and making Cordelia grateful for her rough voice.

It feels impossible to her that she will ever go back to work, that her world will ever not be in complete chaos. How can any of this get better? She has given up hoping that Garth will suddenly just appear with an explanation. She knows too much. He's obviously been involved in something and with someone.

'Well, you get well soon. If you are still unwell next week, you will need a medical certificate.'

'Okay,' says Cordelia, and she is ashamed that her throat clogs and she feels like she's going to cry.

'Chicken soup,' says Jacinta. 'It works wonders for a terrible cold.' And then her boss hangs up.

Cordelia curls up into a ball. She feels hungover but she knows she's not. She rarely drinks to excess and has only been hungover a few times in her life. But her head is pounding and her mouth is dry.

Getting off the sofa, she heads for the kitchen and drinks down two glasses of water and makes herself a coffee and a piece of toast.

She wishes she hadn't sent her mother away and at the same time knows that it was the right thing to do. She would like to text her and ask her if she has found out anything at Garth's firm but she also never wants to speak to her again. The things she's done are crazy. Is there actually a man following her or did her mother just make that up so that Cordelia wouldn't be upset that her mother was spying on her? Can she believe her mother about anything? Can she trust her at all?

It is maddening to feel this way after everything she has been through. She is seventeen again with her life in chaos and she can't believe it's happening.

The answer to what Garth is doing, to where he is and who he's with, must be somewhere here in this apartment, she decides.

She just needs to find it.

The first place she goes is back to his bedside drawer, emptying everything out and even searching under the drawers. Her search yields nothing except two more letters about the unpaid tax bill. From there she moves to his cupboard, throwing everything out and onto the floor, taking some pleasure in the mess she is making, despite knowing that she will be the one to clean it up. His pile of snow-white shirts grows on the floor, soon covered by navy suit jackets and pants. She checks in every pocket but finds nothing. Garth likes to keep his suits in pristine condition and only ever slots his phone into one of the pockets. He has pocket squares to match all his ties, a look that irritates Cordelia for some reason, and she tosses all of them out of a drawer, the vibrant reds and yellows and blues joining the pile.

She pulls out his underwear drawer and turns it upside down, disappointed when all that falls out is underwear.

In his sock drawer there is a card at the bottom and she pounces on it, only to find that it's the last birthday card she gave him. *Thank you for being there for me every day and making my life better in every way.* Cordelia feels herself cringe as she reads the trite words, but last year, she really meant them.

Garth's birthday is on the first of August, and last year she took him to their favourite Italian restaurant and gave him a pair of silver cufflinks with GSB intertwined. She'd had them made for him and they had cost her a lot of money, but he loved them and Cordelia can remember that as they shared cannelloni and squid ink pasta, she felt a moment of perfect contentment. That time feels very far away now. Natalie joined the firm a month or so afterwards and Garth was suddenly detached and distant.

Shaking her head, Cordelia lets go of the memory and climbs on a small step stool to grab everything at the top of the wardrobe, opening boxes that contain his collection of wallets and cufflinks, finding the pair she got him lying with all the others. The fact that he has left them and just disappeared stings as though he has left everything that could remind him of her behind.

There's not a lot to look through but then Garth didn't bring everything he owned with him from the UK. When he moved here, it was with only a few suitcases and boxes of stuff. It had always been the intention that he would go back once he was a partner in the firm and that Cordelia would go with him. She thought she would one day return to the UK as his wife.

She stands still for a moment, stunned at everything she once believed about her future. She thought she would be a clothing designer and dress the rich and famous; she thought she would marry an Australian and have two children; she thought she would watch her parents grow old. She's not naïve enough to believe that everything you want for your future comes to you, but she is shocked to find that every single thing she has ever wanted has been taken from her.

And it's all her mother's fault. Cordelia allows herself a hot, fierce minute of hating her mother before she admonishes herself to let go of the useless emotion.

She leaves the mess in the bedroom and goes to the spare room. There is a desk and chair in the room, for both her and Garth to use. Cordelia puts anything they receive in the post on the desk, and she goes through the envelopes quickly. Most of it is addressed to Garth and she never thinks much about it, assuming it's stuff from the UK or junk. Their bills come via email.

Now she sits down in the chair and opens everything,

including handwritten letters from his mother and an aunt. His mother writes him long letters on pale blue paper, and Cordelia scans the first one.

Dear darling,

The weather is terrible right now and of course the leaking roof isn't helping...

She drops the letter, knowing that it will say nothing else of value. Why can't the woman just use email?

Some part of her worries that he will be angry with her when he returns but she dismisses her fear. She will welcome his anger if he returns, welcome it and reflect it back to him. How dare he do this to her? She opens bills from the UK, junk mail from clothing stores and wine stores, a letter from his dentist telling him he was overdue for a check-up, another letter from his mother in which Evangeline rambles on about the house and everything that needs fixing and tells him that as her only son it is his duty to return to the UK and sort everything out. Evangeline sends a letter like that to Garth every month, and Cordelia knows that he feels very guilty that he is not there to help his mother, hence his daily phone call. 'I just want to make partner and then I will be in a better position with money to help her,' he has explained to Cordelia. But she has no idea how he will ever make enough money to repair his family home. It would need hundreds of thousands of pounds to fix it.

The desk has two drawers, which she opens, but there is nothing in them except stationery. Cordelia sighs and stares at the desk, touching a half-moon brass handle in the centre that is just there to balance out the look of the desk, matching the two handles on each drawer at the side.

Unless it's not just for looks... Cautiously, she pulls on the handle and is surprised when a wide, flat drawer pulls out.

There is only one thing in the drawer, another letter from Evangeline. Why isn't it with the others?

Cordelia pulls it out and opens it.

Dear darling,

Just a quick note to say thank you so much for the money. I know twenty thousand pounds is a lot but you always come through. It helped enormously. You can't believe how wonderful it is to have proper hot water again. I know it's really hard to have to help but you are so lovely for doing your best. I hope you can help with the roof as well.

Love, Mum

So, Garth has been sending his mother money to fix the house. She remembers the conversation about the footballer who cost Garth 'thousands'. Garth could be gambling to get money for his mother. Even though surely she wouldn't want him to be doing that… and is that why Cordelia has been paying for everything?

Why hasn't Garth said anything to her and how long has this been going on? Could Garth be in trouble because of his gambling? Has he borrowed money from someone bad?

She will have to show this to the police.

Her phone is on the desk and it pings with a text, causing Cordelia to jump and drop the letter.

Janine has given me the number of a lawyer named Nicholas Blake. Apparently, he's very good.

Cordelia doesn't reply. Misery and shock settle over her like a scratchy blanket she can't push off. Garth is sending his mother money and making Cordelia pay for their lives. She thinks about how many times he's mentioned her trust fund, about how adamant he is that she should forgive her mother, and she wants to be sick. Is he just with her for her money? Is it possible he knew who she was the day they met, knew who her mother was?

No, he loves me. He loved me?

Maybe he grew impatient with waiting for her to inherit money and started gambling to help his mother. Cordelia wonders if anyone else, if anyone at the firm, knows about this. He spends so much time with them. Maybe they know more than she does.

Now what? Cordelia thinks about marching over to Garth's office and demanding that someone tell her what they know. But she would never do that. Her mother did things like that, things like calling Tamara a whore in front of the whole office, something that Cordelia heard about at her mother's trial. Her mother doesn't have an assistant anymore or a business. She has nothing but regret and some money. Cordelia doesn't want to end up like her.

She will never behave like her mother. Her mother was crazy, and even now she is still doing strange things, but as Cordelia leaves the spare room to get something to eat, she wonders if perhaps she may need someone in her corner who's willing to do crazy things.

This whole situation is so weird and it's making her feel like she is actually going mad.

Is this how she felt when she burned down our house? Is this what it was like for her, this out-of-control desperation?

She reads her mother's text about the lawyer again and responds.

Thanks. I'm sorry about this morning. Please come over tomorrow night so we can talk.

She's not hungry for anything so she leaves the kitchen and climbs back into bed, turning over and returning to sleep because that's all she can think of to do.

What the hell has happened to my life? she thinks and then she can't help her tears when she realises that she had this thought six years ago, and here she is again, in chaos and despair with no idea how to fix or change anything.

Her phone pings again and she picks it up, meaning to tell her mother to stop texting her, but the message is not from her mother.

I need to speak to you. I know what's going on.

It's from Natalie.

Cordelia drops the phone as though it's burning her hand and she covers her mouth.

Then she picks it up again and looks at the message. She has no choice. She has a thousand questions but she wants to see Natalie's face when she asks them.

EIGHTEEN
GRACE

Friday

As the elevator doors open on the office floor, I realise that I am nearly two hours late for work, and I hope the car trouble excuse will not be a problem.

'Grace,' says Tristan when he sees me, 'that took ages, what happened?'

'I know,' I reply, nodding. 'Roadside assistance took forever and it was so cold waiting for them. It's ridiculous that it's this cold in autumn. I really need a coffee.'

'Of course you do,' he agrees with a smile, and I move away from him and to my office.

I drop my bag on my desk, checking my phone first to see if I have anything from Cordelia, knowing that there will probably be nothing but feeling heartbroken when that's the case.

And then I go to the bathroom. When I'm washing my hands, Natalie walks in, a tissue in her hand as she dabs at her eyes. She is obviously crying, and when she sees me, she darts into a stall.

'Is everything okay?' I say, expecting her to just tell me that it is, but instead she comes out again, blows her nose and grabs another tissue.

'Is this about... Garth? The man who's missing?' I ask.

Natalie nods and sniffs.

'Do the police have any idea what happened to him?'

She shakes her head. 'They think... I mean they kept asking about his relationship with his girlfriend.'

'Really,' I say, a slight ringing in my ears. 'I wonder why that is. Do you know her?'

She nods her head slowly, bringing a hand up to flick her hair over her shoulder and surreptitiously scratch her neck, where I can see red welts appearing. 'I get hives when I'm stressed,' she says softly.

'I understand,' I say. 'It is a very stressful situation.' I want to repeat my question about her knowing Cordelia but I know better than to push. People will tell you all sorts of things if they think you're willing to listen and if they think you have no skin in the game.

Natalie doesn't have to know that I am very much in this game, and that I need to make sure that my family wins.

'His girlfriend is very sweet actually. Probably a bit too young for him, and I think very naïve.'

'Oh,' I say.

'Yes, and I don't think she has any idea about what he's really like.' She shakes her head.

'Does he...?' I hesitate to ask the question. Will she wonder why I'm asking it? Will it make her question who I am? But then I am the nosy assistant. And people jump to conclusions all the time.

'Does he cheat on her?' I ask, watching her face carefully.

'I wouldn't know about that,' she snaps, clenching her fists. 'I need to get back to work.' I can see I've upset her. Well, if she's been sleeping with my daughter's boyfriend, she should be upset, she should be suffering.

'But if he has been cheating,' I say, 'surely the police should be told that?'

Natalie narrows her eyes at me. 'I don't think that's any of your business,' she says. 'And anyway, I don't know much about his personal life.' She turns to leave but not before I catch a scarlet flush on her cheeks and then see her scratch desperately at her neck. She's lying, obviously.

Natalie quickly grabs another tissue and opens the door, just as Kelsey is walking in. She bumps the younger woman as she pushes past her.

'Rude,' says Kelsey.

'Probably just a bad day,' I say.

'Everyone is having a bad day,' she says and she sounds almost gleeful. 'I've sent my dad an email to tell him I'm dropping out of university but he hasn't even responded because he's too caught up in all this,' she says, waving her hand.

'Did you know him, Garth?' I ask her and she rolls her eyes.

'I know everyone. I've been working here since November last year.'

'And what did you think of him?' I question her casually but she's not falling for it.

'Don't you ask a lot of questions for someone who's only worked here for a few days, Grace? You've heard that old saying, haven't you? About cats and curiosity.'

'Oh, well,' I say, feeling myself flush. She is very outspoken for someone so young. 'I think that everyone wants to know what happened.' I lean forward and look in the mirror as I speak, checking my make-up and refusing to answer her rude question. 'But I'm sure you had very little to do with Garth.' I shrug like it doesn't matter to me at all.

'That's not...' she begins and then she shakes her head. 'I really need the bathroom and I'm sure you need to get back to work.' She goes into a stall, and when I hear her turn the lock on the door, I know that it's time to give up on getting anything else from her. She's an intern and the daughter of a partner. She probably knows a lot more about what's going on here than she's willing to tell me. But I know I will get no more from her today.

So, I return to my office. I get to work, knowing I have to wait until lunchtime to call Janine. Even if Cordelia never wants to speak to me again, something I hope will very much not be the case, I still need to help her find a lawyer.

'Grace,' she says when she answers the phone, and I can hear the question in her voice.

'I'm fine,' I say, 'but I need your help for Cordelia.' Janine is not one for chit-chat.

'Because?'

'I'm in Melbourne, where she lives now. Her boyfriend is missing. They found a knife in her car. And someone saw the car leaving her building at 2 a.m. on the last night she saw him. He was supposed to be working late on Monday, the day after, but he didn't go to work and never came home.'

'Hmm,' says Janine and I know she is taking notes as I speak.

'And how long has he been missing?'

'Five days now,' I say.

'Right,' says Janine. 'Leave it with me. I'll look up my contacts and send you some names.'

'She didn't do anything to him, obviously,' I say.

'Of course not,' agrees Janine. And I remember when I had my first appointment with her, still shaking and sweating as I detoxed from alcohol. 'I didn't mean to do it,' I told her. 'It was an accident.'

'Of course it was,' she said, nodding her head and then pushing her glasses up so they sat closer to her eyes. 'It was absolutely an accident. But now you need to tell me everything that led to the accident.'

I didn't tell her everything, of course. I told her I lit candles and fell asleep. I never mentioned finding a letter from my husband's lover and burning that. Lawyers and police don't need to know everything. No one ever really needs to know the whole story.

I work through the rest of my lunch hour to make up for lost time, getting a text from Janine just before I get up to make myself another cup of coffee.

Nicholas Blake – very good criminal defence lawyer, best in the business. He'll cost you but he's a master at the job.

I thank her and send Cordelia the name, not expecting a reply.

I am exhausted from this morning. The drama of the police interviewing people and Garth being missing seems to seep in through my closed office door and I can feel everyone whispering – and I know that some of them are whispering about my daughter. And I know without a shadow of a doubt that Garth has cheated on her and that the woman he has slept with is probably Natalie, just as Cordelia suspected.

As I power through, struggling to concentrate, I am grateful that tomorrow is Saturday. I am in the middle of a spreadsheet when I get a message from Cordelia.

Thanks. I'm sorry about this morning. Please come over tomorrow night so we can talk.

I want to sob with joy. She's giving me another chance and I am so grateful. Perhaps she understands that everything I am doing is for her and her happiness.

At the end of the day, I quickly get ready to leave the office, longing for my hotel room and some peace and a large glass of wine.

I would like to spend some time with Cordelia tonight but I know she needs a little space.

I'm standing up with my bag packed when Kelsey walks past my office, looking in and then stepping inside.

'Going home?' she asks me.

'I am,' I say, 'what about you?'

'Meeting my boyfriend,' she says, her eyes scanning my desk.

'Well...' I say, having exhausted my appetite for conversation.

'Hey,' she says, 'my earring. I've been looking for it everywhere.' She leans down and picks up the earring from my desk. I had completely forgotten about it.

'I found it on the floor... near the bathroom,' I say, stopping myself just in time from saying I found it in Garth's office.

'My dad gave them to me – he would have been so upset if I'd lost one,' she says with a smile. 'Thanks.'

'How long has it been missing?' I ask.

'Hmm,' she says. 'Months, I think. I wore them last Christmas. I was hoping it would just turn up.'

I nod, watching her face, searching for the truth. She's only nineteen – surely there's no way she and Garth are involved? And she says she has a boyfriend.

'Have a good night,' she sings and she turns and leaves.

As I walk in the brisk air, I think about everything I know about Garth and I realise I know very little. For starters, what was Kelsey's earring doing in his office?

Frustrated that I have no answers, I stop in front of a restaurant and go inside, ordering myself a glass of wine while I peruse the menu.

I order a steak and baked potato from a pretty young waitress and I get through two glasses of wine before I force myself to stop.

In my hotel room, I am glad to remove my wig and the glasses and just be Grace Morton again, just be me.

Tomorrow night I will see my daughter and hopefully we can figure this out together.

I run myself a deep, luxurious bath and soak for an hour as I go through everything I know. What do the knife and the car covered in mud have to do with this? Is it possible that Cordelia found out Garth cheated and hurt him in some way? I shake my head at this thought. Cordelia is a lot smaller than Garth and she would have had to work hard to overpower him... and I can't believe she would ever resort to violence. Of course, I would never have believed who I became as I struggled with my feelings over my late husband's affair. Jealousy is the most pernicious of emotions and it can lead to terrible things.

Without being able to stop myself, I dry off a hand, lift my phone off a small round stool next to the bath and text Cordelia.

Are you okay?

Not really.

Should I come over?

No, please don't. I'll see you tomorrow night. I need some time.

There's nothing else I can do now. I have a glass of wine next to the bath, ordered from room service, and I take a deep sip, letting the velvet taste soothe me.

I scroll through my phone for a few minutes before returning to Instagram to check on Tamara, but she's added nothing new. She doesn't even seem to have a job although perhaps if she does, it's not glamorous enough to mention on Instagram. Leaving her page, I go through Garth's Instagram again, wondering if I've missed something that could help me figure out what's going on.

I look at the picture of him holding a glass of beer again, read Natalie's cryptic comment – *Hope it was worth it* – and wonder what she meant.

I look at the date of the picture and see that it was posted on 18 December, close to Christmas, but it doesn't look like a Christmas party. I click on the picture and enlarge it, hoping for something that can tell me what Natalie was talking about.

I can see that Garth is sitting at a table in a pub, can see the wood-panelled walls and groups of people behind him, most of them caught mid-movement so not really clearly pictured.

I study the man who my daughter has been with for over four years, who is now missing and was definitely cheating. My eyes roam from his messy blond hair to his wide smile and face covered in light stubble, and then I glance at his arm, more specifically at the arm and hand that is resting on the table, not holding the beer. I see the side of a woman's hand, long red fingernails. The woman's hand is resting close to Garth's arm, very close, actually touching his arm. Is that Natalie's hand, and if not, whose hand is it? I enlarge the photo some more and then I see the tip of an ear, an earring and some hair. The earring is very distinctive, a small cluster of diamonds with a tiny sapphire in the middle.

It's just work drinks. It doesn't mean anything. Unless it does.

I want to call Cordelia immediately but I caution myself to wait until I know for sure, until I've connected all the dots. I caution myself to wait.

NINETEEN

CORDELIA

Saturday

Cordelia glances around her at the filled café where families sit in groups next to friends just catching up. The vibe is typical of a Saturday morning, with everyone in a good mood in the first hours of the weekend, time stretching ahead of them to do whatever they want. The air is warm and fragrant with coffee and baked goods.

The café is actually one she's been to before with Garth, when she came to visit him at work. She had asked him repeatedly to take her to see his office.

'Why would you want to come to my work?' he'd asked her.

'I just want to see who you work with and where you work so I can imagine you during the day,' she'd said, smiling at him.

'Weird, but okay,' he'd replied, and so she took a day off from university to go shopping and met him at his office, was introduced to everyone and saw his desk, and then they came here for coffee.

But that was at least two years ago, well before Natalie arrived. Would she have been jealous of Natalie even then?

Maybe, but she and Garth were in a much better place then, still loving the idea of being together in the same city, loving being back together. She remembers being so proud of him when she saw his nameplate in brass on his office door, remembers congratulating herself on finding such a handsome, intelligent, lovely man, and she also remembers thinking that nothing was ever going to derail them. How could it? They loved each other and he was so supportive and caring. But here they are. He is missing and she is planning to meet the woman he may or may not be having an affair with.

Natalie and Charles have an apartment near here so that's probably why she picked it.

Cordelia has had a sleepless night waiting for this meeting, everything Natalie could or would say running through her head. It would have been so much better to do it yesterday but Natalie wouldn't agree to it. She had texted Natalie back as soon as she got her message.

Where and when?

Tomorrow morning, Westgate Coffee.

Why not today? I can come to you.

Not today. I'm at work. Tomorrow at 10 a.m.

She agreed because she didn't have a choice.

The door to the café swings open, bringing with it a gust of cool air, and Cordelia looks up from studying the menu even though she's not going to order anything to eat. A man with grey hair has walked in and Cordelia shifts in her chair, thinking about the man who her mother claims is following her, her heart racing as she studies the stranger. But then she sees he's holding the hand of a little girl. Just a grandfather and granddaughter out for the morning. Her mother said the man was Cordelia's age anyway. There is no one following her.

She looks at her watch. Natalie is five minutes late.

Cordelia prepared for this meeting as though she was going on a date, making sure that she blow-dried her hair perfectly straight, that she applied her make-up carefully. Then she selected a pair of grey pants and a silk blouse to wear under her black trench coat. She wanted to look every inch the professional. She wanted to look older than she is and able to handle whatever Natalie is going to say. In truth she felt like a child playing dress-up.

It's a typical city café – bright white walls, stained wooden floor, timber chairs and tables, young people behind the counter making coffee and serving. The walls are decorated with posters of kittens, which Cordelia finds comforting to look at, staring for a few minutes at a black-and-white one playing with a rubber duck. She wanted a cat but Garth likes dogs, and it would be unfair on a dog to have him in an apartment with two parents who have to be at work all day.

Cordelia's coffee is too bitter but the sugar is all the way over on the counter and she doesn't have the energy to get up and get it. Instead, she just sips it and watches her phone. They were supposed to meet at 10 a.m. and it's ten minutes past now. Finally, she sees Natalie walk into the café. The woman looks amazing as always but Cordelia is immediately aware that she is dressed incorrectly. Natalie has her white-blonde hair swept up in a ponytail and is wearing tight blue jeans and a soft blue knitted top. Cordelia feels stupidly overdressed. Natalie spots Cordelia immediately, waves and then goes to order herself a cup of coffee.

'I'm not looking forward to winter,' says Natalie as she sits down opposite Cordelia, who nods, finding the greeting strange, too cordial, too banal for what they are about to discuss.

'I'm listening,' says Cordelia and she watches as a flush rises up from Natalie's neck onto her cheeks and then she scratches at her neck.

'The police have been at the office,' says Natalie. 'They've interviewed everybody, and nobody knows where Garth is.'

Cordelia sits back in her chair, staring at Natalie. 'I thought you said you knew what had happened to Garth. That's the only reason I'm here – because you said you knew what had happened and you were going to tell me. Why have you brought me here if you don't know anything? I already knew the police have interviewed people at the office because obviously they would have.' Cordelia can hear the edge of anger in her words. She wants to lean across the table and slap Natalie but she curls her hands around her terrible cup of coffee instead.

The colour on Natalie's face deepens and she looks around the café, her green eyes darting back and forth. 'I wanted to tell you myself in person because it's going to come out and you might as well know. I just didn't know how to get you here.'

Cordelia feels heat rise inside her and she clenches her fists, her short nails pushing into her palms.

'I knew it,' she whispers.

'You don't know what I am going to say.'

'Yes, I do,' spits Cordelia. 'You're sleeping with Garth. You've been sleeping with Garth and I knew it. Every time I saw you together, I understood that it was happening, but of course he denied it.' Cordelia can taste acid in her mouth. The true awfulness of what she has suspected consumes her, and she closes her eyes for a second, visualising herself grabbing Natalie's pretty blonde hair and pulling it off her head.

Gosh, so much violence, Cordelia, you're sounding a lot like your mother. She hears Garth's slightly mocking voice in her head. The vision disappears as she opens her eyes again.

A waitress in jeans and a white T-shirt appears with Natalie's coffee, and she places it on the table with a quick smile.

'Thank you,' says Natalie, picking up the coffee and taking a quick large sip, and Cordelia can see that it burns going down.

'It only happened once,' says Natalie, not meeting Cordelia's gaze. 'At the company retreat. We were both drunk and it only happened once. But I had to tell the police because they were asking everybody about any interaction they'd had with Garth. I had to tell them.'

Cordelia casts her mind back to the company retreat held four months ago in the spring. The firm hired a beautiful old hotel in the country and took everyone there for team-building and whatever else they did on such retreats. She remembers Garth moaning about having to go: 'I really hate all those stupid trust exercises – it's not like they make me a better lawyer. And the food is always awful, and if you complain, everyone makes you feel like an idiot.'

'Poor baby, will you miss me?' she asked him.

'You know I will,' he replied. Did he seem different when he returned? Not particularly but then Cordelia was not looking for him to be different, just for him to be Garth. Did they have sex the night he returned? She thinks they did and she shifts on her hard wooden chair in the café, feeling a touch of disgust. How could he have done that? Natalie is staring at her, her face still flushed and a look in her eyes like she's searching for forgiveness. Well, Cordelia is not in the business of forgiveness.

'And now you've had to tell me. Are you proud of yourself, Natalie? Are you proud of what you've done? Do you know where Garth is? Do you know what's happened to him or was this just about assuaging your own guilt?' She bares her teeth, hissing the words at the woman sitting across from her.

Natalie takes another sip of coffee, shaking her head. 'No, I want to explain. Please let me explain. It happened once and I realised afterwards that it would never happen again. But you should know, Cordelia, that I'm not the only woman he has slept with at the firm. He flirts with everyone. We all know he's with you, but he still flirts with all the women at the company, with all the women he meets, even clients.'

Cordelia feels like she might be sick. She would like to cover Natalie's mouth with her hand to stop all the terrible truths spilling out.

'And sometimes when he's talking about you, he calls you his...' Natalie looks down at her half-drunk cup of coffee.

Cordelia picks up her own cup, drains the last of it, feeling the granules on her tongue. Darkly bitter like her resentment of this woman and now of Garth.

'His what?'

Natalie closes her eyes as though saying the words is not something she can face. 'He calls you his little credit card.'

'Oh God,' says Cordelia, feeling the physical sting of the words on her skin. She looks round the café, where she can see a mother balancing a toddler on her lap, gently helping him spoon cappuccino froth into his mouth. Ironic but she thought it wouldn't be long until she and Garth were married and had children of their own. She was looking forward to being a family again, to being a proper family, and she was going to do everything differently to how her mother had done it. But now everything is in tatters again, everything in her life is in tatters.

'I can't,' says Cordelia, leaning forward and dropping her head into her hands. She feels like she's being assaulted with words, like she is being battered with everything Garth, a man she thought she knew, has done. She wants to run, to get up and run, but she knows she needs to hear everything Natalie has to say. She lifts her head, fury surging through her. Natalie must be enjoying this on some level. She's trying to come across as kind and concerned but she must be loving the fact that Cordelia has chosen such an awful man to fall in love with.

'And why have you decided to so kindly tell me all this,

Natalie?' asks Cordelia. 'Is it just because you slept with him once or do you have another motive?'

Natalie pushes back her chair and stands up. 'I did it, to be honest, because I thought we were kind of friendly and because I hated the way he spoke about you and I always wanted to say something. The police have been at the firm and I didn't think that you should be ambushed by the stuff he's said and what he's done.'

'What *you've* done with him,' says Cordelia, and Natalie nods her head.

'I don't think I'm the only one,' she says.

'Who else?' asks Cordelia, her voice rising in the café so people turn to look at her.

'I don't know, I don't know... not for sure,' says Natalie. 'Look, I wanted to tell you because you're not a bad person. You're sweet, and he's taken advantage of you. He takes advantage of anybody who will allow him to.'

'Who else has he slept with?' she asks again.

'I'm not saying anything. A lot of rumours about Garth and women fly around the firm.'

'Rumours that you were prepared to keep to yourself, that you would have had to keep to yourself along with your own indiscretion if he hadn't gone missing,' says Cordelia.

'You're right and I am sorry. All I can tell you is how sorry I am.'

She looks down at Cordelia with a pained, searching expression. There is pity in her eyes. A small, tiny part of Cordelia knows, really, that Natalie is doing what she thinks to be right, but that doesn't help her now. It doesn't stop her wanting to scream and it doesn't stop the hate she feels in this moment.

Natalie carries on. 'I just wanted to prepare you, that's all. I can see that was a stupid idea. I should just have let the police tell you everything. I'm going now. I'm sorry about what happened at the retreat. I wasn't myself and it's not something I would ever do again.'

'And what if I told Charles about it?' asks Cordelia, looking up at her. 'What if I just called up Charles and went, "Hey, did you know Natalie and Garth slept together at the company retreat?"'

Natalie clutches at her top, shaking her head. 'I told Charles after it happened. I was so guilty I told him and he forgave me. But you do what you want, Cordelia. I apologise for wanting to protect you from just how horrible Garth is.'

Natalie turns to leave.

'Are you lying for him, is he hiding and you're just lying for him?' Cordelia blurts out.

'No, obviously not,' says Natalie, shaking her head. 'I'm sorry, Cordelia, really sorry,' and she walks away, leaving Cordelia slumped in her misery.

She wants to get up and move, wants to leave the café with its stifling heat filled with people who have nothing to worry about but what kind of cake to order. But her legs won't obey her. Her entire body feels heavy as the knowledge of who Garth is and what he has done settles over her.

As the clatter and chatter of the café fades, she tries to put into words what she is feeling, just so she can explain it to herself. Devastation? Yes, that seems right. Humiliation? Absolutely. Fear? That works as well.

He's cheated on her, he's used her to pay bills while he sends money to his mother, and he's lost money gambling, maybe even more than just the thousands he mentioned about the footballer.

What? How is such a thing possible? How did I let this happen to me?

Did he know all this was going to come out and just run away? In her search of the apartment, she didn't see his passport. Sitting back in her chair, she shakes her head. She didn't see his passport. Why didn't she specifically look for that? Why didn't the police ask for it? Would they know if he had gotten on a plane? Probably. The same questions she has been asking herself for days go round and round in her head: *Would he just run away from me, from work, from his mother? Who is he cheating with? Who is he? Who actually is he?*

She pictures him now, on a beach somewhere, sitting under a hot sun looking out over a perfectly blue ocean. He probably has a cocktail in his hand and a beautiful woman next to him, and he is probably laughing at her, at the police.

Anger, fury, rage? Yes, those words work as well.

She takes her phone out of her bag and thinks about calling her mother. Does Natalie have any idea that her mother is working at Garth's firm? Have they interacted at all?

She knows that her mother is likely just waiting to hear from her daughter, and so she finds another feeling. Gratitude. She is grateful she has her mother to rely on, despite everything... bizarre her mother has done. Her mother will understand all the other feelings she has because whether it was true or not, Grace believed her husband cheated. And Cordelia knows that if she had the chance right now to kill Garth, she would. She absolutely would.

Without calling, she returns the phone to her bag. She's not ready to speak to her mother, not yet. She will see her tonight.

Somehow, she manages to stand and then she leaves the café, a gust of wind hitting her in the face, making her gasp.

She starts walking, just walking as thoughts swirl in her head. She walks for two blocks and then three and then four. The wind picks up and she starts sweating, feeling blisters forming on her heels because she's wearing ridiculous shoes to walk in. Going home is probably the best option, and she stops, her body sagging a little as she looks around her to figure out where she is.

She's right near her work and she has no desire to get caught out and about, even though it's Saturday. Jacinta has a habit of going into work on the weekend and then making sure that everyone knows this by sending emails on a Saturday.

Turning abruptly, Cordelia catches a glimpse of a man in a black leather jacket and she stops, watching as he spins around and moves in the opposite direction as though she has caught him following her. Did she just imagine that? Is this the man her mother was talking about? Has he actually been following her all along? She needs to get a better look at his face so she speeds up to catch up to him, thinking she will tap him on the shoulder and then say she thought she recognised him. Moving quickly, she tries to get to him but the faster she goes, the faster he goes. 'Hey,' she calls, trying to ignore the terrible burning of her heels.

The city is full of people and a whole lot of them stop to stare at her but she ignores them. The man is moving quickly now, almost running away from her, and Cordelia speeds up. 'Hey,' she calls again.

He turns down a side street that Cordelia knows is a dead end because there is a café at the end called the Bottom of the Road Café.

'Ha,' she says triumphantly. She'll catch up to him now.

She keeps going, catching another glimpse of the leather jacket, although this time the man looks shorter, but she runs up to him as he stops at the café and touches him on the shoulder. 'Hey,' she says and the man turns around. 'Hello, hi,' he says. 'I speak no English, thank you.' He has a neat brown beard and he smiles widely.

Cordelia stops, feeling her mouth open and close stupidly. This is the wrong man. He is shorter and older and she's pretty sure the other man didn't have a beard although she did not get a really good look at him. 'Sorry,' she says as she backs away and looks around her. The man in the black leather jacket is gone.

He has simply vanished as though he never existed at all. Did she imagine him?

I am not going crazy. I am not going crazy.

Pulling her phone out of her pocket, Cordelia calls an Uber. Her heels are burning, her body is covered in sweat and the thick make-up she put on to meet Natalie is caking on her face.

She moves to the street slowly to wait for Jack, the Uber driver, who will be here in two minutes. Leaning against a wall, she closes her eyes and lets her body rest. She is exhausted, completely exhausted, and the only logical thing she can do now is sleep the rest of the day away.

Her mother will come over tonight and perhaps she will know what to do.

Her phone vibrates in her hand and she answers the call in case it's the Uber driver.

'Yes?'

'Hi, Cordelia, this is Detective Ashton. I just want to make sure that we will see you on Monday at the station.'

'No, I don't have a lawyer yet,' she answers. 'Can't it wait?'

'I'm afraid we do need you to come in as soon as possible. I will give you until Tuesday to present yourself to the station for a formal interview.'

Cordelia feels her stomach twist as she hears the threat in the detective's voice, and she covers her mouth, afraid that she will throw up on this street in front of all these people who are just having an ordinary Saturday.

'Okay,' she says, taking her hand away from her mouth and ending the call without waiting for a reply from the detective.

It's only going to get worse from here, she can feel it.

TWENTY

GRACE

Saturday

I would have preferred to see Cordelia this morning. I need to show her the picture on Garth's Instagram, need to ask her if she's met Kelsey, if she knows anything about Garth and the young woman.

I have sent her a few messages this afternoon, asking her how she is, but she has not replied to any of them, except for one text that simply said:

Please leave me in peace for the day. I will see you tonight.

At 6.30 p.m., I walk into her building, ready for whatever she may have to say, ready to confront her with what I know and to finally get her to tell me everything she knows.

I have no idea if Cordelia has called the lawyer Janine suggested. I have no idea about anything. And because of that, I feel like this situation is completely out of my control.

I am carrying takeaway Thai food, having chosen a mix of vegetarian dishes. I know Cordelia loves a green curry with tofu, and I love the stir fry with chilli and garlic. I've added some extra mixed vegetable dishes so I can leave the food for her to eat over the weekend. I know she's not nourishing her body as she should.

When she opens her front door, she looks so fragile, so broken, I can't help a gasp of shock. She has obviously been crying.

'Oh, darling,' I say, stepping towards her, but she steps back towards her kitchen, where she grabs some plates for the food I'm carrying. I notice that the half-drunk bottle of red wine is still on the counter and my craving for a drink is so strong, I actually have to grab a hold of her countertop and squeeze for a moment.

'Are you okay?' she asks.

'Yes, just... I haven't eaten since breakfast, and I get a little nauseous when I don't eat,' I say.

'I haven't eaten at all,' she says, shaking her head. 'What a pair we are.'

'I know,' I agree with a small laugh and I am grateful to see a smile on her face.

We serve ourselves from the containers, piling our plates high and taking them to the glass dining room table, where we sit and eat in silence for a few minutes.

'Do you want a drink?' asks Cordelia.

I know how I want to answer, but I also know that's the wrong answer. 'Whatever you're having is fine,' I say and she brings a bottle of mineral water and two glasses to the table.

'I met with Natalie this morning,' she says.

I stop eating for a moment, my last bite of broccoli refusing to go down until I gulp some water.

'Oh,' I say.

'Yes, and she... told me some stuff, just...'

'I'm listening,' I say, finishing my water and pouring myself some more.

I push my food around my plate as she explains about Garth and Natalie sleeping together.

Cordelia eats mechanically as she tells me the whole story, including that Garth is sending money to his mother and making her pay for rent and that he's called her his 'little credit card', a phrase that makes my blood boil.

When her plate is empty, she goes to the kitchen to refill it. I am glad she's eating but I can see that she's not even hungry anymore, just filling the hole that has been created inside her by the certain knowledge that Garth cheated on her with Natalie and that he has probably been sleeping with other women as well. I remember this feeling, the shock, the horror, the questioning. I poured alcohol onto it to drown it, something I hope Cordelia never resorts to.

'So that's it. I thought he was and he was and it's even worse than that and now he's missing and the police think that I had something to do with it and that detective told me I have to come in by Tuesday, and... I just... don't know what to do now.'

She eats while we sit in silence as I struggle to think of what to say, of exactly how to help her.

'I spoke to Natalie yesterday,' I tell her now because it's important that she knows.

'What? Why didn't you say so before?'

'I was obviously going to tell you but most of what she told me is what she told you. She didn't mention sleeping with him, obviously, even though I gave her a chance to. She just kept saying he wasn't a good guy.'

'I don't even know when he has time to cheat. He's so busy with work and trying to make partner. He was so busy,' she says, blinking back tears.

'I think people find time for the things they want to do, especially the things they know are wrong and that they are keeping a secret from those around them.'

'But he loves... loved me,' she says. 'I thought he loved me. I thought we had no secrets. I told him everything about my life, about you, about the fire. I told him everything. Why would he keep secrets from me?'

'I think...' I say, wondering if I should bring this up now, wondering if she needs to know this at all.

'You think?'

'I think he may have also slept with a young woman named Kelsey – she's an intern at his office. Her father is one of the partners. She's only nineteen.'

'What? How do you know?'

I explain about being in Garth's office and the earring and then I show her the picture on Instagram.

'This proves nothing, it was a work function, it was...' She shakes her head. 'I don't think it's possible. Garth wouldn't... he wouldn't. No, I just don't believe that.' She leans forward and grabs more food, shoving it in her mouth, shoving away the possibility of Garth and a young girl and I know it's not the time to push my theory.

I close my eyes, summoning Grace Enright, the woman who cannot be toyed with, lied to, manipulated and hurt. I understand her confusion and her despair.

'I don't have an answer for you, my darling. But I'm here to help. Tell me what you want to do.'

'I don't know,' she says in a small voice, still eating. 'I would love to just leave, just like pack up my stuff and leave, but I'm in this now and I have a feeling that he's run away but I don't know why there is mud on my car or a knife in my car... It's just weird and you say I'm being followed and that he spoke to you.'

'He did,' I say, 'and you are.'

She sits back in her chair, putting her hands on her stomach because she's obviously feeling uncomfortable. 'I thought someone was following me today. I was walking and then I turned around and I thought I saw someone but I chased after him and... it was just some guy who didn't even speak English.'

'I need to show you pictures I took of the man,' I say.

'But why, and what does this have to do with Garth going missing?' She stands and takes our empty plates to the kitchen, drops them on the counter and starts pacing, pushing her hands through her hair.

'We need to think calmly about this, Cordelia. We need to not panic and just think,' I say, wanting her to stop her furious pacing. It's making me feel nauseous.

She stops and looks at me; a flicker of loathing appears on her face and then disappears quickly. 'You haven't been out of the clinic for very long. It's only been what... three months? And now my boyfriend is missing and someone is following me and you? What more did you do, Mum? Is there someone else whose life you've screwed up?' she spits. I remember this about her, how she changes moods with lightning-quick speed. But the last time I saw her she was a teenager and behaved as a teenager did. She's an adult now but behaving like she's still a child.

I raise my palms to her. 'No, Cordelia, I haven't upset anyone,' I say, even as I think about Melody, who worked for Ava and wanted to destroy Ava's life, and the people she must have left behind when she died.

And then I think about Ava, who doesn't even know she is my daughter. But Ava wouldn't have me followed, even if she suspected I was somehow involved with what happened to Melody. And what would any of it have to do with Cordelia anyway? Ava had no idea who I really was, and Melody may have known I had a daughter, but Melody is gone.

'Everything was fine until you got out, you know – my life was fine,' she yells, stepping up to me, fury making her cheeks flush a deep red.

My anger rises to the surface again. 'You and I both know that's not the case,' I yell back. 'Garth's cheating had nothing to do with me.'

'Maybe I got paranoid and pushed him into it. Maybe you getting out made me all... crazy and he—'

'Cordelia, stop,' I snap. 'This has nothing to do with me. He cheated with Natalie and maybe with... others. He obviously has a problem with commitment. It has nothing to do with me, and believe me when I tell you that it has nothing to do with you.'

She bursts into tears, her shoulders heaving, and she sinks down onto the sofa. 'Where is he?' she sobs. 'Why did he leave me? What is wrong with me?'

I sit down beside her and hold on to her until she calms down.

'Sorry,' she says. 'I know, logically, that this has nothing to do with you. I know you're just trying to help.'

'I am and I will help, I promise. Have you called the lawyer?'

'No, I didn't... I don't know, I just thought it would go away.'

'Okay, then that's the first thing we need to do.'

'I can't now, it's nearly eight on a Saturday night. I'm sure he's with his family or something.'

'Just call and leave a message so that he can get back to you on Monday.'

'Okay,' she agrees, standing and going to get her phone, which she has left in her bedroom. I hear her making a call and then I hear her speaking for longer than I thought she would. I am very tempted to go and stand outside her bedroom door and hear what she is saying, but I busy myself with tidying up and wiping down the kitchen counters. One swipe of the cloth and the spilled sauces disappear and the white marble is perfectly clean again. If only it were so easy to fix a life. My mind strays to the knife block with one empty space and I see the rust-brown spots on the knife held by the detective, feeling myself shudder at the thought.

After ten minutes she comes out. 'I have a meeting with him

on Monday morning at nine. He answered his phone and was actually expecting my call. He said to tell the police that he's my lawyer if they try and speak to me and not to say anything else to them unless he's with me.'

'Okay.' I breathe a sigh of relief. Someone with more knowledge than me is in charge now. Hopefully he can make sure that Cordelia isn't charged with anything. I finish wiping her kitchen counter, hating Garth with everything I have for a few minutes. How could he have done this to this young woman? Why would he hurt her like this? Why did Robert hurt me? He had so many reasons but none of them made it okay. Cheating is never okay.

Screw you, Garth.

'Right,' I say as I look around the clean kitchen, 'what about a cup of tea?'

Cordelia nods as she reaches into the freezer for a tub of ice cream. 'Do you want some?'

'No,' I say, shaking my head. 'We need to discuss this man following you. You need to look at the pictures I have.'

'Okay,' she says, sitting down and looking at my phone, which I have open to my gallery. She is silent as I swipe through all the photos I have.

When I am done, she looks at me, and then she shakes her head.

'Who is that, Mum?' she asks.

'That's what I'm asking you. He's the one who's been following you. He's the one who spoke to me about something that you were supposed to be doing. Do you know who he is? Do you recognise him at all?'

Cordelia sighs and for a moment I feel like a child irritating a parent. 'That's just some random guy, Mum. I don't know who that is. He's not following me. He's just someone you took photos of on the street.' As she speaks, she is looking at me not with anger but with something else. It takes me a moment to realise what it is. It's compassion, sympathy. My daughter feels sorry for me. She thinks I've made this up, that this is all just some weird delusion.

'That's no one, Mum,' she repeats. 'No one is following me. And I don't think anyone spoke to you. I believe you think they did but...' She shakes her head again.

And I realise that my child, my daughter, this young woman who should know me better than anyone, thinks I'm crazy. She actually thinks I'm crazy.

TWENTY-ONE
CORDELIA

Saturday

She feels like Alice in Wonderland, like she has fallen through the looking glass and into another dimension or back into her past when her mother spent her nights drinking and muttering about affairs. She seems so normal, so well. How has she just taken pictures of some random guy on the street and made up this story? And the story about Garth and a young intern has to be wrong. Garth is thirty-three and the girl is nineteen. Whatever he has done, it's not possible that he would actually sleep with such a young woman.

'Maybe Garth has simply run away,' she tries, hoping to get her mother to look at the situation logically instead of inventing things.

'If that was the case, why are the police looking into you? Why was there a knife in your car covered in blood?' her mother asks and Cordelia catches a look that crosses her face quickly and disappears.

Her mother doesn't trust her. Her mother thinks she's hiding something.

And so here they sit, mother and daughter, both convinced the other is either lying or crazy.

Cordelia closes her eyes. It feels like she and her mother have been discussing this for hours and hours, but when she looks at her phone, she sees it's only just after 9 p.m. Last Saturday night at this time she was with Garth. They had cocktails at a small bar before they went to dinner at their favourite restaurant.

'But it's very expensive,' she told Garth when he said he'd booked, 'don't we save it for celebrations?'

'I think we should celebrate every day,' he told her with a kiss. Even though she had accused him of cheating and she couldn't let go of the idea, she was still trying to make things work and so was he. And now she remembers thinking that perhaps he was trying to apologise in his own way.

She wanted to confront him about it but then decided to just have a nice night out. She was still questioning herself all the time, going back and forth over what she did or did not know for sure.

At the restaurant they both ordered the prawns for main course and they shared a bottle of wine. Cordelia had already indulged in a cocktail and she rarely drank more than that but she was feeling unsure of herself, of their relationship, of her future, and so she had a couple of glasses of wine. When the bill came, she was well past tipsy and so didn't register that his card had been declined and he had to use another one until she remembered it the next morning.

'That was brilliant,' he said as they left the restaurant and he held her arm to keep her steady.

'Thank you for dinner, kind sir,' she giggled and he laughed along with her.

'I love you, Cordy, remember that. I know you're troubled by some things but I do love you. You can trust me, I promise.'

She remembers those words clearly.

But you were lying. Have you always lied? Have you been lying to me since I met you?

Last Saturday night, did he know what was going to happen to him or what he was planning to do? He must have known. It was a last dinner, that's what it was. She would like to sit down and cry, but she realises that her mother is looking at her.

'I'm telling the truth, Cordelia,' says her mother.

'I know you think you are, Mum,' says Cordelia gently.

Careful, Cordelia, she hears in her mind and she touches her chest. Somebody spoke to her, outside work. They told her to be careful. They used her name. Who was that?

Probably just someone from the office and she just hadn't registered. There's no one actually following her. That's ridiculous.

Cordelia looks at her mother, who is staring out at the city lights.

Who are you? Who are you now? she thinks, but she has no idea how to ask the questions. She needs her mother's help with this, but can she trust her to be of help? Or is her mother just here to make everything much, much worse?

TWENTY-TWO
GRACE

Saturday

'Maybe it's time to call it a night,' Cordelia says and I know that she wants me to leave, but I still think we can figure this out, that if we can trust each other, we can figure out what is going on here.

'Maybe his mother knows something,' I say.

'If she knew anything, she would have told the police.' Cordelia sighs and shakes her head.

'We know that he's sent a lot of money to his mother and that he has done some gambling, probably in the hopes of increasing that amount.'

'And we know that he's missing now,' adds Cordelia, 'but knowing all these things is not helping.'

'Do you think his mother might be able to tell us exactly how much he's sent her? Is it possible that he has borrowed money from the wrong sort of people?' I ask her, even though that seems very unlikely. Surely Garth would not be that stupid.

'I can call her,' says Cordelia, and I hear a touch of hope in her voice at the idea that Evangeline may be keeping a couple of secrets of her own, secrets that could help find Garth and release my daughter from this whole terrible situation.

'Maybe she knows something she's not telling us, or the police. Maybe she knows where Garth is.' There is a sudden eagerness to her, as though she might have the solution, and before I can tell her that this is not the case or we would know, she's calling Evangeline. Cordelia taps the screen and puts the phone on speaker so I can hear the conversation.

'Cordelia,' the woman answers, her voice carrying into the room, clipped and cold.

'Hi Evangeline, I just… I'm trying to figure out where Garth might have gone and I know that he sent you money to fix the plumbing and maybe the roof and I just… Do you know where he got that from because he doesn't really earn enough to…' Cordelia's voice fades into silence and I can see her questioning her decision to call Garth's mother. She bites down on her lip as she waits for the woman to reply.

'What my son has done for me and for our family home is none of your business,' sneers the woman. 'My son is a good boy, a good man, and whatever he has done has been to save his family home. And that has absolutely nothing to do with you. You have your little trust fund but Garth has to work for his money. You know nothing about what we've been through as a family, nothing.'

'Evangeline, I'm just trying to figure out what's happened to him,' says Cordelia, and she sounds so desperately sad, I can't help touching her on her shoulder, trying to offer some comfort, but she shakes me off.

'I know what's happened to him and so do you, Cordelia Morton,' snarls Evangeline. 'You've done something to my son and you will pay for that. I know what the police found in your car. Where is my son, Cordelia? You won't get away with this, you know. The police will catch you.'

'I haven't done anything to him,' protests Cordelia. 'I love him as much as you do and I just want him to come home safe.'

'Love!' shrieks Evangeline. 'You have no idea about love. You were raised by a criminal. You have no idea how to love and you have never loved my son enough, never supported him enough. Don't you dare talk to me about love.'

I open my mouth to say something but Cordelia shakes her head at me. She obviously doesn't want the woman to know that I am here.

'Evangeline, if you know more, you need to tell me now,' says Cordelia.

'I will tell you nothing, nothing,' spits Evangeline. 'And you will pay for what has happened to my son, you will surely pay for it with your life.' She ends the call, and Cordelia and I are left staring at each other, more confused than ever.

'The man who's following you...' I don't finish my sentence because there's no point. She's seen the pictures and yet she still doesn't trust me. My daughter doesn't trust me. And I don't blame her. I can't blame her.

'Perhaps it's best if I leave now,' I say, and Cordelia nods.

'Yes,' she says. 'Perhaps it's best.'

TWENTY-THREE

CORDELIA

Saturday

In bed she lies still, hoping that sleep will somehow come and claim her. The apartment is a mess with drawers upended and stuff everywhere.

But she has found nothing that can help her figure out where Garth is.

Cordelia closes her eyes and shakes her head. She feels completely alone. She never wanted to have to trust her mother again, and now she has to because she has no one else. As her body finally gives in to sleep, she wonders if she will ever feel safe again or if she is doomed to live this endless cycle of build-up and destruction of her peace.

And if she is, who is to blame for that? Because it can't just be her mother. Maybe this is all her fault. Her fault for choosing a man like Garth because she was so desperate to be with someone who understood her. But did Garth understand her or was he just looking for an opportunity?

It's possible but not something she wants to believe. But

then she has little idea what to believe anyway. No idea, actually. No idea at all.

TWENTY-FOUR

GRACE

Sunday

I wake up the next morning and try to decide what I can do today that will somehow help my daughter.

Next week I have two days at the firm and then the usual administration assistant will be back from her holidays. I wish that I had more time to go through Garth's office. I'm certain that I would have been able to find something there, something tangible that Cordelia could take to the police. The police have gone through the apartment and found nothing except Garth's phone, and they've gone through Cordelia's car and found the knife.

Would the police have searched his office? I can't imagine a group of lawyers would have allowed that without a search warrant.

I need to get into his office without a lot of people being around. It's Sunday but I know that many of the lawyers go in on the weekend. The office will be open.

Determined, I throw off my covers and get myself into the

shower, all the while preparing my excuse if someone asks me why I am there on the weekend.

I think I've made a mistake on one of the timesheets, I hear myself saying, *and I knew I wasn't going to be able to rest until I checked.* Is that enough? Will anyone be suspicious of that?

Probably not. People, in general, move through the world enclosed in a lovely protective bubble, believing that they are good and that good things will happen for them, and because of that, they rarely suspect anyone, particularly a lowly administration assistant, of something nefarious. My excuse will be believed because why would I lie?

I was never in that kind of a bubble growing up, but after I met and married Robert and my company grew and I experienced success, I think I formed that bubble around myself. When it popped and my whole life was upended, one of the promises I made myself was that I would never allow myself to drop my guard again. I will remain suspicious of everyone around me. That makes me different to most people in a terrible way but right now I am grateful for it.

It's a quick drive in an Uber through the city to Garth's office because the traffic is much lighter on a Sunday. It's actually a lovely day. The sun is out and the air is warm as though Melbourne has embraced summer again.

The doors to Garth's building slide open, which I am grateful for. On the seventh floor, the reception desk is obviously unattended and most of the office is in darkness except for light coming from Max Blum's office.

I debate with myself for a moment on whether I should go and greet him or just try and get into Garth's office without being seen.

I decide on just getting to Garth's office but as I walk along the corridor, Max's door opens and he comes out into the hallway.

'Grace?' he says.

'Yes, hello,' I reply and I give him my planned excuse. He barely even listens to the explanation, his mind obviously on something else.

'Why are you working on the weekend?' I ask him before he can question me further.

'Well,' he says with a shrug, 'we're a man down and very behind so I had to come in. My wife is livid of course but it can't be helped.'

'Have you heard anything more about... Garth, is it?' I ask, hesitating on purpose so he thinks I'm searching for the name of the missing lawyer. It's not something that has anything to do with me after all.

'Nah,' he says with another shrug. 'I'm off to grab myself a coffee in the hope that it will help me keep going. Can I get you anything?'

'Oh no, thank you, I'll only be a few minutes. I hope it's a productive day.'

He shakes his head. 'As productive as a Sunday can be,' he says, moving towards the elevator.

I glance around the office but there is no one else that I can see. I know I have to be quick.

Darting into Garth's office, I use my phone as a torch so that Max doesn't return and see lights on. And then I begin searching his desk, one drawer at a time. I start with the bottom drawer, actually removing it and searching underneath as I remember finding a letter from Tamara to Robert, finally confirming what I had known all along, that my assistant and my husband were having an affair.

There's nothing there so I move on to the next drawers but they yield nothing but stationery and notes about cases.

I flick through the book on his desk but the rest of the pages are blank, and then I look over at his bookcase against one wall, stuffed full of law books. There doesn't seem to be anything useful there but I have to be sure. I start moving the books, pulling one out and then pushing the others back and forth so I can see behind them.

I hear the ding sound of the elevator opening and start to sweat with panic. I cannot be caught in here.

Then I hear voices.

'Bloody unfair of him,' says a woman who I recognise as Natalie, 'this is the last place I want to be but he's just disappeared, and everyone has to pick up the slack.'

'Leave it, Natalie,' I hear Max reply. 'I'm tired of talking about the dickhead, let's just get this done and get home.'

I freeze in place, my heart racing.

'I'll check if he's got the file in his cabinet,' I hear Natalie say and I feel my knees go weak. If she catches me in here, there is no way I can talk myself out of it.

'I've already got it,' Max says, and mercifully, Natalie doesn't come into the office. I only have minutes before I'm caught and I move from the bookcase to the filing cabinet, moving files aside as quietly as I can.

By the time I get to the bottom drawer, I have given up hope. I'm not going to find anything and now I just need to get out of here as quickly as possible. I will have to go into my office, turn on the computer and just sit there, and then I can tell Max, and now Natalie, that I've fixed the problem.

I move my hand through the drawer and I feel something, an envelope that I pull out and look at.

Cordelia Morton is written on the front along with the address of their apartment. It's a padded envelope and, feeling it, I know it has something small and hard in it. The envelope is sealed and I don't have time to look at it.

I silently slide the drawer closed and shove the envelope

into my bag, and then I stand by the office door, opening it with agonising slowness as I check the corridor.

No one is there and I dart out, closing the door quietly, and make my way quickly to my office. I'm covered in sweat, everything made worse by the wig I'm wearing, and I can feel my make-up running, but I make it to my office and sit down behind my desk, flicking the switch of my computer.

I pull up Friday's timesheet and peer at it. There are no mistakes, but then I don't make mistakes.

'Oh, Grace,' says Natalie and I jump, knocking my bag, the envelope spilling out and landing on the carpet.

I look down in horror but it's upside down and there is no writing on the back.

'Sorry,' she says, 'I startled you.'

'I was just concentrating,' I say with a small laugh, bending down and scooping everything into my bag. 'I was just leaving.'

'Oh,' she says, sounding disappointed. 'I was going to ask if you would mind doing some photocopying for us. I know it's the weekend but—'

'It will be my pleasure,' I say. 'I'm here to help.'

I stand and take a thick sheaf of papers she is holding from her and she turns away. Throwing my bag over my shoulder, I make my way to the copy room and do what's needed, feeling like the envelope is actually heating up in my bag.

It takes twenty minutes, and when I'm done, I take the papers over to Max's office.

'Is there anything else?' I ask, and Natalie opens her mouth, obviously to ask me to do some more work, but Max sees that I have my bag over my shoulder and shakes his head. 'No, Grace, thank you so much. I hope that didn't keep you too long.'

'Not at all, I have lunch with a friend in the city so I had the time.' I want to make sure that nothing else is requested of me.

'Thanks, that's good of you, enjoy your lunch,' he says and I nod and smile, closing the office door before Natalie has a chance to say anything at all.

In the elevator, I text Cordelia.

I've found something.

She replies instantly.

What?

It's a padded envelope but it's addressed to you.

Are you on your way here now?

I am.

TWENTY-FIVE

CORDELIA

Sunday

She is cleaning the windows in the living room when the doorbell rings, signalling her mother has arrived. She has been up and cleaning for hours, unable to lie in bed as she has questioned everything Garth has ever said to her, every memory of their relationship, every good and bad time. What was true? What was a lie? What is she going to tell the police? What will they find out about the knife? As part of her cleaning process, she has gone through the whole kitchen, dumping out utensils from their drawers and carefully going through everything. The knife the police found is definitely from the knife block in the kitchen. And she was the last person to use it, she's sure. She does most of the cooking when they eat at home.

Dropping her cloth, she runs to buzz her mother in and then opens her front door, waiting for her to come up in the lift. She is aware that she's sweating from all her work and is dressed in an old black T-shirt that used to belong to Garth and yet another pair of tracksuit pants and socks. Her hair is tied back in a ponytail and she didn't even bother to brush it this morning.

When her mother appears, Cordelia can see that she's had a rough morning as well. Her usually neat copper-coloured hair is in disarray, pieces falling out of her chignon, and she looks hot and uncomfortable.

'I went into his office this morning. I knew I had to look through it again,' she says before Cordelia can say anything.

'But didn't the police go through his office already?'

'Probably not. I mean, they would need a warrant and right now they seem to be concentrating on you,' she says, and Cordelia nods.

'I need some water,' says her mother, and she goes to the kitchen, drinking down two glasses in quick succession.

'Let's sit and you tell me what you've found,' says Cordelia, and they sit down next to each other on the white leather sofa.

Her mother takes a small padded envelope out of her bag and hands it to Cordelia.

'You didn't open it?' she asks as she studies it, and her mother shakes her head.

'I... thought I should leave it to you. Do you want me to stay?'

'Definitely,' says Cordelia. She cannot do this alone. Her heart is pounding in her chest as she runs her hands over her name on the envelope, recognising Garth's handwriting, and then she tears it open, tipping it upside down. A small black mobile phone falls out. And with it a single piece of paper with a typewritten sentence:

IF YOU CALL THE POLICE, GARTH DIES.

'Oh,' gasps Cordelia.

There is nothing else in the envelope.

Cordelia picks up the phone and touches the button on the side, expecting that it won't turn on, but the screen lights up, the battery at fifty-five per cent.

It's an older phone but still a smartphone, and she swipes her finger across the screen, expecting it to be locked, but it opens up and she can see that there are the usual apps that all phones come with these days.

There are also notifications for five text messages. Cordelia shakes her head as she and her mother stare at the phone in silence.

'Are you sure you want me here for this?' asks her mother.

'I'm...' Cordelia has no idea what to say. Maybe these messages are private and something she wouldn't want her mother seeing, but why are they on this phone instead of being sent to her phone? 'Just stay. This is so weird, I need you here,' she says.

Her mother nods and Cordelia opens the messaging app, holding the phone closer to her mother so they can both read what's written.

The first message is from Tuesday last week, the first day she started to worry about Garth because he didn't come home at all or send her a text.

Hi Cordy,

I am writing this from a new phone so you won't recognise the number. I've left my phone at home because things are a bit tricky at the moment. I want you to know that I love you, Cordy, I really do but I've made some real mistakes, really big mistakes.

I have a problem. I did something, something bad, something stupid. I borrowed money from someone to help my mother. It was only to help her, I promise. You saw my family home and you know how badly it needed to be fixed. I couldn't just tell her to sell it, I couldn't, not after I left her alone in the UK. I know my sister is there but they're not close and she would never go to my sister for help. I promised my father before he died that I would take care of her, and I couldn't just leave her to suffer. The bank wouldn't lend me the money because I haven't been here in Australia for very long and I don't have any assets and the money I do have goes on rent and... I just didn't know what to do or how to help her so I borrowed money from some people who like to be paid back. People who are not good people. I know that you don't have access to your trust fund yet and I know you would have helped me when you did. But these people want their money now, they want it now or they're going to hurt me.

Please don't be angry at my mother. She needed the money. The old house is falling apart, as you know, but she would be devastated to have to sell it since it's been in my family for generations. I had hoped that one day you and I would raise our children there.

'Oh,' says Cordelia, a sob catching in her throat as she reads the words. She jumps up with the phone in her hand and grabs a tissue.

'Are you sure I should be reading this?' asks her mother and Cordelia nods.

She forces her eyes back to the phone and keeps reading.

I owe these people three million dollars. I don't know what I was thinking. I've screwed everything up and I am so, so sorry. I need to pay the money back, Cordy, or I may lose my life. I have had to go into hiding to save myself.

I know this is something so huge to ask that you may not be able to do it, but you need to ask your mother for some money to pay off this debt. I know she must have it. I know you never wanted to speak to her again but only you can help me, Cordy. If I don't pay it back, they will kill me. I have no doubt about that.

I love you, know that I love you.

I will text again tomorrow so you've had time to think. I am thinking about you every minute of every day and all I want is to get back to you and our lives. If you can do this for me, if you and your mother can do this for me, I will spend the rest of my life making it up to you and paying her back. I promise you that.

Cordelia puts the phone down on the coffee table, and she covers her eyes because a fierce headache has taken hold of her. 'I can't,' she says and she feels her mother's light touch on her shoulder.

'You can,' she says kindly. 'We need to read it all so we know what's been going on.'

Cordelia lifts the phone and, taking a deep breath, scrolls down to the next text, which was sent on Wednesday.

You haven't replied and that's okay. I assume you're shocked. I know I would be. No one knows about this but you, Cordy, no one. I have had to cut myself off from everyone, even my mother, as I struggle to figure out a way to get this done, but there's nothing I can do but hope you'll find it in your heart to forgive me for what I've done and to help me. I know that means forgiving your mother as well, and that was something you were never going to do, and I know what a difficult position I am putting you in by asking you to speak to her. In the last few weeks, you've accused me of cheating when I've told you I'm working, and you told me that I seem distant, but I have never cheated on you, I promise you that. I have been living in fear for my life. Trying to work out how to get enough money together so that I could pay them back. I even tried gambling. But there's no chance of me getting the money together, no chance at all. I have no actual assets, only a house in the UK that's falling to bits and that belongs to my mother. I hope you respond. Please let me know if you can help me. I want to come home to you more than anything else.

'So, he's lying even as he pleads for my help,' Cordelia says. 'I don't understand. And why not just text my phone? Why this phone, and if it was meant to be posted to me, why hasn't it been?'

'I don't know,' her mother says with a shrug.

Cordelia scrolls down to the next text, sent on Thursday.

Please answer me. Please. I can't stay where I am for much longer. They're looking for me. They will find me soon. Please answer me. Can you help?

Cordelia feels sick. He sounds desperate. And if she had received the phone, she would have answered him, would have tried to help, and even as she thinks about it, she knows that she would have contacted her mother and asked for the money. But now that she knows he has cheated on her with Natalie, and is probably cheating with someone else, she's not sure. Is this all a lie?

'Let's read them all and then talk,' says her mother quietly and Cordelia scrolls down.

On Friday, Garth sent:

I can't believe you haven't replied. I have to move again. They've found me. Please, Cordy, I'm begging you.

The next text is from yesterday.

Cordy, they have me... they found me. They've given me two days. I don't want to die. I'm begging you. I don't want to die.

'Is the last one from today?' asks her mother.

'No,' says Cordelia, her voice a whisper because she can barely speak. 'It's from yesterday.'

'I need... a drink,' says her mother, standing up and going to the kitchen. Cordelia follows her with the phone in her hand, watches as her mother fills the kettle. 'It must be hard to not be able to drink alcohol,' she says, 'especially now.'

Her mother shrugs. 'There are always going to be hard things in life. I have to be able to get through them. I know that this feels impossible right now but we will get through it.'

Cordelia has the out-of-body feeling again, the feeling that she is above herself, watching what's happening. She can see her messy blonde hair and her sweaty T-shirt and she can see the phone that she's clutching so tightly she may snap it in half. The phone is her only link to Garth.

'I don't want him to die,' she says, the words coming in a rush, a desperate pain over her heart. 'I know what he's done but I don't want him to die.' Her voice breaks and she feels her body crumple onto the floor as tears come thick and fast. She imagines him alone and scared, hiding somewhere, waiting for her to reply, and then she sees some faceless man bursting into a room and grabbing him, hurting him and threatening to end his life.

Is that who has been following her? Is her mother actually right? Is there a man who wants money from Cordelia to save Garth? Does the man who her mother has taken pictures of work for the people who Garth owes money to?

Garth must have told them that he was sending these messages, that all that needed to happen was for Cordelia to respond and then speak to her mother, and then the money would be paid back. This is all a chaotic mess. She has imagined a debt, imagined a worst-case scenario of a hundred thousand dollars – but three million? It's more than her whole trust fund. It's an impossible number to even contemplate. Why would he have borrowed so much? Did Evangeline even need that much?

She feels her mother next to her, feels her put an arm around her and hold her while she cries. When the tears stop, Cordelia gets up and finds a tissue. She is so sick of crying, of feeling powerless, of not knowing what to do.

'What do I say to him?' she asks her mother. 'How do I reply to this?'

Her mother stands as well and returns to the kitchen for her coffee. 'I have no idea. If I hadn't found this phone, you would never know that this had happened. Why was it in his office? Why wasn't it sent to you if Garth wanted to use it to communicate with you? It's all so strange. I know that whoever is texting says he's Garth, but is it?'

'You think it could be someone else?' asks Cordelia. 'You think this is some kind of scam?' And if it is... how does that make her feel? If it is a scam, where is Garth? In another country already, or dead?

'You need to insist that you speak to him,' says her mother. 'You need to be sure, absolutely sure that everything he's saying is the truth.'

'And if it is him?' she asks.

'Then if you want me to, I can get the money. It will be very hard, and I will need some time, but I can get it. But I want to hand it over to the person who he actually owes the money to.'

'To the man who's been following me, the man who spoke to you. I'm sorry I didn't believe you, I'm sorry,' Cordelia says, shaking her head.

'I... I understand why you would have questioned it,' her mother replies, 'it seems impossible, but I promise you he is following you and he did speak to me, and if he's working for these people, then I want to look him in the eye and be able to make sure that this will be finished when I hand over the money.'

'You have that kind of money?' asks Cordelia. She has never thought about how much money her mother sold her company for. She didn't care at the time. She was mourning her father, in shock and devastated over what her mother had done, and she knows that Janine told her that her mother had sold the company but never for how much.

'I do,' says her mother. 'I can pay off whoever he owes money to but you have to be sure that this is what you want.'

'Of course it is, I love him,' yells Cordelia, fear and anger making her voice wobble. 'If he doesn't pay them back, they'll kill him. His life is worth that. Isn't it worth that?'

'He cheated on you,' says her mother. 'And he's lied about it.'

'Maybe... maybe it was just the once or twice and he's sorry,' says Cordelia. 'I could forgive just once. I love him, Mum, and I don't want him to die.' She knows that she has been thinking about killing Garth but it's all abstract, not real. In reality she loves him and still wants to make a life with him despite his failings. Maybe if her mother pays these people off, they can start again, rent somewhere cheaper, pay her mother back slowly, and when her trust fund kicks in at twenty-five, she can just give it all to her mother.

'We could just go to the police with all this, show them the phone and the pictures.'

'But what if they hurt Garth? They told us not to call the police. We don't know what they're capable of.'

'All right, tell him you need to speak to him,' says her mother, indicating the phone.

Obediently, Cordelia types:

I only just got this phone. I don't know why you didn't contact me on my phone. I can get the money but you need to call me. I need to know it's you.

She shows her mother the text message, aware in this moment that she could be a child again. Her mother holds all the power now because her mother has the money. Cordelia is torn between resentment and gratitude. She will be forever in her mother's debt, even if she does manage to pay her back. What will this cost her emotionally? She wants her mother back in her life but she is still not able to fully forgive her. She wants to be able to make the decision for herself, not be forced into a relationship over money.

'I need the bathroom,' she says, putting the phone down on the kitchen counter. Will he call? If it's a scam, he won't call. She thinks about his voice, his perfect English accent and the deep tone. Will she know it's him? How could she not? 'You'll come get me if it rings?' she says.

'Of course, Dee Dee.'

She uses the bathroom and then because she is sweaty and hates the feel of her clothing against her skin, she gets into the shower, throwing everything she was wearing into the laundry hamper. Under the hot water she considers what she said to her mother, that she still loves Garth. Does she still love him or is she just very afraid for what has happened and what might happen to him?

If he is being held, and if her mother gets the money and he comes home, will she still want to be with him? He's made such a mess of everything.

Right now, this feels like the middle of a crisis, intense and awful, but if she takes a moment, she can see that there will be a time after this when she will have to consider her relationship. She wants Garth to be alive because if you have the chance to save a life – even the life of a liar and a cheater – surely you should take it? But does she want to be with Garth, who is lying even when he should be telling her the truth about everything?

Turning off the shower, she steps out and grabs a towel, wrapping it around herself.

If he had called, her mother would have come to get her.

She puts on fresh clothes and brushes her hair, applies

cream to her face, taking comfort in the soothing movement of her hands over her skin, even as they shake.

And then finally she leaves her bedroom. As she does, she hears an unfamiliar ringtone, a generic tinny sound.

The phone from the envelope is ringing.

TWENTY-SIX

GRACE

Sunday

When Cordelia goes to the bathroom, I hear the shower start, which I think is a good idea. She has been cleaning, I can see, but I can also see that she hasn't actually completed any jobs. It looks like she began in the kitchen and then moved on to the living room but the counter in the kitchen is still filled with different utensils and I can see that she even took a whole shelf of books out before moving on to the windows. We have some answers now but instead of feeling like I know what's going on, I am just filled with many more questions. I don't know if we can trust anything Garth is saying. I don't know if we should.

I debate with myself for a moment about doing something about the mess, but then I can't just stand here so I begin replacing things into drawers, trying to make it simple so that she can change things around if she wants to, and then I move on to the bookcase, carrying the phone with me so that I can hear it if it rings, even though there is no way I would miss the sound in an apartment this size.

After I have replaced the books, I move back to the kitchen, placing the phone on the counter and filling the kettle to make a coffee. As I flick the switch on the kettle, a low vibration followed by a ringing sound fills the apartment.

I stare down at the phone as it starts ringing, moving a little on the counter. I reach for it as Cordelia comes out of her room, and I pull my hand back.

She takes the few steps to the kitchen quickly, panic on her face.

'Garth,' Cordelia gasps into the phone as she swipes her hand across the screen. 'Garth,' she says again.

'Cordelia, thank God,' he says, 'thank God, thank God.' I can hear him because she's standing close to me, but I need her to put the phone on speaker so I can hear exactly what he's saying. There is something odd about this, about the texts, about the way I found the phone. At the back of my mind is a niggle of worry, something telling me that this is not exactly as it seems. There is something else going on here. And I feel like Natalie may be involved somehow.

'Garth, where are you? The police... There was a knife and my car... Where are you?' Cordelia has so much to say her brain can't make it come out right. She stumbles and stutters, crying.

'Listen, Cordelia,' I hear him say, and I touch her on the shoulder, indicating that she needs to put the phone on speaker. I don't want him to know I'm here so I mouth the words without making a sound.

Cordelia shakes her head and then she seems to reconsider as she takes a deep breath to regain some composure. She puts the phone on speaker and I shake my head at her, telling her not to tell him I am here.

'Why haven't you replied?' he asks, and for someone who is supposedly hiding out and desperate for help, it sounds weirdly demanding.

'I'm sorry,' says Cordelia. 'I only got it today. You have no idea, Garth, I've been so worried.'

'Cordelia, listen to me,' he commands, and I watch my daughter take a deep breath and pull herself together. My suspicions about this man grow even greater.

'I'm listening,' says Cordelia, clenching her fists so that she stays in control.

'I need that money or they will kill me.'

'Who are they, Garth? I can call the police, I can get the police to help if you just tell me who *they* are.'

'No, no!' he shouts. 'No police or they will kill me. I promised them you would be able to get the money and that's the only reason they haven't killed me. They've given me until Tuesday night but I need the money, Cordy. Please, sweetheart, you have to help me. You need to contact your mother. She'll help, I know she will. She'll do anything for you.'

I look around her small kitchen, searching for a pen and some paper, my eyes alighting on the magnetic shopping list on the fridge. Grabbing the notepad, I pull off a piece of paper, and then when she sees what I'm doing, she opens a drawer and gets out a pen to hand to me.

Where have you been hiding?

'Garth, where have you been hiding?' she asks.

'I was in a cheap motel for a night and then I moved to another one, and I was there for the next few days but they found me.'

'And where are you now?' asks Cordelia, and I want to jump for joy because she is suddenly sounding stronger, clearer, as though she has made a decision.

'I'm in...' He hesitates. 'I actually have no idea right now, it's a basement of some kind. They brought me here in a car but I was in the... boot and I've never, never been so scared in my whole life, Cordy. They only gave me the phone back to make this call.'

'Who are they, Garth, do you have any names?'

'No, no, I can't tell you. If I tell you, I put you in danger as well.'

'Can I speak to one of them?' asks Cordelia, and I can hear the curiosity and disbelief in her voice.

'He's shaking his head... they won't speak to you. Please, Cordy, I need you to tell me you'll get the money. Will you contact your mother? Promise me you'll contact her. We both know that's a small amount for her, please, Cordy, I know I've done a terrible thing but this is my life. I had to help my mother. I had to save my home because it will be our home one day, ours and our children's home. You want that, don't you, darling, I know you do.'

'Yes,' says Cordelia, 'yes, I want it.'

'Then why haven't you replied? Why haven't you answered my messages?' he demands again.

'I told you, I only got the phone today. I would have replied but I only got it today.'

'Today? But you were supposed to get it by Tuesday. She said she would drop it to you on Tuesday.'

'She?' says Cordelia, and I watch as she visibly pales, biting down on her lip. The word 'she' was spoken softly and yet it echoes around this apartment. I hold my hand over my mouth to stop myself from alerting Garth to my presence.

'Who is she, Garth?'

There is silence on the other end of the phone. I think about all the things Natalie has said to me, about how she admitted to Cordelia that she has slept with Garth, and it feels like some puzzle pieces are fitting into place. Is Natalie lying to everyone? Is this really about owing some nameless person millions of dollars or is it some kind of game? Are Garth and Natalie trying to extract money from Cordelia and using this as a cover? Is such a thing possible? There are so many what-ifs and possibilities that my mind feels like it's spinning.

'Garth, who is she?'

'Shit,' says Garth and then he hangs up.

Cordelia stares down at the phone, shock making her pale. She swipes the screen and calls the number but the phone rings out.

I watch her type a text, obviously telling him to call her, but she gets no reply. She calls him twice more while I watch her, and she keeps texting him as well.

'Now what?' she says.

'Cordelia, there's something strange about this, don't you think?'

'What do you mean?'

'Well...' I say hesitantly, 'who is the "she" he's referring to? It must be someone at the office. I mean, that's where I found the phone. And why did he hang up right away after he said "she"?'

Cordelia shakes her head. 'I don't... do you think he means Natalie?'

'I think we need to speak to the police. It would be best if you take them the phone and then let them sort this out. Something is odd about this situation.'

'If it's true, Mum, and it might be because I have no idea how else he got the money to send to his mother, but if it's true, they will *kill* him. Do you want Garth's death to be something I blame myself for, for the rest of my life?'

I really have no idea how to answer her and I can hear what she's not saying. I am responsible for the death of the man I once loved. Cordelia does not want to repeat my tragic mistakes. She will save this man's life if she can, regardless of what he's done. Love is not a tap and it cannot simply be turned off.

'Are you sure that was Garth, I mean one hundred per cent sure?'

'I... He sounded a little different but he was afraid for his life. I know his voice. It was him, I'm sure of it.'

The phone buzzes with a text message.

3 million in cash by 8 p.m. Tuesday night. Leave the money on the dining room table in the apartment. Don't be there.

Cordelia grabs the phone and calls Garth again. The number rings out. She texts him and then calls again and again, but he doesn't pick up.

'We need to go to the police,' I say again, certain that this is the right thing to do.

'What if they kill him? What if all this is true and he dies?' she shrieks. 'We have to help him!'

'What if we leave the money here and it gets picked up and he still dies and you get blamed?'

Cordelia shakes her head, holding the phone close to her as though she can touch Garth through it.

'I don't know what to do... I don't know what to do,' she wails.

'I think I need to speak to Natalie,' I say. 'I have a feeling that she will know something else, something more.'

Kelsey – who is only nineteen, I remember, so young – is also on my mind. Does she have anything to do with this?

'I just... can't think anymore,' she says as, on the coffee table, her mobile phone, the one she uses every day, rings.

She moves away from the kitchen and grabs it, answering without even looking at the screen.

'Hello,' she says and then she listens for a minute, and I watch her face pale as she bites down on her lips. 'Yes, yes... I understand, tomorrow. I'll be there but I'm bringing a lawyer. Nicholas Blake. Right.'

With the phone still clutched in her hand, she goes over to the sofa and sits down, dropping it back onto the coffee table and then covering her eyes with her hands, her head drooping forward.

I move out of the kitchen and sit down as well. I am exhausted, a headache is brewing behind my left eye, and more than anything, I want a drink so my thoughts will slow down and I can figure this out.

I don't ask her what was said. I assume she was talking to the detective, who must be very keen if she's working on a Sunday. I just sit and wait. All through her childhood, I rushed in to help whenever I could. I paid for tutors if she was doing badly in a subject and made sure that she never had to cook and clean for herself. If she had an argument with a friend, she and I would strategise on how to make things right. She talked to me about everything, despite the fact that we didn't have much time together. We were close until I started drinking, and then after the fire, we were completely estranged. She has had to grow up very quickly and I cannot simply step back into her life and take over. I need her to ask for my help every step of the way or I may lose her again. She's already angry enough over my working for Garth's firm and following both of them on social media.

'Detective Ashton said that the blood on the knife definitely belongs to Garth. And that they've found traces of his blood in the car, despite the fact that someone tried to clean it all away. She said there must have been a lot of blood in the car. And they want me to come in so they can take my fingerprints. I was going to go in on Tuesday but now she says it needs to be tomorrow.' Her face is impassive, her tone robotic, as though this is all too much to contemplate, too much to take in, and so she is simply disassociating. And I don't blame her for it.

She sits back and looks out of the glass balcony doors into the sunny autumn afternoon.

'How has this happened?' she asks but I know she's not actually talking to me.

'Are you absolutely sure it was Garth on the phone?' I ask her again.

'I think… maybe… I don't know,' she says with a sigh.

'You have to tell the police everything now, Cordelia. I understand how scared you are for Garth but we are in way over our heads. I will try and get the money together but you need to tell them everything.'

'Okay,' she agrees wearily. 'Okay.'

'Should we get something to eat?' I have no other suggestion to make.

'No, Mum, I need some time. I'll leave a message for Nicholas. He said to do that if the police contacted me.'

'Good idea,' I say.

'He charges five thousand dollars, just to start,' she whispers, 'just to even look at my case.' I wish she would look at me. I wish I could find something to say that would comfort her.

'You don't need to worry about that,' I reassure her.

'Okay… I need to rest now, Mum. Can you just… sorry…'

'I'll give you your space. You see Nicholas and the police tomorrow and take the phone with you – show it to him and he will know what to do. I've sent the pictures of the man who has been following you to your phone. Maybe the police actually know who he is and they will know how to find Garth. I'll go into work and see if there's anything else I can find out.'

'Okay,' she says and then she lies down on the sofa, pulling an orange cushion under her head and curling up so that she is as small as a child. I grab the soft orange blanket from the back of the sofa, draping it over her. She doesn't say anything because she is already asleep. And I know that sometimes, sleeping is the best thing to do, the only thing to do.

I leave her apartment quietly, heading for a bar and a glass of wine and some time to work out exactly how I make sure my daughter is safe and that she never has to pay for a crime that she did not commit. And I know that there's no way I'm giving anyone three million dollars. No way at all.

TWENTY-SEVEN

CORDELIA

Monday

'It will be easier to just meet outside the police station,' Nicholas Blake informed her on the phone this morning after she explained everything, including her mother's story about the man following her, and about the phone and speaking to Garth.

Cordelia is waiting in the wind, a black jacket wrapped around her, her blonde hair whipping around her face. She woke up on the sofa in the early hours of the morning with a dry mouth. She had no idea how long she'd slept for but it was obviously not a restful sleep. She wasn't able to get back to sleep, either, instead spending hours going back through her Instagram, looking at pictures of her and Garth from the first one they took together until the last one, taken at least a month ago. When had they stopped taking photos together? And how had she not noticed that?

She studied each photo obsessively, trying to determine when the way he was looking at her changed, when he stopped staring down at her with obvious love in his expression, but she can't work it out. And now every picture must be questioned. *Was he actually happy there or did he smile because I told him to? Is he thinking about another woman as he looks at me like that? Did he buy those flowers for me because he knows I love white roses or because he was guilty about being with someone else?* And round and round in the back of her mind were the questions she needed answers to: *Where are you? Are you lying about everything? Who is the 'she' who was supposed to post the phone?*

Her eyes feel gritty and her head is already throbbing with a headache. She has googled the lawyer and so knows she's looking for a tall man with a full head of grey hair and a beard. She is standing a little off to the side, watching people go in and out of the station, wondering if they are there to be interviewed, if they also have a loved one who is missing, if they are also afraid that they are about to be accused of murder. She shivers inside her jacket even though the air is relatively warm. Garth is not dead. She heard him on the phone yesterday. Didn't she?

'Cordelia,' she hears and she turns to see her lawyer striding towards her. He must be around her mother's age and he has the look of a man who knows what to do in any situation, who can handle himself. She hopes it's the case.

'Now,' he says without any other formalities, 'we are going to allow them to take your fingerprints because there's no point in fighting that, but I want you to know that what they have seems mostly circumstantial and very strange at that. You would be the very worst type of murderer if you hadn't bothered to conceal any evidence, and from what you tell me, it seems some sort of scam is going on here.'

Cordelia feels her stomach twist at the word 'murderer' and she reminds herself more forcefully that Garth is alive, that she spoke to him and that they have until tomorrow night to get the money to the people he owes it to.

'I think we give them your fingerprints and you tell them

what you know so far, and we go from there. But before we go in, I do need to ask you if you feel like you can trust your boyfriend.'

Cordelia begins to nod her head but then she stops and shrugs. 'I honestly don't know anymore. I just don't know what's going on.'

'Right,' Nicholas replies with a nod. 'I know how difficult this must be,' he says, his hand lightly touching her shoulder, 'but let's do what needs to be done now.' Cordelia nods her agreement and walks in front of him, into the station.

Cordelia is familiar with the police station from last week, when she came to report Garth missing and set everything in motion.

It looks innocuous enough but she can't help how jumpy she's feeling, like at any moment she will be grabbed and thrown into a cell and no one will listen to her scream that she had nothing to do with what has happened to Garth.

She and Nicholas take a seat on a brown plastic bench, with a homeless man sitting only a few feet away. Cordelia wrinkles her nose and then tries to breathe through her mouth.

'Cordelia,' she hears and then she sees Detective Ashton coming towards her. 'Nicholas,' she greets the lawyer.

'Emily,' he replies. No one seems very big on the word 'hello'. If the detective knows the lawyer's first name is that a good thing or a bad thing? Cordelia decides to view it as something positive. Her lawyer has obviously been doing this a long time.

'Follow me,' says the detective and it takes only moments until she and her lawyer are seated in a small, windowless room with a camera in one corner and the stale smell of old coffee all around them.

'Can I get you anything to drink?' asks the detective as she and Detective Jameson sit down. Cordelia shakes her head. Her lawyer doesn't even greet the second detective but he does nod in his direction.

Detective Ashton presses a button on a recorder before she starts speaking. Cordelia listens to her state her name, the time, the date and Cordelia's name before the detective looks at her.

'Cordelia is happy to give you her fingerprints but we will not be answering any questions. She has some things she would like to share and then we'll be on our way,' Nicholas says before even one question is asked.

Cordelia has to admit that Nicholas Blake is already worth the money. He speaks with such authority that suddenly this all feels very manageable and she is certain she will be home by lunchtime.

'Well, over to you, Cordelia,' says Detective Ashton with a dramatic raising of eyebrows.

'I got this phone, here, and I was supposed to get it on Tuesday but I got it yesterday, and Garth has been contacting me on it and he's being chased by someone he borrowed money from. It was to fix his home in the UK but he couldn't get a loan and now these people have taken Garth until they get the money paid back. Garth asked me to leave money in the apartment and...' She trails off.

'Perhaps slowly,' says her lawyer, and Cordelia starts again, explaining what she knows and only telling one small lie to protect her mother. The detective doesn't need to know that her mother found the phone in Garth's office.

'And where did you get this phone?'

'It came in the post,' she says without hesitation. It would just be too much to explain about her mother disguising herself and taking a job at Garth's firm. If they ask for the envelope, she will say she's already thrown it away.

'Can I see the phone?' asks the detective, and Cordelia hands it over to her.

The detective scrolls through the messages. 'And you say you spoke to him yesterday?'

'I did,' says Cordelia. The lawyer puts a hand on her arm.

'Well, hopefully he'll answer,' says the detective, so much scepticism in her voice that Cordelia can actually feel it as the woman taps on the number the texts have come from.

'The number you have dialled is not in service. Please check the number before calling again.'

'What?' yells Cordelia.

The detective calls the number again but gets the same response.

'But I spoke—' begins Cordelia, but Nicholas touches her arm again, reminding her to remain silent.

'I think that's enough for today,' he says. 'Can we go ahead with fingerprinting? And then unless you plan on charging my client with something, we'll be on our way.'

'You know, Cordelia, things will be a lot easier if you just cooperate and tell us everything you know. Maybe this is all one big mistake and we can clear it all up,' says the detective, looking at her. 'I mean, you could have bought this phone anywhere and you could have another. You see how this looks, don't you?'

'But it has nothing to do with me. Garth borrowed the money for his mother. You can call her and ask her. They want their money back and Garth knows my mother has money. I didn't do anything wrong,' Cordelia protests.

'I understand,' says Detective Ashton, 'and I have been in constant contact with Mrs Stanford-Brown. She called me this morning to tell me you called her, harassing her about her son and about money. Is that true?'

'What? No, I just asked her if she knew anything else.'

'She told us that Garth had borrowed money from a bank to help her, and we have confirmed that this morning with the bank in question. It is a large loan for two hundred thousand dollars but not a loan that the bank wasn't completely confident Garth could pay back. He earns a lot of money after all. Banks don't usually kidnap people to get their money back, do they?'

'No need to be snide,' says Nicholas as Cordelia feels her mouth open and close without being able to say anything.

'I'm being followed, you know,' she snaps. 'My mother took pictures of a man who spoke to her.'

'And he said?'

'Something about my man and... something I should be doing...' Her words tail off again as she realises that the police are not going to take this seriously.

She pulls out her own phone. 'Look,' she says and shows the detectives the pictures. Both detectives peer hard at the photos and then exchange a quick look.

'We can try and match them to our database but to me that just looks like someone on the street. And when you say he spoke to your mother, it doesn't sound like he said anything particularly threatening, if he did say anything at all. I know your mother has had some... issues in the past,' says Detective Ashton softly.

'She's fine now,' says Cordelia, anger surging through her at the way the detective is looking at her.

'I feel I should tell you that your story is sounding somewhat outlandish. We found Garth's phone in the apartment, the phone you said he was sending messages from on Monday night and now all of a sudden, there's another phone? That's a little too convenient if you ask me.'

'Maybe Garth came home on Tuesday while I was at work and left the phone under the bed,' tries Cordelia desperately. Her lawyer shakes his head, reminding her again to be quiet.

'You're digging yourself in deeper here, Cordelia, and it will be easier to just tell the truth.'

She sounds almost sorry for Cordelia, almost like she's actually worried about her.

Cordelia looks at Nicholas, panic running through her. But he just smiles and shakes his head. 'Emily, you know better than that.'

The detective shrugs. 'I thought that Cordelia was really concerned about her boyfriend, that's all. I mean we have had a John Doe turn up at the Royal Melbourne Hospital... so we are looking into that.'

'What? Oh my God, is it Garth, is it him?' asks Cordelia, her voice rising steadily.

'We're not sure,' says Detective Jameson, finally opening his mouth, 'the body was in a state of... decomposition.'

'This is ridiculous,' says Nicholas. 'Let's go, Cordelia.' He stands up and Cordelia begins to follow but then her knees are weak and she collapses back in the chair, her stomach churning with an image of a decomposed body. Garth cannot be dead. She spoke to him. She spoke to him, didn't she? Nicholas places a hand under her elbow. 'Come on, Cordelia,' he says quietly and she somehow finds the strength to stand.

'Okay, okay,' says the detective, holding up her hands, 'we just need to get fingerprints.'

'Actually, unless you have enough evidence to charge my client, we will not be providing those,' says Nicholas.

'But you stated that you would,' says Detective Ashton, real anger in her voice as she stands up.

'Not when you pull this shit, Emily, you know better than that. Let's go, Cordelia.'

They are out on the street in only minutes and Cordelia feels like she might throw up. She feels the same way she did after her parents took her to the Gold Coast when she was ten and she insisted on riding the biggest roller coaster in the park. Her father gamely accompanied her, holding her hand as she screamed while the car flew down at a nearly ninety-degree angle. When she got off, her knees were weak and she couldn't walk properly. Then her mother helped her over to a bench and bought her some hot chips, covered in salt to help settle her stomach. Now she has no idea what to do, and her mother has gone to Garth's work, something she is terrified of sharing with her lawyer.

'Let's get a coffee,' he says and she follows him into a tacky little coffee shop where her shoes stick to the floor.

When they are seated with coffees in front of them, he says, 'Is there anything you're not telling me? I don't care what you have or have not done, but I need to know everything.'

'I... I...' stutters Cordelia, and then his phone begins to ring and he answers it as she stares down into her cup.

'I need to go home,' she says when he's done with his call because that's all she can think to do. If she can just get home, she can get into bed and sleep and then she can think about the possibility that Garth's body is in a hospital, that it is Garth and that she was not speaking to him on the phone but rather to someone capable of reproducing his accent, of imitating him so that she would believe he is alive when he is, in fact, dead. She pictures his body on a slab in the morgue, blue and cold, decomposing, and she shudders.

Nicholas stares at her for a moment. 'Are you okay?'

'No,' says Cordelia softly. 'No.' Because she's not okay and she will never be okay again.

Nicholas leans across the table, rests a hand gently on her arm and gazes at her with compassionate blue eyes, and for just a moment, Cordelia is reminded so much of the way her father used to look at her that she feels she might explode.

'I'm here for you, at any time of the day. You can believe me when I say that they have nothing substantial on you because they haven't charged you. They may demand fingerprints and then we will have to give them to them. Your fingerprints will be on the knife because it's your knife. It's an argument that I will instantly demolish. They don't have a body, Cordelia. You said you spoke to Garth only yesterday, and maybe you did or maybe you didn't, but until they can prove you did anything to him, they have nothing.'

Cordelia nods as embarrassing tears appear.

'Janine told me about working with your mother,' says Nicholas gently. 'I can only imagine how hard what happened must have been for you, but Janine said her devotion to you was always so clear.'

'I know that,' says Cordelia, sniffing, because she does know this.

'I need to go now. Do you want me to call you an Uber?'

'No, I may just walk.' She needs time and movement to think.

Nicholas nods and leaves, and after she finishes her coffee, Cordelia gets up and leaves the café, walking across the road. She walks a block and then stops in front of a store to look at a beautiful glittery blue dress, floor length with spaghetti straps, and then she turns to work out which way to go and a few feet away from her is the man her mother has pictures of. She recognises him instantly. The man the police don't believe even exists, the man she did not, until yesterday, believe existed. But there he is, large as life. She frantically reaches for her phone to get a photograph, but before she can, he smiles and holds up his arm, taps his watch and then turns and walks away, disappearing into the people walking along the street. Even if she got a picture, they wouldn't believe her.

Cordelia begins to run and she doesn't stop until she is home, opening her front door with trembling hands and then making sure she has locked it behind her.

This is never going to end.

TWENTY-EIGHT

GRACE

Monday

Tristan greets me as I walk into the office on Monday morning; his usual wide smile is comforting after the weekend that I've had. I desperately wanted to go with Cordelia to the police station but I knew it would work against her rather than to her advantage. I have done the only thing I can do and that's to pay Nicholas Blake to take on her case. I wish it were true that money could solve every problem but it solves so very few of them.

'Morning, Grace,' he sings and I return his smile.

'Morning, Tristan, good weekend?'

'Oh, you know, I had to go home and see my parents – Dad always ropes me into helping him fix something and Mum always complains that she doesn't see me enough, but Sunday dinner was lovely so it's always worth it for her cooking.'

'That sounds very nice. I'm sure your parents appreciated it.'

'Do you have kids?' he asks, even as his eyes wander back to his computer and what he's working on there.

'No,' I say, tucking a strand of platinum-blonde hair from my wig behind my ear. Will I be able to be Grace Morton with one daughter when this is over? Will I be able to be the survivor, Grace Enright? I was so clear about things when I left Ava, so certain that all I needed to do was to make sure that Cordelia was okay. I never anticipated any of this. I have two daughters and my dream would be for them to know each other and for us all to be a family, but things are far too complicated for that and far too many people would be hurt by it.

'Ah, well, still time,' he says and I laugh.

'I don't think so but thank you for thinking it could be the case.'

I make my way to my office, wishing I didn't have to be here. But the woman whose job I am doing will be back on Wednesday and that will be all the time I have. If there is anything else to find out about what is going on, I need to use this time now.

As I sit down at my desk, thinking about how to speak to Natalie, about what to ask so that I can find out if she knows anything else, Kelsey walks in.

'Yes?' I ask her, impatient for her to just tell me what she needs and be gone.

'You seem tense,' she says with a small smile. 'Is everything okay?'

'Fine,' I say, 'I'm just...' I take a deep breath. 'How can I help you, Kelsey?'

'I just wanted to say thank you again for finding my earring. It was so good to get it back.'

'My pleasure,' I say and I study her for a moment. Has she slept with Garth, and if I just ask her outright, will she admit it?

'My boyfriend and I are going away,' she says, changing the subject in the same way a child might, and I am reminded again of her youth.

'That's nice,' I reply, my eyes drifting to my computer screen.

'We've only been together for three months but I think he's the one. I mean, he's so cute, see?' she says, turning her phone around and showing me a picture. 'His name is John.'

I glance at the screen and then I look again. 'Oh,' I say, my hand reaching for her phone without my even thinking about it. She hands it over with an impish smile and I study the picture of the young man who has been following Cordelia, the young man who spoke to me. Does she know? Is she involved?

Kelsey leans forward and takes the phone back with a sigh, and then she kisses the screen and looks at me. 'You were asking about Garth, about the lawyer who's disappeared,' she says, and I nod, my mouth dry and my heart pounding in my chest.

'Well, he's an arsehole and whatever has happened to him, he deserves it,' she says with a flippant shrug of her shoulder and then she's gone. I sit stunned and confused at my desk.

In Garth's office is a notebook with only one entry: *Monday 6 p.m. Meeting with J.* John. That's who he was meeting. So that's what this is. It's blackmail.

I stare at my computer screen without doing any work, keeping my phone on my lap on silent, waiting for the buzz indicating a call from Cordelia. Does Kelsey know where Garth is? Does she know who I am? I thought Natalie was involved in some sort of scam with Garth but maybe Kelsey is the one who is involved. Kelsey and her boyfriend? It seems to make sense.

All the lawyers are in a Monday morning meeting in the boardroom and I am waiting for that to end so I can talk to Natalie again. Can she confirm that Garth and Kelsey slept together, and if she can, will she?

It's difficult to do anything but I force myself back to my computer, desperate for the distraction of the monotonous work.

Half an hour later, the phone on my lap begins to buzz and my heart leaps into my throat.

I lift it up to answer the call, which I can see is from Cordelia, but as I do, Peter from HR walks into my office.

'Ah, Grace, could I have a quick word?' he says and I reject the call, hating that I have to do it to her. Right now, she needs to know that I am always available to her. I let her down enough during her childhood. I hate to do it again.

'Sure.' I smile at Peter.

He comes in and stands behind the chair on the opposite side of my desk. 'I know that you're supposed to work until Tuesday but our assistant has returned early from her holiday and she's keen to get back to it. There's a lot of stuff coming up that she's familiar with and so we think it's best. I'm sorry but this will be your last day,' he says with a small, sad smile.

I am instantly relieved. I don't want to be here anymore. I would like to speak to Natalie and ask her directly about Kelsey, and I will have to find a way to do that before I go.

'That's absolutely no problem at all,' I say. 'I have another job starting on Thursday so I'll take a couple of days off. I hope she had a lovely time.' I point to the picture of the older couple that I have left sitting on the desk, liking how happy they seem pictured in front of a white-sand beach on some tropical holiday.

'Oh right, no, that's not her, that's her parents. Tamara says they travel a fair bit.'

'Sorry... what?' I ask, instant queasiness making me dizzy, a ringing in my ears making it hard to hear. I feel like I have been hit with a plank of wood. Pressing my nails into my legs so that I stay present, I concentrate on what he's saying. The name still induces a maelstrom of emotion inside me and I wonder if I will ever be able to hear it again without thinking of her.

'Tamara, our usual assistant, she's back tomorrow. She's only worked here for five months but she's very good.'

'Right, of course,' I say. 'I'll make sure to leave everything in order.'

He nods at me although he looks slightly concerned at my reaction. I just want him out of the office.

It's a common enough name, of course. It doesn't have to be *her* but as Peter walks out, I stare at the picture. Does it seem familiar? She never had a picture of her parents on her desk when she worked for me, but perhaps she showed me one once?

It's not an uncommon name, I remind myself as I begin to open desk drawers searching for something, anything that would tell me who she is. The drawers are neat and tidy because I have made sure to keep them that way, and they're only filled with stationery.

'It's not her,' I mumble as I search through. I pull up the website for the law firm. There is a man pictured under the heading of Chief Administration Assistant and I know there is more than one assistant so they probably don't put all their pictures on the website. Assistants are not really all that important. Or so everyone thinks.

I don't know how to find a picture of her. It's nearly lunchtime so I grab my bag, needing to just get out of this space so I can call Cordelia and ask her what happened at the police station, and then I will come back and figure out if this is just a hideous coincidence.

'Just popping out for lunch,' I tell Tristan, who I can see has just returned from getting himself a coffee. 'Oh, right, I hear Tammy is coming back tomorrow so it's your last day. I hope you've had fun,' he says with a smile.

'I have,' I say, hoping that the heat I feel rising in my body can't be seen on my face.

'Well, I know someone is always going on leave. If you give me your details, I'll try to make sure you get called first.' I know he doesn't have the power to do this and that the next temporary member of staff will come through Bill's agency, but it's sweet of him to say it.

'I will,' I reply and I turn towards the elevator before a thought occurs to me. 'You don't have a picture of her, do you, of Tammy? It's always nice to know whose office you've been working in.'

'Oh, yes, maybe,' he says, not even a hint of suspicion in his voice. 'I'm not really allowed to be on my phone when I'm on the desk but...' He pulls his phone out of a drawer and swipes it open, scrolling quickly as he looks left and right in case someone is coming.

'There you go,' he says. 'We had drinks for my birthday last month. We went to this cute little Mexican place you should try, it's just around the corner. Amazing nachos and the margaritas are extra strong.'

I want to grab the phone out of his hand but I just nod instead. 'I love Mexican,' I say as he turns the phone around.

It's a picture of Tristan and Leah and some people I don't recognise seated around a rectangular table covered in a cherry-red tablecloth. Dishes are crammed into the middle and everyone has a different-coloured margarita in front of them. I glance at piles of corn chips and dips and bowls of salsa as my eyes move from person to person. I look once and then I look again, staring hard, but eventually I have to accept what I'm seeing.

Because there she is, large as life with a smile on her pretty face.

There.

She.

Is.

The woman who worked for me, the woman I supported, the woman who slept with my husband and lied about it, the woman who wanted my company and my life, the woman who testified against me at my trial, the woman who has been nursing her grudges and hatred for six years. All week I have been looking at her email, TR.HWS@harmerwright&sing.com, and I have not thought to put it together. But then why would I have done? Her Instagram page only has perfectly curated pictures of her having a wonderful time.

But there she is.

The dominoes arranged in a pattern all collapse at the same time, and a picture appears.

This has never been about Cordelia.

TWENTY-NINE
CORDELIA

Monday

The ringing of the buzzer drags her out of the black hole of sleep and Cordelia sits up, struggling to figure out where she is.

Looking around her, she sees she's on the sofa, wrapped in the soft orange blanket. She pushes it away, suddenly too hot to be covered. The buzzer continues, insistent, and she drags herself off the sofa and goes to the intercom. 'Yes,' she says, her voice low and raspy.

'Cordelia, it's me,' says her mother and Cordelia pushes the buzzer, letting her in, and then she pulls open her front door, feeling dizzy as she stands and waits.

'You look awful,' her mother says when she sees her.

'Thanks,' says Cordelia, letting go of the door and moving away to the kitchen to get a glass of water.

'I've been calling you for some time. Why haven't you answered?'

Cordelia shrugs. 'I turned my phone off.'

'Okay,' says her mother, wariness in her voice, 'so what happened?'

'They didn't believe me. They called the number that Garth has been texting from, but it's not in service anymore.'

'Have you eaten anything at all?'

Cordelia shakes her head. 'Food won't solve this problem, Mum. I think... They said that a body has turned up at one of the hospitals and it could be Garth but they don't know because of the decomposition. They said that—'

Her mother holds up her hand. 'I don't think it's Garth. There's something weird going on here... there's a lot to discuss.'

Cordelia shakes her head again. 'That's one way to describe it.'

'I'll make something to eat,' says her mother and Cordelia nods, grabbing her phone from the coffee table. It's just after 5 p.m. How long was she asleep? She can't remember getting up to even use the bathroom. Sleep seems to be the only place she can go when the circling thoughts threaten to send her mad.

An image of Garth in a morgue assaults her. Is it him? Has he been dead all along? Her fingerprints will obviously match those on the knife, it's her knife.

She briefly considers the possibility that in a rage, in a moment of madness, she actually did hurt Garth. Could she have done something to him? He's so much taller than her, fitter and stronger too. How could she have done anything to him? And if she did do something, how can she simply not remember? It's impossible.

She goes to the bathroom. *I'm not going mad. I will not let myself believe I'm going mad. I didn't do anything to him. He just disappeared.*

In the bathroom mirror, her face is pale, her brown eyes shadowed. She pulls her hair back into a ponytail, not wanting to look at herself anymore.

Her mother has cleaned the kitchen and Cordelia can smell the sweet sugary smell of pancakes.

'You had very little to use, so I've settled on pancakes,' says her mother as she flips some onto a plate for Cordelia.

'Thanks,' she replies, taking her plate and the syrup to the table and tucking in, aware now of the fact that she has not eaten all day.

Her mother sits down opposite her with just a cup of coffee.

'Aren't you going to eat?'

'I had a late lunch,' says her mother. 'I have to tell you some-thing – well, a couple of things – and I need you to just listen... Don't say anything until I've explained completely, okay?'

'Okay,' says Cordelia.

'It's about Tamara. I mean, there's more than that because I know who's been following you but—'

'Tamara?' says Cordelia. 'Are you serious?'

'Yes, just let me explain,' says her mother, and Cordelia sits back in her chair, knowing that she has to let her mother talk.

And as her mother begins to speak, to explain, Cordelia feels she has entered some kind of twilight zone where the past is suddenly back. After six years, here she is again, back exactly where she was. She remembers her mother's paranoia, the drinking, the accusations and the screaming, and then she thinks about the way her father died and she wonders if what her mother really wanted that night was to kill her as well. Because if she is sitting opposite her saying this stuff, talking about Tamara once again, then surely she is drinking again, surely she has only come back into Cordelia's life to harm her, to finish the job of ending her family. Cordelia cannot figure out how Garth is involved but she can see that her mother, despite looking perfectly sane as she sips her coffee, is actually completely insane.

Tamara cannot be working in Garth's firm. It's just not possible. Tamara is somewhere else, living her life and trying to forget what Cordelia never can.

'I need you to leave,' says Cordelia when her mother is done speaking.

'But... there's more – Kelsey, the intern, showed me a picture of her boyfriend and he's the man who's been following you, the one who spoke to me.'

'God, Mum, can you not hear how insane that sounds? It's just crazy... and Tamara, I mean really, Tamara?'

How can this be happening again, again? How is this happening again? Why did I let her back into my life?

'You have to believe me, Cordelia. This is all connected, all wrapped up together and—'

'No, Mum. I can't do this again. I need you to leave!' Cordelia yells, needing her mother to just stop talking, just stop.

'You need—' begins Grace.

'Get out, just get out!' shrieks Cordelia, standing and gesturing towards her front door.

Her mother nods sadly and stands up. 'This is my fault. I have no idea how she's involved but I know that it has something to do with me.'

Cordelia walks over to her front door and opens it, and her mother picks up her bag and walks out into the hallway.

'Can you tell me the truth about something, Mum?' she says, and her mother nods. 'Have you taken a drink since you left the clinic, even a single drink?'

And what she wants is for her mother to get defensive, to shake her head and tell Cordelia that she will never touch a drink again. But instead, her mother shrugs her shoulders and says, 'It was never really about the alcohol, darling. I knew that.'

Cordelia feels a sob catch in her throat. And she closes the door slowly.

She doesn't know what she's going to do now but she does know that once again she is exhausted and the only place she wants to go is to sleep. She cannot be here again, simply cannot be here with her mother throwing around ridiculous accusations. She can't go through it again.

If the police hadn't told her not to leave, she would get on a plane tonight and fly across the world so she could be away from all this, but she can't leave until she knows what's happened to Garth.

All she can do is lie down on the sofa and close her eyes, hopeful that the morning will bring some answers.

THIRTY

GRACE

Monday

I do not let the hurt take hold. I cannot let it take hold. I thought she would believe me, that she would make the connection, that it would be easier to convince her this time, but too much damage was done just over six years ago. It's not fair. But no one ever told me motherhood would be fair. Cordelia is twenty-four but still very young in some ways. I haven't been there for her for six years but I will not abandon her now just because she told me to go. I'm done letting her lead the way. I need to be in charge now because this is my fault. It's me Tamara hates and wants to get back at, I'm sure of it.

I leave Cordelia's building and go back to my hotel and straight to the bar, where I order my usual glass of red wine. I couldn't lie to her about the drinking. I did think that if I told the truth about that, she would believe me about Tamara.

But she doesn't and I understand why. Tamara is back and seems determined to destroy me, probably through my daughter. Does she know I'm out of the clinic? She must know. The police would have informed everyone involved with my case when I was released. It's something they do. The feeling of unreality that has accompanied me all day since I saw the picture of Tamara returns and I feel slightly dizzy. How can this be happening again?

But it's not happening again, I comfort myself. *You're a very different person this time.* I soothe myself with that thought and then I make a list of the things that I know, that I'm sure of.

I know that Tamara was sleeping with my husband.

I know that she only recently started working at Garth's firm.

I know that I cannot let her get away with this, with whatever she is doing, because it cannot be a coincidence.

I don't know how Garth and Tamara and Kelsey and her boyfriend are connected but I will find out. Is Natalie involved as well? Anything seems possible right now.

I need to start taking some steps to figure this out.

After a quick shower, I catch an Uber into the city and get dropped off outside Garth's office building.

It's late but I can see lots of the windows still lit up with people working. I don't wish to see anyone but I won't need to be there long.

In the elevator, I once again practise an excuse for being there if anyone asks me what I'm doing. But the office is quiet, only a couple occupied, and I make my way to the one I have used for the past week stealthily, praying that I do not meet anyone.

The door is locked, which is frustrating, but at least I have a sealed envelope to slide under the door. I push it through and quickly leave. There is one line written on a piece of paper that I sealed inside a plain white envelope with her name on the front.

I know what's going on. Call me on this number. Grace.

If I'm right, she will call or text. If I'm right? I know I'm right.

As I walk towards the glass doors of the office building, they slide open and I see a man moving away quickly. I catch sight of the leather jacket under the glow of a city streetlight, and without giving myself time to wonder, I dash after him, grateful I have chosen flat shoes to wear for my little expedition to the office.

He moves fast and then he turns, sees me and starts to run. He'll easily outrun me but I'm not giving in and I increase my pace to match his. I must look like a madwoman running through the city, and as I run, heads turn, people curious about what I'm doing. I'm not dressed to be jogging.

He turns down a side street and I know I'm going to lose him but I turn down after him and there he is, just standing still. I glance around, unable to work out why he's stopped, but then I see two police officers talking to a woman. He must have been startled by their presence. If someone is running, if they're being chased, I'm sure a police officer will want to know why.

I march over to him and grab his elbow. 'Don't you dare move or I swear I will tell them you hurt me,' I hiss in his ear. 'And they will catch you and then this whole little scheme is going to unravel.'

'Okay,' he says, lifting his hands a little, 'okay.'

'We need to talk,' I say and he nods.

Still holding on to his elbow, I look around and see an Italian restaurant on the corner.

'Why don't you let me treat you to dinner.' The words are more a command than an invitation, and I thank God for the presence of the police officers who are still talking to the woman.

I hold on to him as we make our way into the restaurant, where there are quite a few empty tables.

We are seated immediately, and only when he goes to sit down opposite me do I let go of his arm.

'Hi,' says a waiter as he hands us menus, 'our specials tonight are...' I tune him out as he speaks, staring hard at the young man who is, as Kelsey put it, 'cute' with red-brown hair and blue eyes. He sits forward and takes off his leather jacket, and underneath he's wearing a T-shirt with some cartoon character on the front. I want to laugh at how young he is, but this is my daughter's life he has somehow gotten involved with. This is no laughing matter. And this boy has no idea who he's dealing with.

I need to know how all this is connected.

'I'll have the puttanesca,' I tell the waiter, 'and a glass of red wine.'

'I'll have um... spaghetti and meatballs,' he says, 'and a beer, yeah a beer, a lager.' He looks thoroughly uncomfortable. I glance around the restaurant. To the other diners, we could be a mother and son having dinner. He is certainly young enough to be my son.

'Wait till our food gets here,' I instruct him, not wanting to be interrupted.

The note I left is on my mind.

What if she doesn't get it? What if she gets it and dismisses it? What if she shows the police? I am not supposed to contact her.

There are too many variables, too many things I can't control, but I can control Grace. I can control who I am and how I react, and I'm not letting that little bitch take everything away from me again.

Not again.

THIRTY-ONE
CORDELIA

Monday

She hasn't been able to get to sleep again, her whole terrible week swirling inside her, making her edgy and restless.

She picks up her phone and searches out the last message she received from Garth.

What are you talking about?

I have to work.

I'm not getting into this right now.

But he was lying.

She is not supposed to leave but the police haven't taken her passport. She had it with her when she went for her interview but things went quite differently to how she thought they would and she and Nicholas left the police station before she handed it over.

She goes to the cupboard and gets her passport out. It's up

to date and she has her credit card. She could go right now, just get on a plane and disappear the way Garth has. They haven't charged her with anything but maybe she would still get stopped at the airport. Surely her name is on some list somewhere. Do the police do that? Have they done it? She can't take that chance and she knows it. She would get into her car and drive away but the police have her car. Defeated, she drops the passport. She is trapped in this nightmare.

She finds herself wondering if he has been cheating on her from the very beginning. They've been together for over four years but in that time they have had many months apart, when he was back in the UK, and who knows what he was doing then.

She goes to the kitchen and looks around for something to eat, something to distract her, and her eyes land on the half-empty bottle of wine that Garth left on the counter on Sunday night, over a week ago.

Cordelia grabs it and then gets a glass, pouring a large amount of the wine and then taking a sip and choking as it goes down. The wine has been open for too long and has a bitter, rancid taste but Cordelia doesn't care. She grabs a bottle of lemonade from the fridge and fills the rest of the glass, creating a sickly-sweet acid drink that she downs, the alcohol immediately hitting her stomach and making her queasy. But she doesn't let it stop her drinking. When it's finished, she grabs a bag of salted crisps and sits on the sofa, scrolling through her phone and eating mindlessly. She's just waiting for the alcohol to kick in so she can fall asleep again when a stray thought attacks her.

What if her mother is telling the truth? What if Tamara is actually working at Garth's firm? It sounds ridiculous and impossible but so many ridiculous and impossible things have happened this week that this would just be one more of them.

She finds her contact list and thinks about calling Ian

because he would know but then she dismisses that idea. Ian likes her and might just try to protect her by lying although she wouldn't have to tell him why she wanted to know. Natalie, on the other hand, will be only too happy to break Cordelia's heart, to tell her everything, after their contentious meeting on Saturday.

She may not answer the call, which will be fine with Cordelia, and then she can just go to bed. Her thumb hovers over the number for a moment and then she presses it.

Natalie answers after the first ring. 'Cordelia?'

'Yes, I need to ask you a question.' Why bother with civilities after everything that has happened?

'What?' Natalie obviously feels the same way.

'Who is Garth's admin assistant? I mean, what's her name or his name?' she adds, ever hopeful that she will be given a name that instantly squashes her mother's insane accusations.

Instead of answering immediately with a name, Natalie hesitates. 'Why... why do you want to know that?'

'I just do and it's a simple question.'

'Her name is Tamara, but she's been away for a week. She's on vacation.'

'And how...?' Cordelia swallows quickly so the wine stays in her stomach. 'How old is she?'

'Around thirty, I think; I mean it's not exactly a topic for discussion. Why are you asking about her?'

Cordelia takes a deep breath and holds it for a moment. *I don't want to know, I don't want to know, I don't want to know. I have to know.*

'Do you know what her surname is?'

'It's... Reed, yes Reed. Why are you asking this?' But there is something in her tone that suggests to Cordelia that she knows there is a connection between Garth and Tamara.

'No reason,' whispers Cordelia.

'There must be a reason,' says Natalie.

Does Garth know it's the same Tamara? Does Tamara know all about Cordelia? Are the two of them just work colleagues, friends, more than that?

Tamara Reed. The same first name could have just been an unfortunate coincidence. But add the surname, and it cannot be. Tamara is working for Garth. And even though she doesn't want to believe it, doesn't want to believe that Tamara would even be in the same city as she is, she has to acknowledge the truth. And she also has to ask the question why. *Why? Why? Why?*

'Is there an intern named Kelsey who works there?' ask Cordelia.

'Why are you asking about her?' asks Natalie cautiously.

'Just... just asking,' Cordelia replies because now she needs to ask all the questions, all the questions she's pretty sure she doesn't want to know the answers to. She didn't believe her mother about Tamara but perhaps her mother is actually right about everything, absolutely everything.

'Look, it was only a rumour,' says Natalie.

'What was only a rumour?' demands Cordelia, and Natalie is silent for a long time. Cordelia takes her phone away from her ear and looks at the screen, thinking that perhaps the woman has hung up.

'Natalie,' she says shortly, 'what was only a rumour?'

'That Garth slept with her,' says Natalie softly, as though this will take the punch out of the words. 'It was near Christmas and Garth had a big night... a lot to drink, but like I say... it was only a rumour.'

'Oh...' gasps Cordelia.

'She's only nineteen and even Garth isn't that—' Natalie continues but Cordelia hangs up the phone. Every time she thinks this cannot get any worse, it does.

She should call her mother and apologise, say something, anything, but she finds that forming words will be impossible. It feels like some hideous circle has been completed but for what reason, she has no idea.

It's after 9 p.m. and her eyes are growing heavy, and once again, she takes refuge in sleep because she simply cannot think about this anymore. She just can't.

THIRTY-TWO

GRACE

Monday

We sit in a silence loaded with questions until our food is in front of us.

'What does Kelsey have to do with Garth?' I ask.

'Kelsey?' he tries.

'Don't even try pretending you don't know her,' I say. 'She told me you're her boyfriend and you must know that Garth is missing, and I know that somehow you and Kelsey and Tamara are all connected, so talk, young man, or I swear I will call the police right now and spill this whole story.'

'No one will believe you.' He smirks and then he picks up his fork, taking a mouthful of his spaghetti and leaving some sauce on his chin as he eats. *Silly child, silly, silly child.*

I leave my food untouched, staring at him until he picks up a serviette and wipes his face, takes a sip of his beer and clears his throat.

'Your son-in-law is an arsehole,' he says.

'He's not my son-in-law,' I reply, 'he's my daughter's boyfriend and a terrible one at that.'

'He really hurt Kelsey, like he treated her like a toy, slept with her once and then ignored her. It pissed her off and you shouldn't piss off the daughter of a partner. And he's old, like he could be... I mean she's only nineteen and that's sick.'

'I agree,' I say, crossing my arms over my chest, protecting my heart from this disgusting information. 'Do you know where he is?'

'We want a hundred thousand dollars,' he says instead of answering me.

'What?'

'Me and Kelsey, we're going to spend the year travelling and we want a hundred thousand dollars so we don't have to rough it. Or Kelsey will tell her dad and Garth loses his job and maybe even worse because... he should not have slept with her.'

I shake my head, confused. How does one hundred thousand dollars become three million? 'Do you know where he is?' I ask.

He shakes his head, takes another mouthful of food. 'I don't. That wasn't my part of things. I just had to follow you and Cordelia, make sure that you were getting the money and put his phone in the apartment on Tuesday, and... that was all I had to do.'

'How did you get into the apartment?'

'Had the keys, didn't I,' he says, lifting his beer to me in a toast of his own cleverness.

What have you involved yourself with, Garth, and why did you think you would get away with it?

'How did you know who I was?'

He shakes his head again. 'We want a hundred thousand dollars,' he repeats.

'What does Tamara have to do with all of this?'

'A hundred thousand dollars,' he repeats, 'or everyone will know what he did.'

'Tell me how this involves Tamara and I'll get you your money,' I say.

He smiles widely, a delighted child. 'You'll get me my money,' he says and he stands up.

'Sit down,' I say.

'Call me when you have my money,' he says, taking a pen out of his jacket pocket and jotting his number down on a serviette, 'and then maybe all of this goes away.' He picks up his glass, drains his beer and turns to leave.

'You know,' I say quickly and he stops.

'Yeah, what?' he replies, turning back, slipping his jacket on.

'I've known Tamara for years. She had an affair with my husband and...' I wave my hand because that's a whole story I don't have time for, 'and I want you to understand that you can't trust her. Whatever she has said she'll give you – she's lying. You and Kelsey will end up with nothing and I will be going to the police, so at the very least life will be difficult for both of you for some time. I can't imagine Kelsey's father will be very impressed to have the police questioning his daughter. Garth is missing and even if the police don't believe anything I say, they will still want to question Kelsey. And then who knows what secrets may come out.'

John stares at me for a moment and I can see that he's thinking about what I've just said but then he leans down and bares his teeth. 'Just get me my money or the police will be taking your daughter to prison,' he says and then he leaves.

I want to chase after him as frustration and anger surge through me but there's no point. I will have to wait for Tamara to contact me so that I can put all of this together, and then I will have to figure out what to do.

Back in my hotel room, I pace up and down as I struggle to fit the pieces together, especially the disparate amounts of one hundred thousand dollars and three million dollars.

Garth is a lawyer and very smart, certainly smart enough to plan this whole little ruse to get money out of me. I have no idea what he planned to do with the rest. Presumably send it to his mother or just leave the country and return to the UK, free of debt and Cordelia. Whatever he had planned, he has no idea that I am not just going to accept what he's done to my daughter. How he's set her up.

I need to wait until the morning to get to the bank. They will question me but I have enough money available so that it will be easy enough to get the hundred thousand. Three million would have taken a few days, and involved breaking some fixed deposits, but now I don't have to do that.

If I go to the police now, will they believe me? They didn't believe Cordelia. I am so tired of trying to tell people the truth and having them question my sanity. I don't need that from the police as well. I'll sort this out myself.

Finally, just after 1 a.m., I shower and get into bed.

I fall asleep with the questions circling my mind and only wake when I get a text message on my phone that drags me from sleep. I grab it eagerly, hoping that Cordelia is open to trusting me, to forgiving me enough to really trust me.

But the message is not from Cordelia, but rather an unknown number. Only three people now have my number – and one of them just messaged me. It's obviously her.

It's two clapping hands emojis and:

Well done, Grace. Pay up or Garth dies and Cordelia goes to prison.

It's just after 8:30 a.m. She has obviously arrived at the office and seen the note.

I read the words over a few times. Is Tamara in league with Kelsey and her boyfriend, John, or is she simply taking advantage of the situation? Whatever the truth is, there is one thing that I am certain of: Tamara has no idea I have spoken to John.

Karma has served her up to me. And now it's my turn.

THIRTY-THREE
CORDELIA

Tuesday

'If you don't come in tomorrow with a medical certificate, I'm afraid that we are going to have to terminate your position, Cordelia. I think you have to agree we have been more than fair but in the absence of any explanation, we will have to make that decision. I urge you to contact me.' It's after 9 a.m. and Cordelia listens to the voice message again.

'I don't care,' she says aloud, because she really doesn't.

She gets out of bed and straight into a shower, unsure exactly what she's going to do with her day aside from wait to hear from her lawyer or the police.

Looking around the apartment, she thinks about the rent that is due in a week and the bills piling up in her inbox.

She is too young to be dealing with this, just too young, and she doesn't want to do it anymore.

Over the past few days, when she has not been worried about Garth or afraid for him or herself, she has been re-examining her relationship with him, going back over all the things he has said to her, including his criticism of her friends and her job and her clothes.

She grew up with a fierce, strong mother who upended her own life over an imagined affair. But today, as she prepares breakfast for herself, Cordelia understands that after the fire, she didn't just abandon her mother and all the terrible things she had done. She also abandoned all the things her mother taught her about how to be a woman in the world.

Cordelia has given up parts of herself and her life to be in a relationship with a man who has lied to her and cheated on her and now probably run away, leaving her to take the blame for his disappearance. And he now needs millions of dollars from her. It's insane.

How has she allowed this to happen? She is smart and well educated. She knows what abuse looks like, but perhaps abuse sometimes comes in disguise. This abuse has left her feeling small and alone, terrified and like she is not good enough, and now she may very well be charged with a murder that has or has not happened. How has it come to this?

Cordelia feels on the precipice of losing her entire life.

Some part of her keeps hoping that, somehow, Garth is aware of what's happening to her, that he knows she's being blamed for him going missing and that he will appear any minute now and apologise for all of this. He owes money but money is not a problem.

And what does Tamara have to do with all of this? Why is she working at Garth's firm? Is it just a coincidence? She feels bad about the things she said to her mother now because her mother was right, but she's also angry at her mother for drinking again. Should she call her? And what about Kelsey and her boyfriend? How are they involved?

A rapping at her front door startles her. She hasn't buzzed anyone in.

Picking up a pair of scissors from her kitchen bench, she

makes her way to the door. Anything is possible now and she wants to be prepared.

'Who is it?' she calls through the door but there's no answer, just more knocking.

Should she open it or just call the police? It could be… Her heart lifts and she hates herself for that, but maybe it's Garth. She pulls open the door quickly, only to see her mother standing there.

She has no idea what to say.

'You need to listen to me,' commands her mother. 'You need to stop acting like a child and listen to me.'

'I'm not a child,' yells Cordelia, sounding exactly like one, but she steps back and lets her mother in.

'Now sit down and listen,' demands her mother, and Cordelia slopes off to the sofa and slumps into it, irritated as she drops the scissors on the coffee table.

'Look,' says her mother, showing her the phone screen.

Cordelia reads the text. 'Who's it from?' she asks.

'Tamara,' says her mother and then she holds up her hand. 'No talking. Just listen.'

Cordelia lifts her hand like a child in a classroom asking for permission to speak, and her mother is so startled by the gesture that she keeps quiet. 'I know it's her,' she says. 'I called Natalie and asked for her name and surname. It must be her and I know it is so I'm sorry but I don't understand why she has contacted you. What exactly is going on?'

And Cordelia leans back against the sofa cushions and pays attention as she learns exactly who she has allowed into her life.

THIRTY-FOUR

GRACE

Tuesday

It's been a very long day. Cordelia and I have spent it together, talking, crying, working through everything. I have no idea who the two of us will be tomorrow, how we will feel, what will have become of us. But whatever happens, it's time to put an end to whatever Tamara has planned. I'm taking control of this situation.

I glance down at my phone, checking the time. It's just before 11 p.m. as I enter Garth's building, Cordelia just behind me.

'So what now?' she asked me after I explained how I thought this all fitted together.

'Now you just have to trust me. I have to speak to John and to Tamara and I will arrange to meet everyone in one place with the money.'

I sent Tamara a text.

I will meet you tonight at the office. 11 p.m. Bring Garth or no money.

She didn't say she had no idea where he was. Because she does know exactly where he is, or she thinks she does.

The next thing I had to do was contact John.

He was reluctant to do what I wanted him to, but when I'd spoken to him in the restaurant, I'd managed to sow the seeds of distrust for Tamara.

I'm sure he and Kelsey have been discussing the possibility that they were used. He doesn't care what happens. He just wants his money. Of course he wants his money, and one hundred thousand dollars is a small price to pay for this to be over. There is no honour among thieves, no honour among those who seek to hurt people. He was easily persuaded to do what I need him to do.

Now Cordelia and I take the stairs up to Garth's offices and walk into reception.

'Are you sure?' she asks me one more time because she is horrified about the plan I have made, and of the necessary decisions that had to be taken.

'I'm sure,' I say.

No one is here, which is good, and we follow the small sliver of light coming from the administration assistant's office.

I am holding a bag that contains one hundred thousand dollars. I just need Tamara to believe that it contains the whole three million.

I have to admit that when I push open the door to the office and see her sitting behind the desk, I am shocked. I expected her and yet I did not. She is as lovely as her Instagram photos, her cheekbones pronounced and her blonde hair perfect.

'Tamara,' I say, and behind me, Cordelia gasps.

'In the flesh,' she says, smiling.

'Where's Garth?' I ask her and she shakes her head.

'Safely tucked away somewhere.'

That's what you think.

There is a strangled sob from Cordelia and I want to

comfort her but I don't turn around, instead shielding her with my body from the smirk on Tamara's face.

'Can you tell me why?' I say. 'What has all this been in aid of?' I clutch the bag tighter to me in case she tries to take it.

'Sit down over there, Cordelia,' says Tamara, standing and pointing to a grey fabric armchair on the side, against the wall.

Cordelia meekly does as she's told. She's in shock, I believe. And I can see her thinking back over everything that happened six years ago, and realising that what her father and Tamara and eventually the court declared an 'alcoholic delusion' may not have been a delusion at all.

I feel such deep sorrow for my child as I watch her visibly rewrite everything that she has known for six years. Because I am right about Tamara now, and therefore I must have been right about Tamara then. I wonder briefly how my daughter will survive this, how she will hold on to who she is.

'What do you have to do with Garth going missing?' I ask Tamara.

'Now there's an interesting story. I knew when you got out, you know. I was told and I think... well, I think that you didn't pay for your crime, Grace,' she says, waving a hand, and then she stops speaking and bites down on her lip as she shakes her head. 'You're a murderer and you should have been locked up forever. And yet here you are, just walking around like you didn't kill the man I loved with all my heart.' Her blue eyes are bright with tears but I feel no sympathy for her at all. He was mine before he was hers. She had no right to steal Robert from me.

There is another gasp from Cordelia. I have a feeling my daughter will learn a lot of unpleasant truths tonight.

I keep a tight hold on the leather bag I have filled with cash, not wanting Tamara to leap across the desk and somehow grab it.

'I have a gift for you,' she says and she turns around and

pulls a bottle of wine out of a filing cabinet drawer. I stare at it, recognising the label. It's a bottle of wine Robert bought for my birthday, two years before everything fell apart. He spent two thousand dollars on it and I have no idea how much it would be worth today. We were saving it for a special occasion, like when Cordelia graduated from university, or his business finally reached its potential, or when I managed to conquer the overseas market, something Liza Hong, my deputy, and I had been discussing before I found out my assistant was sleeping with my husband. At some point Robert took it and gave it to his mistress, a sickening thought.

'Recognise it?' she asks with a malicious little smile. 'I kept it for you. I'm sure I'll have enough money to buy myself plenty more where that came from.'

'I don't understand,' says Cordelia.

'Oh God,' sighs Tamara, turning to look at my daughter, who is huddled in the armchair, 'you're such a silly little girl, Cordelia. It took me all of five minutes to seduce Garth. All I wanted was to take him away from you. Your mother got herself locked up in a clinic so she could conveniently be protected from everything, and I've had many years waiting for her to get out. My whole life was destroyed and I've had to rebuild from the ground up. Your life changed, Cordelia, but then you just carried on afterwards, running away to the UK and finding yourself a "true love".' She uses her hands to put air quotes around the words.

'And I was left alone and devastated and there was no justice for me. I lost out on all the money and on your lovely father and I had to start again. I know your mother adores you and I knew it would hurt her if your little heart was broken. And I knew she would come running if you needed her. She was always so concerned about you.' She looks at Cordelia, who is curled in the chair, pale and close to tears, and she frowns comically. 'Poor Cordy, so in love, so young,' she sighs.

'Why not just come after me?' I ask her. Tamara keeps looking at the door, as though at any moment she will try to grab the money from me and run. Am I right about where Garth is? Is he here or somewhere else? Is he actually locked away or just waiting for his new love to get the money so they can leave together? I have a feeling I know where he is but I am still worried that he will suddenly appear and then Cordelia and I will be overpowered.

'It was just meant to be a little affair,' says Tamara, waving her hand, 'and then wouldn't you know it, I fell in love, and then Garth told me about his little problem – well, problems – with all the money his mother needs and the scheming little minx who was trying to blackmail him. Kelsey and John had no idea what they were doing. They only wanted to punish Garth for hurting Kelsey. And they wanted money to travel. I don't think Kelsey's father even knows about her new boyfriend. But that's not my concern. When Garth told me he was being black-mailed, I came up with a much better plan, one that gets everyone what they want, except you, Grace, and your little daughter.'

A wave of intense hate for this woman rises up through me but I maintain my silence.

'And here we are,' she continues. 'I found a solution to everything. Kelsey and John will run off to see the world and Garth and I will pay off his loan and help his mother and start our lives over. Aren't I clever, Grace?' she asks, wanting me to admire her, to applaud her. The woman is clearly mad.

'You're very clever. Well done, Tamara,' I say, my voice catching in my throat.

'You *owe* me this, Grace. You took everything from me and you owe me this, and if you just hand over the money, Garth will present himself to the police station tomorrow and declare he was lost in the bush or something. And then he and I will disappear and Cordelia can... I don't know, find someone younger or something.' Her attitude is so cavalier, so cruel – I almost can't believe it.

'You were supposed to post the phone to me,' whispers Cordelia.

Tamara smiles. 'Yes, Garth thought of that, but I thought it would be better if you only found it later, after the police had declared you suspect number one. I knew your mother would hate for you to be in trouble with the police after everything that she did. I was going to post it today but then I found your mother's note and the phone was gone. You're clever, Grace,' she says, turning to look at me. 'Not as clever as I am, but... what can you do?' She shrugs. 'I had John following both of you to make you scared. I knew you would come, Grace, even if you didn't want Cordelia to know you were here. I didn't expect you to get a job in Garth's firm but you can't control everything, can you? Your disguise is useless, by the way. I've been watching you since you arrived in Melbourne. Well, I was watching Cordelia and then there you were, dressed up and pretending to be someone else.'

'And the knife with his blood on it?' I ask. 'And the car leaving the building?'

'Oh, that was all John. He and Kelsey were so eager to help, I gave them something to do. Garth wasn't happy about us needing his blood but he knew it was all for the greater good. And he didn't like the idea of the knife and the car either because he didn't want little Cordy to suffer... but he knew it was necessary to really make sure that mummy Grace got involved with her cash. I, myself, quite enjoyed the idea of Cordelia suffering and you, Grace, suffering because she's your child.' She shrugs.

'It's over now. Give me the money,' she says, holding her hands out to me, 'and all of this, including me and Garth, just go away.'

'I don't think so,' I say, and I glance over at Cordelia, who looks very small and sad. It is terrible to hear that the man you love is in love with someone else. It's terrible to hear everything she has heard tonight. But I comfort myself that this is nearly over. If everything I have put into place goes according to plan, it will be the end.

'You ruined my life, you bitch,' Cordelia hisses at Tamara, who laughs.

'Your mother ruined mine. I should have a lovely house and half a company and I have nothing. Now I will have three million dollars.'

'Minus what Kelsey and John want and the loan.'

'Yes, yes,' says Tamara, 'we'll take care of all of that.' And then she looks away, a slight smirk crossing her face, and I know that she and Garth were never going to pay those two stupid children anything at all. They were used and gaslit the same way I have been, the way Cordelia has been. Tamara and Garth were probably not even going to go to the police to let them know Garth is alive.

They were simply going to flee the country and leave Cordelia to deal with the consequences. But I anticipated that.

Tamara reaches out her hand. 'Give me the money, Grace, or your little princess will end up in jail.'

'The police will catch you, you know,' I say, speaking slowly. I glance at a clock on the wall. I only need another minute.

'By the time you explain, Garth and I will be long gone and they won't believe you anyway. I mean, there's so much evidence against your darling daughter. You didn't go to prison for killing your husband. But now you can visit your daughter in prison and it will be almost like you did,' says Tamara, lifting up the wine and glancing at the label. 'Maybe I should open this and we can all have a drink together.'

'You're mad,' I say.

'No, *you're* mad and an alcoholic and you should have spent the rest of your life in jail,' says Tamara, spitting the words as her eyes narrow.

'You need to know that I've spoken to John,' I tell her.

'Liar,' says Tamara with a laugh, and she drops into the office chair. 'I'm not an idiot, Grace.'

'Neither am I,' I say. 'I told him that you weren't going to give him any money, that you and Garth were just using him and Kelsey, and he's only young but he's pretty angry. He feels like he's been toyed with.'

She shrugs dramatically. 'I'm sure you'll sort it all out, Grace, or not. I don't really care. Give me the money.'

'I'm not doing that until you guarantee that Garth will call the police and tell them he's fine.'

'Fine,' says Tamara, rolling her eyes at me. She takes out her phone and I panic because I think she's going to call Garth wherever he is, but instead, she just pushes play on a recording.

'Hi Cordy, it's me. I am so sorry about this. I'll go to the police tonight, before we leave. I'm sorry, Cordy, I'll always love you but...'

'Oh God, oh God,' says Cordelia at the sound of his voice. The words are rehearsed, spoken without emotion.

'... but I believe Tammy and I are soulmates. I've been struggling so hard to be one kind of person, to do everything I need to do for my mother and you and I feel like... it's my turn now. My mother will be fine and I need to take a chance on my own happiness.'

I shake my head at the ridiculous words, at the deranged sentiment and the level of Garth's selfishness.

'Bastard!' shouts Cordelia, jumping off her chair and grabbing for the phone. 'Bastard!' she screams even though Garth can't hear her.

Tamara chuckles. 'He's not here, Cordelia. He's safe and far away... now hand it—' She doesn't get to finish her sentence because suddenly there is the sound of the door that leads to the stairs slamming, a loud thud that echoes through the quiet office.

'Who's that?' asks Tamara, her gaze moving to the office door.

I smile as a man screams, 'Where is my money?'

'What?' says Tamara, paling at the anger in his voice, and now it's my turn to shrug. 'As I told you, John wants his money,' I say. 'He and Kelsey have so many plans, and I told him you were going to ruin them, that you were going to leave the two lovebirds without any money at all. They want to travel and I said I would help. I'm happy to give them the money. They can enjoy a year on me.'

I step to the side as we hear the sound of doors being smashed open and John roars, 'Where are you? Where's my money?'

I told him to make it very dramatic. To scream and shout and smash things. He has followed my instructions to the letter.

And now it's my turn to smirk.

THIRTY-FIVE

CORDELIA

Tuesday

She leaps off her chair at the sound of cracking wood and smashing glass and huddles into a corner. Tamara looks frantically around her and then grabs the wine bottle, holding it above her head to use as a weapon. Cordelia watches her mother move to the side, still clutching the bag of money as Tamara darts around the desk, the bottle held aloft. Cordelia can see how panicked the woman is as the sound of more things being smashed echoes through the office.

'Where are you, where are you?' John is screaming, his voice loud and rough with fury.

'Bitch,' Tamara hisses at her mother as they all hear stomping footsteps, and suddenly the office door opens.

Tamara swings the bottle of wine, a grimace on her face as she puts all her force into the swing.

'Bastard,' Tamara yells, the bottle connecting with his head as he comes through the door.

A low thunk sound fills the air and he drops forward, onto his knees and then onto his face. Blood appears, heavy and thick, metal-smelling, and begins to sink into the grey carpet, and Cordelia thinks she may be sick.

She wants to close her eyes, to not see this, but she cannot help but look. Holding her hand over her mouth, she peers down at the man lying on the carpet. He is dressed in a collared blue shirt and chinos.

And he is not John.

Even from behind Cordelia can see that this is not John, Kelsey's boyfriend. That young man had broad shoulders and red-brown hair.

The man on the floor has sandy-blond hair and he is smaller, narrower.

The man on the floor is Garth.

It is Garth lying on the floor, blood pooling around him from the head wound created by being hit with a full bottle of wine.

Not missing, not somewhere else, but right here, waiting for his lover to get three million dollars from Cordelia's mother.

It's Garth.

'Garth,' she wails, her stomach churning, her eyes filling with tears. 'Garth,' she says again as she goes to him and drops to her knees, touching his shoulder, shaking him to make him move.

She still loves her version of him, still loves the Garth she met in the UK who was so kind and stable and supportive, who became her everything.

Her mother crouches down beside her and physically pulls her away from him. 'No, leave, leave now and I'll sort this out.'

'But Garth,' cries Cordelia, reaching for him.

'Cheated on you and lied to you and was in love with someone else and willing to let you go to jail. Leave now,' her mother says again, a wild look in her green eyes.

'Garth, oh my God, Garth, baby, wake up, baby, I'm sorry,'

yells Tamara, crouching down beside him, and in that moment, Cordelia realises what is happening.

Two women who love Garth are crouching next to him, but Garth only really loves one of them, and the other one is the woman he was using. That was her. That is her.

'Go now,' her mother screams and Cordelia obeys her. Pulling the sleeves of her hoodie over her hands, she flees to the staircase because her mother said not to use the lift and runs down seven flights of stairs until she is outside in the cold autumn wind.

She starts running, just running, not even thinking about where she is heading although she knows she needs to get home.

Her mother told her what to do, told her she would know when to run, but Cordelia had not imagined this.

Garth is lying in an office with blood seeping out of his head. Garth was sleeping with Tamara? How is this possible? Nearly seven years ago, her mother started drinking, accusing her father of sleeping with Tamara, and then things escalated until her mother set their house on fire, killing her father, who was sleeping inside. And from that moment on, Cordelia was certain that she knew exactly who the enemy was, exactly where blame lay. But she was so sure of the enemy that she neglected to look at those closest to her. Garth knew everything, understood everything. How could he turn into the enemy?

She feels so stupid, so angry, so heartbroken.

She keeps running, turning down a side street so that she is heading in the right direction, her breath burning in her lungs, her stomach churning and her heart broken.

'I'm going to sort this out,' her mother said, but after everything that had happened, Cordelia didn't believe her. She still doesn't. How can her mother sort this out?

But she can't do anything right now except run, her lungs on fire, her eyes tearing up, her soul crushed.

She can only run.

THIRTY-SIX

GRACE

Tuesday

'Oh my God, oh my God,' she shrieks, 'I didn't mean to. I didn't mean to.'

Blood is pooling on the ground around his head, sinking into the plush grey carpet. She hit him on the side of his head. He looks like he's dead although he may just be out cold. But there is a lot of blood.

A knock on the head doesn't have to kill you. But perhaps a knock on the head with a two-thousand-dollar bottle of French wine might if it's swung hard enough, if there is fear and anger behind that swing.

'Of course you didn't mean to,' I say, stepping forward and almost touching her gently on the shoulder, stopping just above her pale blue silk dress. I don't want there to be any evidence of my being here. I wiped the office down thoroughly before I left here yesterday, making sure to eliminate traces of Grace Morton or Grace Enright.

Suddenly she is just a young girl again, waiting for my help and my guidance, just the way she was when she started working for me.

'What now – what am I going to do now?' She sinks to the floor, wraps her arms around herself, clutching the bottle of wine tightly to her. 'What now?' she keeps repeating. 'Garth, Garth, are you okay, are you okay?' She drops the bottle of wine and crawls over to him again and touches him, flinches and pulls her hand back.

'Is he breathing?' I ask.

'I don't...' she says, tears appearing.

'Turn him over and check,' I say. 'We need an ambulance.'

'No, wait... no, don't call them, he'll be fine. I think he'll be fine.' Even in her despair I know she can feel her lies and this scheme unravelling if the ambulance comes, if the police arrive. Pushing with all her strength, she turns him over, struggling with the dead weight of him. His eyes are closed but I can see the slight rise and fall of his chest. His skin is ghostly pale and his breathing very shallow. 'Garth, wake up, wake up, baby, please. It's your sunshine girl, it's me.'

The words sicken me, my past and my present colliding. She needed to be someone's sunshine girl. Robert is gone so she took Garth from Cordelia and turned herself into his 'sunshine girl'. The longing for a bottle of something to wipe it all out almost overwhelms me, but I shake my head, forcing myself to concentrate, to be here now, to sort this out now. That's the plan.

'You have to help me,' she sniffs. 'You know what to do, please help me,' she whines, looking up at me.

'Don't worry, it's going to be fine. I'm going to sort everything out,' I say. 'I promise you it's all going to be fine.'

I don't tell her that my heart is racing and my palms sweating. I need to seem calm and in control.

'You just stay there,' I say to her. 'I'll be back in a minute.'

'And you'll help me?' she asks, her blue eyes wide, more tears snaking down her cheeks. 'You'll really help me?'

'Of course I will,' I say. 'Don't move.' And she does as she's been told, amazingly, stupidly. She just stays there believing that I will help her. I am still holding the bag of money, its weight in my arms beginning to hurt.

'Think,' I tell myself as I step out of the office and close the door behind me. 'Think.'

I stand in the silence of the empty space for a moment and stare at the nameplate on the door.

Turning away I walk along the corridor until I see them.

They are standing outside Garth's office, where the door is hanging off the hinges, just standing quietly as though they have all the time in the world.

I glance into Garth's office and I can see that everything has been destroyed. The computer is lying on the floor, the screen cracked, a filing cabinet is on its side, and the book that was on the desk is gone.

Kelsey watches me study the destruction. 'He's an arsehole,' she says, 'and he deserves whatever he gets.' Garth had little idea who he was dealing with when he discarded this young woman. She has not fallen apart but rather enlisted a new boyfriend for revenge. She should never have gotten involved with Tamara but none of them should have tangled with my child, with me.

'Here you go,' I say, handing John the bag. Both he and Kelsey are still wearing gloves as I instructed them to.

'What went on in there?' he asks.

'Nothing you need to worry about,' I say.

'Oh, I'm not worried, Grace,' he says with a quick laugh, 'we have what we want.' He lifts the bag slightly. 'Nice bag,' he says of the leather satchel that I hastily purchased this afternoon. He glances inside.

'It's all there,' I say. 'And it's not to protect Garth, you understand that, it's because you did what I asked you to do. It's payment for bringing him here.'

'Yep.' He nods. 'We're leaving tonight, aren't we, babe?'

Kelsey smiles. 'My parents are going to freak,' she says.

'When the two of you get back, you had better not come anywhere near me and my daughter. I promise you I will be on the lookout for you,' I warn them as John grasps Kelsey's hand, their childish excitement obvious.

'Well...' He shrugs.

'I've recorded our conversations, John, all of them. Blackmail is illegal.' I'm sure Kelsey knows that, being the daughter of a partner.

'We won't bother you again,' says Kelsey, some worry in her eyes at the news that I have recordings.

John offers me a quick nod, his smile not so wide now, and then they leave, using the stairs. My heart is racing but I take some deep breaths and try to calm my body. The slam of the door to the stairwell helps me relax. They're gone. They have the money and they're gone. Can I trust them to stay away from me and Cordelia? I have no choice. Both Cordelia and I trusted the men closest to us, the men we loved with all our hearts, and both of us have been betrayed.

I need to move quickly so that she can't clean up, so that she is caught.

I grab an office phone, dialling triple zero and holding my shirt over my mouth to muffle my voice. 'Someone is screaming like they're being hurt. They're in an office on the seventh floor of the Landmark building, 33 Nicholson Street,' I say into the phone.

'Okay and could you please tell me—' says the man who answered the phone.

'I think they're being hurt,' I say and then I put down the phone, wiping the handset.

'Grace, Grace, where are you?' I hear Tamara call.

'Coming,' I shout, 'just stay there. It's all going to be fine.'

I can hear her crying and moaning, 'Garth, are you okay, Garth, can you wake up?' I imagine she is shaking him and trying to get him to open his eyes.

I move towards the reception area, listening to her calling Garth's name over and again, and then I leave the offices of Harmer, Wright and Sing, taking the stairs down to the lobby and ducking outside even as I hear sirens scream along the empty city street.

I wonder if she hit him hard enough to kill him. I wonder if they will catch her still there or if she will have the sense to run.

The air is cool and I wish I had a jacket, but as I walk along the street towards a place where I will be able to wait for a taxi, that I will pay cash for, I feel suddenly and completely filled with joy.

I'm free now. Tamara will be caught even if she runs. She will go to jail.

She will finally get everything she deserves.

Cordelia will be fine because any case the police have against her will disappear. Her heart is broken but she will recover from that. I did, and I will help her move on.

I never imagined it would end like this. In my pocket, my phone was on record the whole time I was talking to Tamara so that I would have evidence. I didn't think she would hit Garth.

This is so much better than I hoped. How silly of Garth to be hiding out in Tamara's apartment. But it's exactly where I thought he would be. John has been watching them for hours. I wasn't entirely sure I was right before I walked in there, but the vibrating in my pocket of my phone as John sent three short texts to tell me I was right made me aware of exactly how long I had to keep Tamara talking for.

I asked John to find Garth and bring him here. That's what he was being paid for.

I didn't tell Cordelia. It will take her a long time to stop loving him completely. It took me years to stop loving Robert, and sometimes, I'm not sure I have fully succeeded.

Tamara should run now but perhaps love will keep her sitting there. Love makes us do such strange things. I know because my broken heart nearly destroyed my entire life.

But I've taken it back now, taken control.

As I've always believed, it doesn't matter if revenge is served hot or cold. All that matters is that it's served.

And Tamara has been well and truly served.

THIRTY-SEVEN

The Lawyer, the Assistant and a Bottle of French Wine

Police are still trying to piece together a strange case involving a senior associate with the prestigious Melbourne firm of Harmer, Wright and Sing, Garth Stanford-Brown, and his administration assistant, Tamara Reed.

Triple zero received an anonymous call from the offices just after midnight only to find Garth Stanford-Brown unconscious in the administration assistant's office and his personal office trashed. Ms Reed had struck him with a bottle of French wine, since valued at over three thousand dollars, causing a serious concussion injury.

Ms Reed is currently under sedation in hospital and police have declared her to be not fit for questioning. An anonymous hospital source says that Ms Reed appears to be repeating the phrase, 'Grace did it, Grace did it.' Investigations have uncovered a relationship with Grace Morton, a former CEO of Wax to the Max, who accused Ms Reed of having an affair with her husband six years ago.

Garth Stanford-Brown was reported missing just over a week ago by his girlfriend, Cordelia Morton, who happens to be the daughter of Grace Morton, but while police initially suspected that Ms Morton may have been involved in his disappearance, this has since been proved untrue.

Five years ago, Grace Morton was declared not responsible for the accidental death of her husband in a house fire and she has, until recently, been in a criminal psychiatric facility. She is believed to be living in Sydney and did visit her daughter, who lives in Melbourne. But sources in the police indicate that she has never met Mr Stanford-Brown or been to the offices of Harmer, Wright and Sing. She could not be contacted for comment.

CCTV for the building was disabled that evening. Security teams are investigating how this occurred.

Mr Stanford-Brown remains in an induced coma and therefore cannot testify as to what happened but Ms Reed's fingerprints were found on the bottle and she was the only person present when the police arrived. She was also holding the bottle and confessed immediately to the police, saying, 'I didn't mean to.'

Investigations into this bizarre case are ongoing.

EPILOGUE

Cordelia

She picks up the last box and looks around the apartment. It looks exactly the same as it did when she lived here, which is surreal. Everything in this apartment was bought by Garth. Her few pieces of furniture from her rental apartment were put into storage before she moved in here because Garth felt they didn't work with the space.

'That should have been a clue,' she mutters.

'What?' asks Evangeline, coming out of the bedroom with a blue scarf in her hands.

'Nothing,' says Cordelia.

'Is this yours?' asks Evangeline.

Cordelia nods and Evangeline places it on top of the box. 'I have everything now,' says Cordelia.

'Right, well, best of luck,' says Evangeline, but Cordelia can hear the bitterness in her voice.

The rent for the apartment has been paid until the end of the month and Cordelia has no idea what Evangeline will do after that.

Garth is still in a coma and no one has any idea if he will wake up or not.

Evangeline is horrified that Cordelia has chosen now to leave. 'If you love someone, you stay no matter how difficult things get,' she told Cordelia when she arrived in the country and came straight to the apartment to find her packing up her things.

'Not if that someone was willing to destroy your life,' Cordelia replied.

Evangeline didn't want to hear about her son's lies, about his cheating.

Cordelia has not talked about what happened at Garth's office, about Tamara. She was at home, after all, just like her mother was. They shared a dinner of stir fry beef with noodles, even argued over how to make the sauce and then they fell asleep on the sofa, watching Netflix. Both she and her mother have been clear on how they spent the night with the police. It has surprised Cordelia how easily these lies of self-preservation have tripped off her tongue as she has spoken to Detective Ashton. The detective seemed uninterested in further questions anyway. Garth is no longer missing and the woman who hurt him confessed. It appeared to have nothing whatsoever to do with Cordelia.

'I suppose you should be on your way then,' sneers Evangeline, and Cordelia tries to find some sympathy for the woman.

Cordelia asked the police to call Evangeline, told Detective Ashton that she would not be sitting by Garth's side, waiting for him to wake up, that she will, in fact, be returning to Sydney.

And now she has everything crammed into her small car downstairs. The furniture from her storage unit is sitting on the pavement, waiting for the rubbish collection tomorrow, although some of it is still new so there will be people who will grab it before it's taken away.

In Sydney, her mother has rented an apartment while she

looks for something to buy. 'Something with an ocean view and big enough for the two of us to not be in each other's space,' she said.

'I won't want to live with you for long, Mum,' Cordelia told her.

'Of course not, but you need time to heal, to recover, and then you can decide what's next.'

Cordelia has no idea what's next but she is grateful to have the time to think about it.

'I hope he gets better,' she says to Evangeline as she makes her way to the propped-open front door.

'Spare me your sentiments, Cordelia,' says Evangeline, and then she follows Cordelia and shuts the door behind her.

Cordelia stands in the hallway, closing her eyes for a moment and taking a deep breath.

She's only twenty-four but she feels like she's lived a whole lifetime. That can be a good thing or a bad thing according to the therapist she had a Zoom call with yesterday. She will see Isaac in person next week in Sydney, but she just wanted to have a chat first, before she embarked on the long drive back to Sydney and left her whole world behind again.

She will never again allow a man to do to her what Garth did, and that may mean being single for a long time, but first she has to deal with everything that has happened and therapy is the best place to start.

Pushing the button for the elevator, Cordelia looks around her one last time. 'Goodbye, Garth,' she whispers, and then because she can feel how much her life will change, 'Goodbye, Cordy.' He was the only one who called her that and she hated it. She will never be Cordy again.

She is Cordelia Morton and she will survive this, just as she has survived everything else.

The elevator doors slide open and Cordelia steps inside, never to return.

Grace

'Ms Enright,' says the real estate agent and I realise that I have been standing on the balcony for quite some time, staring at all the yachts moored in the small bay. It's a hot day for the end of March, the sun beating down on my head, warming my whole body.

'Yes,' I say, turning around to face him. He's struggling to conceal his eagerness for a sale. The apartment is big and old and has been on the market for some time because of all the work it requires but it is in the perfect location.

'It needs a lot of work,' I say. 'I mean, I will have to redo the entire thing.' I gesture around the living room, where the beige carpet is stained and the walls are covered in green floral wallpaper. The generic new furniture brought in to help sell the place clashes with the décor.

'Yes, but the location makes it a premium property, even at this price.'

'And yet you have been unable to sell it.' I smile and he flushes slightly. 'I'll think about it, but I have to go now. I have an appointment with another real estate agent,' I say, lest he think the time I have spent here means I am a sure thing.

'The owners are very open to negotiation,' he says quickly.

'Of course they are,' I say and I leave him, taking the stairs because the building is only three floors high in a position right over the water, the views never to be built out.

I have already made my mind up to buy the apartment. I can't wait to get started on the renovation, colours and finishes for a new kitchen and the bathrooms are running through my head as I move into the street.

I am not meeting an agent to look at another apartment but rather to look at warehouse and office space for Cordelia. I have not told her about the space. It will be the perfect place for her to start her own line of clothing. She may not want to and that will be fine. I'm just taking the preliminary steps for her. She may want control of her life again after ceding it to Garth without meaning to, but I think she will want to do this. I hope she will. And perhaps she can concentrate on the design side and I can take care of the business side. I am prepared for her to tell me that this is not what she wants, and then I will look into something else. I have money and many years ahead of me to build something new. I did it before and I know I can do it again.

I take a deep breath, breathing in the autumn air and the smell of roasting coffee from a nearby café.

I feel... free, that's the right word for it. I am finally free of my past. I am Grace Enright now and perhaps Cordelia will want to change her surname as well. It's up to her.

The press have covered what happened, or what they think happened, but they have also moved on quickly. Perhaps when Tamara goes to trial, if she ever does, which looks unlikely given her fragile mental state, the story will be revisited, but that's months away, years maybe. Cordelia will be stronger by then, more certain of herself.

I decide to stop in the café to grab myself a drink, choosing a delicious-looking slice of carrot cake to accompany it. I am content to people-watch as I eat and drink. Truthfully, I am content with everything now. I have my daughter back and that's all I wanted. She is safe and she is no longer with a toxic man. My other daughter, Ava, the child who will never know she is my child, is thriving from what I can see on her social media. Every morning, I contemplate what it would be like to see Cordelia and Ava together but it is just a little fantasy I allow myself. I can't have everything. I worry slightly about running into Ava again without meaning to, but Sydney is a big city and I am sure we will not come across each other. I can follow her from afar and celebrate her life quietly by myself.

I am following Kelsey on Instagram now as well, watching

her post pictures of her travels around the world. I will keep a close eye on her and John in case they feel I may be a future source of revenue.

Life seems full of possibilities now. I have even started to think about dating again, about perhaps finding a man to go out to dinner with, just some company.

I am still young enough to start again and I am stronger than I ever thought possible.

And after everything that has happened, and everything I have been through, I know that nothing will stop me doing exactly what I want to do. Nothing.

Getting in the car now. I'll be there soon.

I smile as I read the text from Cordelia. I would have liked to be there to help her pack up and move but it was something she needed to do herself.

But soon she will be here and she can move into the rental apartment with me and we can both start again, both of us survivors.

Both of us women who can't be stopped.

A LETTER FROM NICOLE

Hello,

I would like to thank you for taking the time to read *A Mother Always Knows*. If you enjoyed this novel and want to keep up to date with all my latest releases, just sign up at the following link. Your email address will never be shared and you can unsubscribe at any time.

www.bookouture.com/nicole-trope

I am so glad that readers got another chance to spend time with Grace. She is a fierce mama bear who will do anything for her children. Cordelia is very young but she has been through so much and has emerged stronger and more resilient, just like her mother.

I admire Grace's ability to understand Cordelia's pain and to acknowledge it and accept that it means she has to work harder to earn her daughter's trust back.

I hope for a wonderful future for the two of them, and I do think that Cordelia will embrace a new career in clothing design. The mother–daughter relationship changes over time, and Grace and Cordelia have had to deal with more than most, but I hope readers never doubted Grace's love for her daughter.

As always, I will be so grateful if you leave a review for the novel, especially if you loved the book and can avoid those pesky spoilers.

I love hearing from my readers – you can get in touch on social media. I try to reply to each message I receive.

Thanks again for reading,

Nicole x

facebook.com/NicoleTrope
x.com/nicoletrope
instagram.com/nicoletropeauthor

ACKNOWLEDGEMENTS

My first thank you goes to Ellen Gleeson. Every book is different and this one took some twists and turns, and I was grateful to have your support throughout the process.

I would also like to thank Jess Readett for all her enthusiasm and for helping me get my novels into the hands of many eager readers.

Thanks to DeAndra Lupu for the copy edit and Liz Hatherell for the very thorough proofread.

Thanks to the whole team at Bookouture, including Jenny Geras, Peta Nightingale, Richard King, Alba Proko, Ruth Tross, Mandy Kullar and everyone else involved in getting my novels out into the world.

Thanks to my mother, Hilary, who is an excellent beta reader.

Thanks also to David, Mikhayla, Isabella, Jacob and Jax.

And once again thank you to those who read, review and blog about my work and contact me on social media to let me know you loved the book. I love hearing your stories and reasons why you have connected with a novel.

Every review is appreciated and I do read them all.

PUBLISHING TEAM

Turning a manuscript into a book requires the efforts of many people. The publishing team at Bookouture would like to acknowledge everyone who contributed to this publication.

Audio
Alba Proko
Sinead O'Connor
Melissa Tran

Commercial
Lauren Morrissette
Hannah Richmond
Imogen Allport

Cover design
Aaron Munday

Data and analysis
Mark Alder
Mohamed Bussuri

Editorial
Ellen Gleeson
Nadia Michael

Copyeditor
DeAndra Lupu

Proofreader
Liz Hatherell

Marketing
Alex Crow
Melanie Price
Occy Carr
Cíara Rosney
Martyna Młynarska

Operations and distribution
Marina Valles
Stephanie Straub

Production
Hannah Snetsinger
Mandy Kullar
Jen Shannon
Ria Clare

Publicity
Kim Nash
Noelle Holten
Jess Readett
Sarah Hardy

Rights and contracts
Peta Nightingale
Richard King
Saidah Graham

Milton Keynes UK
Ingram Content Group UK Ltd.
UKHW041909021224
3275UKWH00002B/93